Year

of the

Ginkgo

Books by Sharon Dilworth

The Long White
Women Drinking Benedictine
Year of the Ginkgo
Two Sides, Three Rivers
My Riviera

Year

of the

Ginkgo

Sharon Dilworth

Carnegie Mellon University Press
Pittsburgh 2022

Cover design by Connie Amoroso

Library of Congress Control Number: 2022942529
ISBN: 978-0-88748-681-4

10 9 8 7 6 5 4 3 2 1

Year of the Ginkgo was first published by Unbound Press, Glasgow,
Scotland in 2010.

First Carnegie Mellon University Press Classic Contemporaries
Edition, October 2022

Chapter One

It's the female ginkgo tree that smells. The male trees are odorless. But get a berry from one of the females caught in your shoe tread and the smell of vomit and rotting eggs will haunt you all day.

I am in love with my neighbor, Allan. He's Scottish with dark hair and black eyes and he speaks with that incredible burr. He's got salt and pepper eyelashes and a jaw line that begs you to pull him into you and kiss the skin on his neck until it bruises.

The ginkgo tree dates back 200 million years. It's one of the few specimens still living from when dinosaurs walked the earth. Magnolias and cockroaches also number among the survivors.

I can't do anything about my neighbor, besides fantasize. It's not just that he's married, or that I'm married, or that we both have kids – there are real complications. For one thing he's married to Maggie – someone who I actually like. One of the things no one mentions when they complain about middle age is how difficult it is to meet people who aren't deadly dull.

Allan's wife Maggie is interesting; she speaks all these odd languages like Malaysian and Thai. She was a Luce Fellow – studied low-income housing on the effects of childhood diseases in Indonesia and then traveled extensively in the Far East. I would feel funny sneaking around with her husband when she's off doing something fascinating, which she always is. Everyone wants her help and she's entirely selfless in giving it. She's not the type to talk about herself or her problems. She just does things. Last year when there was that hoopla over the Malaysian scandal, Maggie was quoted in every news story. She was at the trial, translating for the dead man's wife, who steadfastly claimed no knowledge even though they suspected her not only of embezzling funds, but also of sleeping with her brother-in-law, and because of that had most likely had her husband killed. Rather than sentence her, they deported her to Kuala Lumpur. Maggie accompanied the wife to the airport and there were photographs of the two of them hugging goodbye.

"I don't think she hired anyone," Maggie said.

"You think she's innocent?" I asked.

"Just the opposite. I think she did it herself," Maggie said. "She's quite capable with a knife. I think she slashed his throat all on her own. She wouldn't have wasted money paying someone to do something she could have done so easily."

If she weren't so nice, she would intimidate me.

Right now, Maggie's helping our neighbor Barbara adopt a baby girl from China. Mandarin is one of Maggie's languages. Barbara, in my opinion, is a case in point – someone who does nothing but talk about herself. Non-stop and in English so there is no chance you'll miss what she's saying. She came over a week after she had moved to the street and handed me two hefty garbage bags filled with what looked like Goodwill donations. "I'm sure your boys can use these," she said. What would teenage boys do with red and yellow cable-knit sweaters or size 9 faux leather pumps?

I think Maggie's out of her mind to get involved with Barbara, even if she is the only person Barbara knows who can understand the documents the Chinese government sends over. I'm the only one who doesn't like Barbara; everyone else thinks she's just great – so full of energy and charisma. I don't see it. She talks a lot. I'll give her that much. She's continually talking about what she's going to do – what we all should do – camping in the Laurel Highlands, picnics on the Allegheny, season tickets to the opera, the flower show at Mellon Park, movies, fund raisers, cocktail parties. On and on it goes. There's nothing she doesn't want to do. Everyone finds her simply charming and full of great ideas. I took an instant dislike to her. My husband thinks that's unfair, but normal considering my current state of being.

It's the end of August. Unemployed since April, I am now a member of the leisure class. I get up every morning, see my sons off to basketball camp. I read both papers – the *NY Times* and the *Pittsburgh Post-Gazette*. Then I walk to the coffee shop with the classifieds. I started the habit of the coffee shop because I thought it would motivate me to see other people going to work every day. Instead what I've found is a great number of people who seem to be in my situation – not much to do with the day. We regulars guard our tables. We sit and drink and watch the others who run in and out without much connection, empathy, or envy. I listen to the kids behind the counter, who are incredibly mean-spirited about the customers. They rip on everything – but concentrate on people's habits, which they abhor.

"Who orders a triple shot latte? No one needs that much caffeine."

"She never throws out her stir sticks. She leaves them right on the counter as if we're trash collectors."

"He buys that muffin for his mutt."

I'm curious to know what they say about me and wonder if they would find me odd if I asked them what I do that annoys them. But then I couldn't go back. That would put me into the weirdo category. I leave after two or three refills. Home to rearrange the house. I have moved almost every piece of furniture on the first floor. I'll start on the second just as soon as I'm satisfied with the living room. I'm still not sure about the couch under the window. My husband says the way I have it arranged now is not conducive for socializing. I say, so what? At least it's different.

I go to the computer and check my E-mail – mostly spam – and then I go onto my websites. There are two that I check daily – one is about ginkgo trees, the other about Scotland.

These sites send me periodic updates – and now I'm learning everything I want to know about these two fascinating subjects.

The summer has passed quickly. Much more quickly than it would have had I still been working. Now a few days before Labor Day, Barbara phones me frantically. "I need Maggie," she says. "Have you seen her? Do you have any idea where she is?"

Maggie has just stopped by. She's collecting toys for the Ronald McDonald Family House picnic that she throws for the family members staying in town over the holiday weekend. She does it every year – chicken wings and potato salad for sixty at Mellon Park.

"Barbara's looking for you," I announce, letting Maggie decide if she wants to hide from her.

"I should go over and talk to her. I'm sure it's something to do with the Chinese adoption," Maggie explains.

Maggie agrees to go over to Barbara's and I tag along because I'm curious to see what's going on. Two weeks ago, Barbara was desperately seeking a husband. I guess she's going to skip that step.

"Barbara's really going to adopt a baby?" I ask.

"Yes. Isn't that wonderful?"

"It's interesting." I'll give her that much. "She doesn't strike me as the mothering kind."

"Were any of us the mothering kind before we had kids?"

We walk down the street to Barbara's apartment. Barbara opens the door and sighs as if we're late. "Here you are," she says. "Thank God." Barbara ushers Maggie over to the cluttered desk and asks her to translate a letter she's just received from the Chinese agency that is in charge of all adoptions in some remote province in China.

I'm slightly suspicious. Wouldn't an agency have someone to translate their documents for their clients? Wouldn't that be an obvious step in the process? Maybe Barbara is doing something illegal. Maybe this is a black market adoption. My suspicion turns to curiosity.

Barbara explains her impatience. "I've waited two years for this," she says. The process, a very slow but very good one, has been made even slower for single women wanting to adopt because of a change in policy with the Chinese government. Maybe all her noise about finding a man/husband was simply a shortcut to a baby. I study Barbara for a few minutes. She has a big-time job at as director of development at one of the big hospitals in Pittsburgh. It's Joe's hospital but he says he has absolutely nothing to do with development. She works with the administration and operates on their level far from the physicians. Joe says he reads about their decisions and plans like everyone else in the city – in the newspapers. It's a big job and I don't know how Barbara handles it. Maybe that's where she puts all her smartness and energy, into her work because socially she's not so sharp.

And I'm the one without the job. It does make one curious.

"My Mandarin is a bit rusty," Maggie apologizes humbly, but her admission agitates Barbara.

"Do you understand it or not?" Barbara asks, reaching for the papers. Maggie's busy reading and doesn't hear the bitchiness in Barbara's tone. Though maybe she does and chooses to ignore it.

Barbara actually stomps across the room in a huff as if this is going to make any difference to anyone. I roll my eyes. She's such an idiot. I can't believe she's contemplating motherhood. I feel like I should tell someone she's an unfit weirdo. Give her a kid and she'll probably flush it down the toilet or give it away in those garbage bags. The spotlight rarely leaves Barbara for long – I don't know how she's going to compete with a kid.

Barbara stands. "I need this done today. Should I find someone else?"

"Like every third person in Pittsburgh is fluent in Chinese." This from me.

"Caroline, do you ever do anything useful with that sarcasm?" Barbara asks.

Maggie looks up. "Allan thinks she's hilarious."

I blush and smile, then an odd noise comes out of my mouth – I realize it's a giggle. I cover my mouth and force myself to stop. Thirty-eight year old women do not giggle, but I am so pleased that I find it impossible to stop.

"I can think of other things I might call her," Barbara says.

Maggie asks for a pen. "I need to make some notes," she apologizes.

"Allan thinks I'm funny?" I'm not proud; I fish to hear the compliment again.

"Hysterical," she says. She is bent over the desk writing furiously.

Those words don't necessarily mean the same thing. I suddenly have hope that she'll sabotage Barbara's adoption process.

I attempt to ask Maggie for clarification. "When you said . . ."

Barbara shushes me. "Leave her alone. She's trying to work here."

Either way – hilarious, hysterical – Allan at least talks about me, which is more than I knew before and with this bit of encouragement, I'm off to dreamland – a place where neither Maggie or Barbara are ever invited.

There are other reasons why my fantasy concerning Allan exists solely in my head. One of the biggest obstacles is Allan. I don't have much evidence that these obsessively passionate yearnings are shared, though I did have some indication – a spark that got the whole thing started. Now I'm not so sure. In fact, there are times when I'm not sure Allan even likes me, which is why I am so pleased to hear that he thinks I'm hilarious. Most people consider humor a positive trait –I'm thinking that Maggie's hysterical for hilarious substitution was simply a slip of the tongue. Barbara's awkward social skills get everyone worked up.

On the other hand, his feelings about me don't really change anything. I lust after him steadily and seriously. I work full-time at this profession of fabrication. I've become so accustomed to my fantasy that any reality like his feelings for me doesn't actually come into play. The stories I construct about Allan have nothing to do with our real lives. In my imaginings, it's just him and me. There are no kids or wives. There are no husbands, no laundry, no indigestion. No veins, no weirdness. There is nothing uncomfortable; nothing needs to be negotiated. We're not sneaking around. We're not hurting anyone. We're just together. Two single people, patrolling the world for love. Miraculously he finds me. And he admires me greatly before I fall in love with him. We talk about love. Then we make love. He declares his love for me, then we make love again. In my fantasy I'm incredibly attractive, with long wavy brown hair. I have a model's figure and I'm intriguing. In most of the scenarios, I'm an agent for the government, an important one. In others, I'm a spy. I grew up during the Cold War and the world of trench coats, berets, and Russian accents has always been a part of my romantic fantasies.

Despite the circumstances of risk, menace, and danger lurking at every corner, Allan and I always manage to have a great time. The settings are beautiful, lots of seascapes, waves and wind; the bed covers are goose down duvets. The sex is wonderful. There is always red wine in glasses that don't tip over no matter how wild the sex. There are candles. I am extraordinarily skinny.

I come home from Barbara's thinking not about China or babies, but about Allan and the back of his neck. I sat behind him two weeks ago when some of the girls in the neighborhood put on a violin concert. The oldest musician was 12 and the concert was painful, but the hostess had made tea and little cucumber sandwiches and I sat directly behind Allan. He shaves or gets it shaved back there. He has a tiny line of white that shows through – making me think he'd look terrible bald. He has a few freckles, and once when I got too close, I could see the tiny white hairs stand up where my breath brushed his skin.

He swatted as if a fly had landed on him. I sat back and acted as if I was enjoying the music, which I couldn't really listen to. Allan seemed particularly sexually enticing that day – I wonder how everyone isn't throwing themselves at him – and all my senses were focusing on him.

The doorbell rings. I don't jump to answer it. The kids in the neighborhood have been particularly aggressive about door-to-door sales this year. Suddenly they're all little capitalists. They're all selling things for good causes. Tins of popcorn to help the soccer team get to Denmark for the international championship. Wrapping paper so the church group can go to Ecuador to help build churches in the mountain villages. The boy scouts, girl scouts, everyone needs something. But finally, because I have two sons who go door to door, I answer the bell.

It's Allan. I stammer out a hello. He's obviously here to whisk me away. He's madly in love and though he's been fighting it with all his might, is unable to do anything anymore to conceal it.

He apologizes. "I hope this isn't a bad time," he says.

I stare, trying very hard to discern if he is really there or if this is still part of my imaginary life.

"I was hoping I could talk to Joe," Allan says.

I struggle to think of something witty to say. Nothing comes to mind, so I continue staring at him.

"Joe," Allan repeats.

The screen door that separates us makes him look a bit fuzzy, much like the grainy quality of the movies I imagine us in.

"Joe?" I ask.

"Your husband."

"Oh, right." I remember him.

"I've got a couple of medical things I need to ask him."

Joe's a doctor – an E.R. physician and our friends often use him as a neighborhood emergency Mini-mart. Open 24/7/365. Allan is not one of Joe's usual customers.

"Am I interrupting something?" Allan asks. "Are you busy with dinner?"

He clearly doesn't understand my world.

"Hysterical?" I whisper, coaching him through the screen to bring the world into my control.

"Do you have a cold, Caroline?"

Men like healthy women. "I'm never sick, Allan."

"Bravo for you," he says. "You must save a fortune in cold tablets."

I have to remind myself not to be too crazy in front of Allan. I don't want him thinking I've lost my marbles. The struggle is mind-boggling. My ruminations of Allan are so fueled by my imagination that the reality of him jars my daydreams. In my made-up world, we are exceedingly close and obviously intimate; it's confusing to actually see him and act naturally. I'm afraid I'm going to say something that doesn't belong in reality.

We're still on daylight savings time and the evening air is rose colored. I invite him in and offer him a drink.

"That would be great," he says and comes in rubbing his hands. He does this a lot – an anticipatory gesture that I don't know how to interpret, but I take it as a positive sign – that he's overwhelmed by my presence and excited to see me. I lick my lips trying to determine if I'm still wearing lipstick. It doesn't seem like it.

13

We sit in the living room – which actually is fine for socializing as long as there are only two. He doesn't look ill. Maybe this is a ploy. Maybe he's really come to see me and is using Joe as an excuse.

Why do we pay so much attention to commitments we made to the State? Shouldn't there be a separation between current lust and nuptials that were made fifteen years ago?

He sighs.

"Tough day?"

"Unendingly problematic," he says. "Made even more so once I came home."

"That's too bad," I say. He's trying to confide in me. I have to listen carefully so I don't sound like a dimwit.

"Americans are emotionally fraught creatures, aren't they?" he asks.

"You're telling me." I nod.

"They're actually quite mad."

"And loud," I add.

He pauses, puzzled. "Who said anything about loud?" He separates his legs and leans back into the couch. He smells like pine. Or maybe that's from Tony, my male maid. Wednesdays are his day, though he's not at all reliable.

"You did," I say. "Last April you told me Americans were loud. This June we were fat and last week we were incredibly stupid."

"I hope you're not taking it personally," he says.

"Me? Take anything personally? How could I?" I ask.

His wife is American. "From Idaho," he always jokes. "Moscow, Idaho. Isn't that ridiculously brilliant." Being from such a place absolves her of the sins the rest of us suffer by association.

I've never been to Scotland, but from what I've gathered from Allan, the Scots are perfect. They have an astute knowledge of history and culture. Most can recite Robert Burns, Greek mythology, Shakespeare, and Racine. I'm not sure why Racine, but that's the way it is. Unlike Americans who can't name another country's president or prime minister, the Scots are current on all matter of political concerns. Like Allan, they're dark and good looking and have sarcastic opinions on everything under the sun. Not all of them have wives.

"Did you say yes to wine?" I walk over to the cabinet where we have a great deal of wine stocked. There are even clean glasses and a corkscrew – almost as if I had planned this.

"Whisky, wine, a gigantic hammer," he says, that huge grin on his face. His teeth are quite small and very white. I wonder if he's used a whitening process. "I'll take whatever blurs the senses."

See how well we could get along?

I pour out two glasses of wine. This is very familiar to me – something I've done over and over again in my head. Though there, I'm usually sitting in Allan's lap. I opt for the chair across the way and sip my wine.

"Is Joe around?" Allan asks.

I explain that I've just come back from Barbara's. "She's really serious about this baby thing."

He rolls his eyes.

He and Maggie have two daughters. I don't think he's anti-children, so I'm thinking he's anti-Barbara, and with this I agree. She is an eye-roll. "You're not kidding." I nod, staring at his face. His lashes, as I might have mentioned, are very dark with flecks of gray giving the impression that he's just walked in from the snow.

He drinks incredibly fast. Maybe he's as nervous as I am, though he hides it better than I do. "I'm sorry, is Joe home?"

I shrug. That's the fifth time in five minutes he's brought up Joe. Is it really necessary that we talk so much about my husband? I drink and pretend that we're having a conversation about our love, but then see the odd expression on his face and force myself to be a normal human being.

I explain that Joe has been jogging to work these days, so a car in the drive isn't any indication of who's here or not. I walk into the hallway and call up the steps. "Anyone home?"

Nothing but silence, which is also no indication that the house is empty. I have two teenage sons and they never answer their mother's call. They ignore me until they need me.

"Do you ever talk to your husband, Caroline?"

"Am I supposed to?" I ask.

I replenish his wine glass.

"Cheese? Crackers?" I offer. A candle-lit soak in the claw-footed bathtub?

The light is just leaving the room. Allan drinks his wine in two swallows. I get up to refill his glass and he says something about drinking in the dark. "I could bring over a few light bulbs," he offers.

"That'd be great," I say and turn on one table lamp. I don't see any reason to flood the room with harsh lights.

"Which Americans are mad?" I ask.

"All the ones I come in contact with." Allan says. "They really are out of their minds." He finishes the second glass of wine. At least I get that part right in my ruminations.

"Are you okay?" I ask. I'm not this dull in my daydreams, but I'm worried that Allan might be here to ask Joe about an irregular heartbeat or about blood in his urine. Has his primary care physician given him a three-month sentence? How can I live without him?

"What do you mean, Caroline?"

"Health-wise," I clarify.

"Do I look okay?" He leans forward, but he moves into the shadows and I can't see his face.

"Yes." You look great. You're one of the most handsome men I've ever met. You have this incredible mouth, perfect lips. I'd like to be the wine in your glass, the glass in your hand, the pillow near your arm.

"I've got a couple of questions for Joe," Allan says. I stare at him. I'm good with questions.

Allan mistakes my silence for curiosity. "I'm sure he'll fill you in when I leave."

"Joe won't tell me a thing," I say. "He's incredibly discreet."

"That must be why I like you two so much," Allan says. "You're not like the rest of these pests."

I hear praise in that sentence. He is using the plural; I'm included in that compliment.

Joe comes home. He's wearing hospital scrubs and his running shoes. Allan stands up and I don't think I'm imagining the flash of guilt moving across his face. He shouldn't feel guilty. Emotions are unruly – crazy things – we believe we're in control, but it's not always the case.

Allan and Joe shake hands. "You golf today?" Allan asks.

Joe shakes his head. "Couldn't get away." Joe doesn't golf, but Allan doesn't seem to know it. He talks to Joe frequently about golf and golfing problems. He complains when the weather isn't good enough for golf, when he thinks he should be playing instead of doing whatever it is that he's doing.

"You got a minute?" Allan asks.

"Sure, sure," Joe asks. "Let's sit."

Maybe to prove to Allan that there really is more than one discreet American, or maybe because I don't like to see my husband and my 'lover' in the same room, I leave the two of them to have their discussion in private. Joe takes over my wine glass and I go up to our bedroom and flick on the television. I turn down the sound, and listen to the cadence of Allan's voice. But I'm too curious. I am not by nature a discreet person. I put my ear to the heating vent and strain to hear what they're saying.

It's not clear. I hear part of their conversation. Allan's talking, but I can't make out what he's saying. Joe's voice booms – Allan is right on that one – Americans *are* loud.

"Let me check on that for you," Joe booms.

"If it's not too much trouble," Allan answers.

"Not at all."

My son, Max, age 12, comes in and flops on the bed. He grabs the remote and flicks on the television. The sound booms, then echoes in the room. I stand.

"Jesus Christ," he says and jumps up as if I'm going to hit him." Have you flipped? What are you doing on the floor?"

"I dropped my earring," I offer, but don't feel I need an excuse. It's my room. I can do what I want.

He stares at me, trying to figure out what I'm really doing. I stare back; the conversation continues downstairs. I won't hear any of it.

"Are you okay, Mom?" Max asks.

"Just fine," I say. "Go ahead, watch your program." I motion for him to get back on the bed.

But he doesn't.

Ever since I lost my job, the kids have been nice to me. It's a strain, not their first reaction, and I should bask in their care, but I feel it's a stretch for them. Joe must have talked to them and told them that they should be more considerate. And at times, they are. But it's not natural and makes us all a bit awkward.

Max leaves rather than stay in the same room with me.

The front door slams and Allan is gone. I turn to the window. Night is settling. I see his dark shape walking towards his house. He stops, lights a cigarette and smokes by the trees. I rush downstairs.

Joe sits in the living room, his head back against the chair, eyes closed. He's lit the room with the overhead lights – harsh, insensitive yellow lights. I flick them off.

"You didn't invite him for dinner."

"What's that?"

"Allan. You should have told him to stay for dinner."

"Why? Did you cook something?" Joe yawns. I know my husband, he suspects nothing of my fantasies.

Unemployed, I have no interest in cooking. Now that I have the time, I don't have the inclination. I had planned to call Wheel Deliver and order Thai noodles. I'm not sure how Allan feels about take-out food. We don't eat out a lot in my dreams. Food is not a big issue – maybe because I'm so skinny.

"What about his family?" Joe asks. He talks with his eyes closed.

"Oh," I say. "Are they home?"

I take Allan's glass into the kitchen. There's a sip left. I drink it and think about some sort of Catholic ritual of drinking from the same chalice. *You are unstable*, I tell my reflection in the window over the sink. I vow not to think of Allan for at least two hours – go over to the refrigerator and dial the number for take-out. "Dinner will be ready in 45," I shout to the house.

Later that night I ask Joe if everything is all right with Allan.

"As far as I know." He doesn't look up.

He has his laptop in bed, balanced on his knees. He's writing a mystery novel. It's about a man who kills his wife and gets away with it. He spends all his free time researching methods and reading published mystery novels. The house is now decorated with stacks of current best-selling thrillers and cop novels.

I've read the first few chapters of Joe's book. I read them quickly, which Joe took as a positive sign. "You liked it?" he asked.

"I did," I told him.

"You really did?"

"I did. Really." And it's true. What he has is really good and I'm proud that he's doing it.

There are only four characters: the dead wife, the husband, and the two police officers.

"It's got to be the husband. You don't have any other suspects," I say. Then I try to think like Joe. "Unless it's one of the cops."

"Why should you trust anyone?" Joe asks. "Cops aren't always good. They've been known to go against the law when provoked."

"But they didn't know her," I tell him. "Wouldn't they need a motive?"

"That's what you think," Joe says.

Joe was an English major as an undergraduate. He tells me a lot of doctors majored in the humanities. Lots of doctors are clandestine writers. They have the material. It's too bad more of them don't write. Joe refuses to have doctors or hospitals or lawyers in his mystery. "It's going to be different than other detective books."

"He's in good health?" I ask.

"The cop?"

"Allan," I remind him who we're really talking about.

"In good health?" Joe stops typing. "Why?"

"I was just wondering." People usually come to talk to Joe about their ailments.

"He didn't say anything about his health."

"Then what did you two talk about?"

"His wife," Joe says.

"Maggie?" I'm intrigued, but puzzled. It seems an odd reason for Allan to seek Joe's medical expertise.

"I think he's only got one," Joe says. He looks out at me over his readers, not puzzled, but bemused.

"That's right," I say. "As far as I know, he's only got the one wife."

But there are others who love him. Madly, hysterically, as is our emotionally fraught American way.

Chapter Two

I first realized my devotion to Allan at a neighbor's June barbecue. Karen and Greg were spearheading a neighborhood coalition to protect the empty lot at the end of the block. The lot belonged to the house on the corner – directly across from Allan and Maggie's. The owner of the house, a mentally handicapped man who worked at the bakery in Shadyside – he made deliveries on his bicycle – was put in a rest home ten years ago. His will stipulated that the property was not to be sold until his death. Mellon Bank was in charge of the estate. They mowed the grass, planted flowers, weeded, and cleaned the sidewalks in the winter months and no one ever cared who played in the empty lot. Two acres of mowed lawn – the boys grew up on it. It was a meeting place for the entire neighborhood, our own little park in the middle of the city. When they were really young, we went over in the early evening and caught fireflies in glass jars. When they got older, it was theirs – a place to find a friend, then another and another until enough kids had gathered for a game of soccer or baseball. They played for hours. If they weren't in the house, they were over there.

This spring we learned that the owner had died and the bank was going to sell.

Karen and Greg thought that it was a crying shame that the most likely scenario of the sale was that the land would be developed. "Space is vital for a vibrant neighborhood," they insisted. They thought the best idea was for everyone involved to come together to talk about other solutions. "We won't have any say in what some crazy contractor will build on it. It could be a monstrosity."

I used to work in the county executive office: I was the assistant director of city planning and knew that our entire street is an open zone, which means that something awful could be built there. Karen and Greg were right. A monstrosity was a real possibility. Developers built a huge ugly thing over on Fifth and Kentucky – a 25-unit condominium structure that ruined the pretty tree lined corner of those blocks.

A neighborhood coalition wasn't going to help if a developer was set on buying the property. The bank had probably been counting the days until they could dump the place and there was little that could be done to stop the sale, even if it went into auction. It was hard to think of an individual buying such an expensive piece of land. I mourned the sale too and was glad that my boys had had the use of it for so many years. They were getting older now and were busy with school activities. Still it was something that was being taken from us and I was saddened by the loss.

Karen and Greg have this gigantic house with all sorts of adult children moving in and out. Greg calls them his boomerangs and tells me that he's never going to get rid of them, no matter how hard he throws them away. Allan and Maggie live right next door, though in June I wasn't thinking in those kinds of geographical concepts.

Karen and Greg are in chaos. They're enthusiastically crazy and always have been. They're wonderful neighbors. The kind who go overboard for holidays. Their house at Christmas looks like a theme park. In October they buy orange and black garbage bags and spider webs for the trees and bushes. Karen's a scream. She tells everyone that the 12 step-program saved her life, which might be true, except it did nothing to curb her alcohol consumption.

Greg had recently purchased a new grill and the backyard was quickly filling with smoke that smelled of burned barbecue sauce and advice about how to correct the problem, when Allan came in.

I've known Allan ever since he and Maggie moved to Pittsburgh two years ago. I liked her tremendously. He was more of a neighbor – we talked, complained about our kids becoming teenagers, their two girls being the same age as Max and Josh, but I never considered him anything but Maggie's husband.

But that night changed everything – I didn't fabricate a thing that night. I didn't have to. It was perfect just the way it was.

Allan walked across the backyard to the bar that was really a wobbly card table decorated with a paper Christmas tablecloth – green and red holly. He poured himself a large glass of wine, then came and handed it to me.

"Already have one," I said, and held up my own glass.

"Would you mind holding it for me?" he asked.

"Careful, I may pour it down my throat," I warned.

"In that case, I won't swim for long."

I opened my mouth, a perfect O of surprise. "You're going in?" Karen and Greg have this double kidney-shaped built-in swimming pool that's much larger than most backyard pools, but it doesn't scream: use me.

"Does it look dangerous?"

"Most definitely." The pool was perfectly calm, the surface, a dark indefinable color.

"I don't think I'll run into sharks."

He pulled off his shirt, then turned, and with a step or two dove into the pool. Everyone watched as Allan surfaced. "Wonderful," he shouted out. He shook his head, much to the delight of the dog, then climbed out. Dripping wet, he came back for his wine glass. He drank it in two swallows.

"How's the water?"

"Very warm," he answered.

"And dirty?" I asked.

"It's cleaner than the ocean," he replied.

"I wouldn't bet on it," I said.

"No major companies are draining pollutants into it. There aren't any dead fish. No one's crapped in it."

"As far as you know," I said. "Karen and Greg have kids. You never know when kids are involved."

"You think they'd mistake a pool for an outhouse?"

"Get a tetanus shot tomorrow."

"Does Joe have any extra laying about the house?"

"He might," I said. "I'll look."

"Speaking of," Allan said. "Where is the old man?"

"Watching the Pirates lose another game," I said. "He took the boys. They at least like the hotdogs and fries."

"The hot dogs *are* good."

The city of Pittsburgh spent millions on two new sports stadiums and the only thing people rave about are the hot dogs, the French fries, and the view. The view is fantastic, but I'm not sure you'd get all of us unemployed ex-city workers to agree that it was worth it. This is Western Pennsylvania. They lose the sports teams and there will be massive migration. People would be at a real loss as to how they would spend their weekends. They seem to ignore the fact that the city is in debt to the tune of 80 million dollars. I harp on that note too often. I really do have to find something new to talk about. Don't talk about your own problems, I told myself that night. Go somewhere else. Which in the end, is exactly what I did.

"Summer agrees with you, Caroline," Allan said.

I misheard and told him that I thought the summer was too hot.

"That wasn't what I said," Allan said. "I meant that you've got a lot of color," he said. "You look nice."

Allan and I were not the kind of neighbors who complimented each other, so I felt myself blush under his gaze, but he seemed genuine and I accepted his words of praise without a sarcastic remark.

"More wine?" I asked. "We should refill before the lecture begins."

Karen and Greg had promised a short informational talk, but I knew my neighbors. They were fired up about the empty lot issue and would probably talk all night.

"Good thinking," Allan said. He took my glass.

"Hey there," I said and held it tight.

"I'm going to refill it," Allan said. "If that's all right with you."

"Sorry," I said, and handed it over.

"My pleasure," he said and stood up. He had not redressed. His chest hairs were lighter than the hair on his head. Some gray. I watched him walk away, admittedly a bit puzzled. Maybe Allan had started cocktailing before coming over. That would explain the dip in the disgusting swimming pool.

Drunk or sober, it didn't matter to me – not then – it was nice of him to get me more wine.

He came back and stretched out on the chaise longue next to me.

"Is this going to be dreadful?" he asked.

"Worse," I answered. "You have no idea." Karen and Greg had called me several times to get advice. I still had some access and information on planning and development. I explained what they would need to save the lot. "Something just short of a miracle," I said honestly. "On the other hand, there are so few city employees still working it could take ages for anything to happen."

Their plan was for the neighbors to come together and buy the property from the bank. It was to be co-owned – a communal property, which was a difficult thing to manage in Pittsburgh. I cared about the lot, but sometimes you have to know when to throw in the towel.

I told Allan what I knew and he groaned. "At least the food is good," he said.

Greg and Karen got up to explain their point of view on the vacant lot. They started out saying that, like everyone else, they thought the land should be protected – for the good of the fine people of the neighborhood.

"It's like they're trying to save the wetlands," I whispered to Allan. "We should get your daughter in on this one."

Allan laughed.

"Do you golf, Caroline?"

"I'd rather kill myself," I said.

"Death squad or hitting a little white ball and you'd go for the execution?"

"Not a doubt in my mind," I nod.

"Seems a bit extreme, doesn't it?" he asked. "It's just a game."

"I don't bowl either," I said. "And when I think that golf and bowling are televised, I know the world is insane."

"Too bad," he commented.

"That I don't golf?"

"The men in this neighborhood are awful," he said. "Present husbands exempted." He nodded towards the group of men standing near Greg. "These are the guys I golf with," he paused. "And none of them are even that good."

The men in the neighborhood are awful. They're pharmaceutical reps and Westinghouse or what-was-Westinghouse executives. They're dull. Like their wives, they're caught up in their own concerns and rarely talk about anything interesting that doesn't involve them at the center.

"At least you'd be funny."

"Principles," I said. "Can't golf. Can't drink beer. Can't care about football."

"You're definitely not Scottish."

"Was there some doubt on that?"

"Your accent's pretty Mid-western."

"I resent that," I told him. "I was born and bred in New York."

"And that isn't the Midwest?"

"You have a lot of nerve," I said and he laughed.

The one thing that I miss about being unemployed is the conversation with adults. In a normal workday I bet I talked to thirty people. Jobless, I ask the baristas at Starbucks for my coffee. I say hi to a neighbor, I might call Julie. I talk to Joe. The boys were in their summer mode – all sports, no confidential talks about girls or how much they hate their teachers. It's not a lot of stimulation.

That night felt different and I told myself it was just what I needed. Allan and I were stretched out on matching lawn chairs, staring up at the evening sky as if sunbathing on a beach. The wine was excellent. I sipped slowly.

Greg came over. He had a petition he wanted us to sign. There were already a dozen signatures.

"How many more do you think we'll need?" he asked me.

"This looks good," I lied.

The petition was useless. The mayor received a thousand of those every week.

"There's a Power Point presentation in the living room," Greg explained. "You'll have a better understanding of how your contributions will save the land. Karen's also drawn a little sketch of her idea of what the vacant lot could look like with a bit of work. She thinks a few benches, some flower beds. We'll give it just the right feel."

Allan put his hand on my thigh. I yelped.

"We'll be right there," he told Greg. "Give us a minute."

"I'll circle back," Greg said and went off to the next group of people. The night was all light and warm sunshine, one of the longest days of the year.

It came to me slowly but once I wrapped my head around it, I thought I had it right – Allan was flirting with me.

I smiled at that thought.

He had paid me two compliments. One that summer agreed with me, and two, that I would be a fun person to spend the afternoon with. I put down my wine and sucked in my stomach.

My head was swimming a bit. I was not used to attracting attention from men.

It took me a few minutes to realize but I was happy. I was enjoying myself – the first time since I got fired.

I didn't want him to leave. I tried to think of something captivating to say, but the best I could come up with was to ask him if he was enjoying the summer.

"God no," he sighed. "Things couldn't be worse."

Wrong question. I should have asked him something about being Scottish. Men like to talk about themselves. But he had more to say about the summer that he was not enjoying at all.

"It's been a horrible month," Allan said.

"Tell me about it," I sighed.

"You too?' I wasn't agreeing with him. I wanted him to tell me about it. English is a tricky language, especially when you're trying to converse inter-continentally.

"It's not been the greatest summer," I offered. But I didn't fill in the details. I loathe people who talk about themselves. One of the mothers on Max's basketball team did nothing but talk about her lousy life. She was outrageously negative and therefore offensively boring and hard to be around. I worried about becoming like her. I wouldn't bore Allan with my problems.

"A terrible summer," Allan said and with his accent his complaints sounded like miniature jokes.

"What seems to be the problem?" I asked. I looked around for Maggie, but didn't see her. The wine tasted great. I drank forgetting that I was unemployed and unable to find something to do with my days.

"What do you call it?" he asked. "Worse than dreadful." Allan's hair was dark, even darker when wet. On a woman you'd know immediately that it was dyed. On him, I was simply suspicious of his claim to be Scottish. Where was the red hair, the kilt? The bagpipes? He didn't look typical. But I was just starting to notice that he did look sexy.

I stopped staring at him. "Your daughter?" I asked. "Is that the problem?"

"She's one of them."

Allan's eldest daughter, Jane age 16, was spending the summer in a sycamore tree in front of their house protesting global ignorance. She had climbed up there in June and had continued her vigil every since.

"She thinks everyone is stupid," Maggie had tried to clarify Jane's position for me. "Not just the president of the United States but all of them."

"Them being?" I ask.

"The leaders of most of the other countries in the free world."

Jane hoped to get her photograph in the local newspaper, after which she thought the story might go into syndication. "But even if it doesn't, I have to do something. Standing around doing nothing but complaining makes me just as guilty as the pigs I'm blaming for this mess."

She had a few good points. I always liked her spirit. I remember two years ago, she protested the dress code at her public school. She thought the girls dressed like sluts and that everyone, not just the boys, were distracted. She wore sandwich boards to protest then. "WORLD'S OLDEST PROFESSION MIGHT JUST START IN JUNIOR HIGH." And on the back. "COME SEE FOR YOURSELF."

When I wasn't on the internet searching for facts about ginkgo trees – the interest in Scotland obviously came later – I spent a lot of time at my desk staring out at my neighborhood. I was gathering a great deal of information about the neighbors. For instance, Carl and Rachel, who live across the street, have a dog walker who comes way too often for it to be legitimately about the two dogs who are too old to need that much fresh air. She comes at 9, then again at 11, and then again at 2 and once more at 4. I want to ask them about it, but don't want to give the impression of spying on them.

But mostly I watched Jane. I worried about her balance.

Allan wanted me to know that she wasn't just wasting her time up there. "That wouldn't be in the spirit of the protest."

She was catching up on the traditional literary canon because her public school only taught minority progressive literature.

That night at the barbecue Allan explained that Jane was currently reading the Russians. "Big fat Russian novels," he said. "Nothing slim or insignificant."

"I loved *Anna Karenina*," I said. I had read it as a teenage girl, maybe a few years older than Jane.

"That's one she's not reading," Allan said.

"Not fat enough?"

"She's more interested in the big *moral* dilemmas," he explained.

"Adultery is a moral dilemma," I said.

"Is that what the book is about?"

"It's about a woman who cheats on her husband," I explained. "She's madly in love with another man, but can't tell her husband. It finally drives her to suicide."

He was still grinning, and when I think back that I talked to him about the plot line of *Anna Karenina* without falling all over myself, I'm amazed.

"Jane is in an anti-love, anti-romance phase in her life. She thinks marriage is a constraint of the bourgeoisie. She's more concerned with life and death, good and evil, God or no God."

"All while she's up in the tree?" I asked.

"Protesting global stupidity," he said.

"You sure she won't fall?" I asked.

"She's pretty determined."

We finished our wine and night was creeping slowly into the summer sky. They hadn't turned on the backyard lights, which meant that the party was coming to a deliberate end.

Allan sighed and the conversation seemed to drain out of us.

"I'm sorry about your troubles," I said. I told him that I admired Jane. At least she had principles worth going up in a tree for. My boys, granted a few years younger than Jane, would only protest the absence of Play Station or if the refrigerator was suddenly empty of juice.

Allan closed his eyes and kept them closed. "Are you okay?" I asked. "Has the pool water finally gotten to you?"

"You should save me," he said.

"Me?"

"I'm drowning."

"I didn't realize the waters were so deep," I said. At the time, I thought we were talking about Jane and her tree sitting. Little did I realize how much I was being deceived.

"They are," Allan said.

He didn't seem drunk. Tipsy maybe, but he was Scottish. We had only had two glasses of wine.

"I'm in terrible trouble," he said.

He sat up and bent forward, his head going down to his knees. He was still bare-chested, the night no colder than when we had started.

He swung his legs around to my side of the chaise longue. "Oh help." He knelt as if in prayer.

And then he leaned over and put his head on my shoulder as if looking for support. He groaned. I could feel his breath, warm and teasing on my T-shirt. I held my breath and he groaned again, his breath coming faster and to my now discombobulated mind, faster.

I have been in love ever since that moment.

People's lives are changed by such little things. I'm overwhelmed by how the barbecue, which didn't do a thing to save the empty lot, transformed mine. Entirely.

I've read Updike. I've read Cheever. I know middle-age angst isn't a fictitious concept used to sell movies and books to the baby boomers. I'm aware that with advanced age comes a certain restlessness and anxiety, that another path might have been more satisfying. I knew all this and yet it happened to me. And when it did, I welcomed it. I embraced it as if I had been waiting for something like this all my life.

I think back to how calm I was the night of Greg and Karen's barbecue. In fact I return there often to that moment when I was sitting in that chaise longue and Allan was telling me how summer agrees with me. I'm amazed how I was just sitting there, not all that invested in Allan and his bare chest. Neutrally sitting there inches away from his salt and pepper lashes, the skin on the back of his neck, his head on my shoulder, talking affairs, talking sex, talking about men and women coupling. Now I can barely string together a sentence when he's around.

Now if he took his shirt off, I think I'd have a heart attack. It is the end of summer. The empty lot has been sold to a developer and there's no reason for Karen and Greg to have another barbecue, though I really wish they would.

I'm not reckless or courageous enough to abandon my family. I'm not contemplating infidelity. I don't even want to cheat – but what happened at the barbecue happened and now I'm a foolish prisoner to the world of my own make-believe. Ever since that night, when he put his head on my shoulder and asked me for help, I've given up sanity. I'm helplessly in love. I finally understand what that means. It means you can't do anything.

Allan is a civil engineer. I love this job title. Civil as in well-mannered, urbane, gracious. Engineer as in problem solver, someone who gets things accomplished. Perhaps as in someone who has dreams, someone who sees things that might be – someone who could build a bridge over to my inadequate and boring life.

There are a great number of bridges in the area – too many to count is what most people say. The city controls some, the county some others. The State owns the rest. That's what brought Allan here. There are more bridges per square mile in Pittsburgh than in any other American city.

It also for some crazy reason has a lot of ginkgo trees.

I'm the one to blame for Barbara living in our neighborhood. A few days after the barbecue at Karen and Greg's a friend called and asked if I knew of any place where this great woman, someone we were all going to love, could live. I should have said no. Instead I told her that there was a great building on the end of the block that had three apartments that were built as luxury apartments around the turn of the last century. Each had working fireplaces in two of the bedrooms and in the living room. There was a solarium and a porch that looks out onto the street. They had original wood floors and new appliances in the kitchen. My friend said it sounded perfect. She would have Barbara call the landlord.

Like I said, I don't know why I got involved.

My friend whose name is Julie is a reporter for the *Pittsburgh-Post Gazette.* She had known Barbara's sister in Philadelphia. It seemed that Barbara had called her and asked her for help in finding a place to live. Then Barbara went on to tell Julie that she knew no one in town. "Absolutely no one." She was counting on Julie to do something to amend that situation. "I love people. All kinds of folks," is what Barbara told Julie during that initial conversation.

Julie said she felt oddly responsible for this woman's well being. It's not in Julie's nature to care much about others so I was surprised when she said she had decided to have a get-together to welcome Barbara to town.

Barbara was moving to Pittsburgh because of a great job, head of development for one of the hospitals, which made sense. The only people moving to Pittsburgh work either for the universities or for the hospitals. I disliked her without even having met her. I didn't want to meet people who had jobs. They seemed privileged and made me feel ignorant. How would I introduce myself? "Hi. I'm Caroline. I used to do something. Now I'm a loser who doesn't do much of anything. I could tell you something interesting about myself. I'm madly in love with my neighbor who is married with two daughters, but then you'd think I was off my rocker."

Julie, a talented well-published and well-respected writer, is unbelievably neurotic about most things, but mostly about herself. Her biggest obsession is her weight. She used to be very thin, but now that she's nearing forty, she's put on a few pounds. Maybe it's more than a few. Maybe it's more like fifty. She looks like a lot of women our age; but she laments the loss of her youth and when she's had a glass of wine, talks about nothing else.

The night of the party, Julie answered the door wearing sweat pants and an old T-shirt. The house did not look ready for a party. I sighed, wishing I hadn't come, but had no excuse not to. Julie opened some wine, and then brought out a gigantic bowl of potato chips and some store-bought French onion dip. A few minutes later, she brought out a ten year old photograph of herself. She passed it around.

"Can you believe that I once raced in the marathon?" Julie asked. "I even had a good time."

"Running in a race was a good time?"

34

"Finishing time," she clarified. "It was under four hours."

The photograph is a shot of her coming across the finish line. She's wearing short-shorts and a skimpy mesh shirt. The marathon is in May – it's always phenomenally hot, someone usually dies of dehydration. She's extraordinarily fit. You can see that she's ecstatic to be finishing the race. After all those miles, anyone would be glad to be done.

I had been meaning to talk to Julie. The fact that she brings out these photographs only emphasizes her weight gain. It's hard to deny that ten years ago, 50 pounds lighter, she did look better. The photograph was passed around the circle, then someone put it on the coffee table next to the chips. Julie picked it up again and tried to circulate it. "This is what I used to look like," she said. "Wasn't I beautiful?"

"You certainly were," I say. "You were beautiful."

The other women were reporters at the newspaper. They had seen all the old photographs. Everyone in Pittsburgh has seen them.

I've noticed that middle age crisis in women usually manifests itself in a desire for weight loss. But all this talk and they take very little action. There's no battle cry. There's no running for the front lines trying to recapture youth in any way that would matter. They simply believe that if they could lose the excess pounds they'd be where they want to be. I admire men who are at least active, albeit destructive, in their disgust with the passing of time

"I should train for this year's marathon," Julie said.

"Can't," I say.

"I could," Julie says. "If I really set my mind to it, I could do it. I know I could."

"There is no marathon," I told her. "The mayor canceled it. No more funds."

"I thought the hospitals were going to save it," Julie said, though I sensed that she was relieved not to have to put her mind to a 26-mile road race.

"Hasn't happened yet," I said. It felt like I was gloating – reveling in giving others bad news about the city. "Doesn't look like it will."

"I'm sure something good will happen," Julie mused.

I kept my mouth shut. No one likes a gloomy soul.

We ate and waited. They talked office politics. They were good story- tellers but after awhile of not knowing who they were talking about, it got boring. The bowl emptied. Julie refilled it.

I liked these women. Most of them were like Julie, reporters for the newspaper. They were forceful and opinionated, bold and intelligent. I had called most of them after I was laid off. I don't know what I was looking for, but the advice we got was to circulate. "Let our situation be known, so that others could help."

They were union members and said it was regrettable that the city employees had never unionized. They gave me advice, most of which I took, but it didn't get me anywhere. One of them suggested I see someone – a therapist – I guess she sensed that I was somewhat fragile. I went. The therapist was a wonderful woman. She and I talked about everything – she was quick and funny – sarcastic without being condescending. I told her I made lists of people who had lost their jobs. Jimmy Carter, Margaret Thatcher, Napoleon, the Disney Guy etc. She added to the list. Knowing that others had also been made unemployed did little to lift my spirits and I stopped going because she said my reaction was normal and I didn't see paying $75.00 an hour to be normal even if I did enjoy our conversations.

Barbara arrived late. Over an hour, which seemed, at least to me, incredibly rude. We were there to meet her and she waltzed in like she was a Hollywood star coming down the red carpet. No apology or explanation; she just came in with this huge burst of energy, talking about how great she thought Pittsburgh was.

"It's amazing," she exclaimed.

Everyone laughed and she smiled broadly.

"Just amazing."

Julie offered her a glass of wine. It was hard to read Barbara's response. She obviously had things she wanted to say. Julie poured her some and handed the glass to Barbara.

"A real gem of a place," she continued.

"Certainly you're in the minority with those opinions," someone said. But it was nice to hear compliments about the city in which we lived. If she had left it at that, I might have believed her enthusiasm. But she kept gushing and after a while her talk seemed less than genuine.

"This place is a golden secret no one else knows about. I, for one, am thrilled to be here."

There are many things to admire about Pittsburgh. It's got beautiful homes – many with stained glass windows built at the turn of the last century. There was opulence here and the neighborhoods reflect times of golden plenty. It's hilly – the same topography as San Francisco. There are parks, plenty of green space. It's easy to get around. There's a bus system that works and plenty of downtown parking. You can go to a movie without waiting in line. There is a symphony and a ballet, an opera and some regional theater. There are two major universities and hospitals galore.

And still the city has been steadily shrinking since the 1970s. For a while everyone talked Renaissance. We were having a high tech boom, except that suddenly, though in retrospect it was really more steadily than suddenly, the city was 80 million dollars in debt. The public schools were a mess and the local police force was corrupt, the emergency medical workers had been cut, the firemen were getting pink slips. The mayor cut street cleaning and rodent control. The annual marathon was canceled and the downtown, after 5pm, looked like a ghost town.

"I am just really thrilled to be here," she said again, only this time she held out her arms as if embracing us.

I wondered for a few minutes if Barbara excelled at sarcasm. Maybe this was her idea of a break-the-ice-joke.

She had more of these.

"You've got to find me a man," she said. She did, I swear. She crossed her arms under her chest and demanded that we, a group of women she had never met, find her a man.

Pittsburgh had one of the country's oldest demographics, second only to Palm Beach County, Florida. The average age was 65. Between 1985-1995, there had been a 36% jump in the 85+ population, which didn't make sense. Older people don't move anywhere except Florida. These people weren't long time residents but newcomers. That was the one that stumped the mayor's office. How could that many people in their late 80s/early 90s, move to Pittsburgh? Did they take the bus? Did they come for the rain? It was growing too. The older demographics were forecasted to increase by 7% in the next decade – this was much higher than the national average.

There were very few young people, even fewer single people, living in the city. They counted them every other day. You wouldn't have wanted to live here if you weren't married. The chances of meeting a mate were lower than being killed by hot volcanic ash.

"I really need to find someone nice," she said.

A few of the women smiled as if they were just waiting to start the chore she had assigned them. I sneered.

"New city. New job. It's time I got myself a new man."

We were tired from the wine, bloated from the chips and dip. No one knew what to say so I spoke up. Someone had to break the awkward silence. "That'll be easy," I said. "There are dozens of men in this city." I didn't know why Barbara rubbed me the wrong way. Maybe it was her enthusiasm, her stylish black pants, or her haircut, which seemed incredibly cute.

"There are?" she asked and clapped her hands. Then she laughed. I had never heard anything quite like her laugh. It was deep in her throat and it went on way too long, like perhaps she was choking.

"You can have my husband," one of the woman offered. "I'm tired of him."

Julie was still looking at her old photographs. "Fifty pounds should be easy to lose. Don't lots of people do that in half a year?"

"They lose it and then they gain it right back," I said. "Gain the fifty back and then some."

"I wouldn't want to do that," Julie said. "I definitely wouldn't want to do that."

"I think I'll try and concentrate on someone who's single," Barbara announced.

"Single men? Under 65?" I said. "Oh, is that what you're looking for?"

"That's kind of what I had in mind."

"That'll be a bit tougher," I said. There was Allan, of course. Problematic, of course, seeing that he was mine and married.

The chips were gone. Julie, uninterested in talking about something other than her body, got up and refilled the bowl again.

Barbara stayed 47 minutes. She talked the entire time. She wasn't introduced to any of us. She didn't ask any of our names. She simply put down her glass and stood up.

"I'm so sorry," she said. "I have to go." In front of five women, she pulled the dramatic gesture of looking at her watch and then being totally surprised. She let out a bit of a squeal. "Oh dear. I really must fly."

I couldn't help myself. "Are you going to the airport?" I asked.

She looked puzzled, then laughed. It was a strange sound that morphed into something alien-like. Then in a flurry of *I'll-call-yous,* and *thank-yous,* and *see-you-soons,* she left.

"Pittsburgh? Tuesday night? 10pm?" I threw out. "Probably had a dentist appointment."

To my surprise the other women seemed to have liked her. They sympathized with her plight and seemed eager to help her. "It's hard to move to a new city."

"Especially this one," someone answered.

"Especially when you're single."

I considered my aversion to Barbara. It was her overly enthusiastic attitude that had rubbed me the wrong way. She liked things she hadn't experienced, didn't know. Maybe Joe was right. Maybe I was too negative. Maybe I was too bitter because of my job loss. I hated to think that my judgment was so affected by employment status. I tried to imagine myself after a long day at work, frantically trying to get everything done before coming to Julie's. I was pretty sure that my feelings for Barbara would be similar to what I was feeling. And yet I was in the minority. I had a quiet panic attack. It lasted several minutes. Steady there, I warned myself. You met someone you didn't like. It's not a big deal. That thought kept me steady and I drank another glass of wine. Things were okay. I could forget about Barbara. Let her enjoy Pittsburgh. Let her enjoy her new job. If she stayed long enough the mayor might even give her the key to the city. He was desperately seeking good public relations with the citizens of his bankrupt fiefdom.

Someone suggested ordering a pizza, but Julie said no. "I'm on a diet," she announced. "Pizzas are no longer welcome in my house."

That ended the party. We all went home.

I have to watch myself. I'm not as nice as I used to be. Joe blames it on my current job situation. I thought for a while it might be age, but now I blame it on others. I just don't meet the right kind of people. Barbara put me off. There was something odd about her. I wasn't thrilled with the idea of her being my neighbor.

In college it's easy to meet people. You walk out of your dorm room and there's someone in the hallway. You meet people outside of a lecture, meet friends of friends, it's all you do in college. Meet people. I had the most absurd friendships when I was in college.

Nowadays, I rarely meet anyone I'd like to talk to let alone share a transcontinental car trip with. There's Maggie, and her husband. Though I wouldn't want them both to be in the car with me. People have either become incredibly dull or my husband's right – losing my job has made me incredibly bitter.

A few weeks later Julie called to thank me for helping Barbara find the apartment. Julie's not one to waste time with these kinds of social gestures, so I knew she had something else she wanted to tell me.

"I emailed Barbara's sister the other day." Julie got to the point quickly enough. "She and Barbara no longer speak."

"Really?"

"Barbara never said a word about their fight," she said.

"Maybe she was embarrassed," I said, though Barbara did not strike me as the type.

"She talked like they were close. As if they had talked all the time," Julie said. "I don't think I misunderstood that part.

"It seems Barbara's estranged from her entire family," Julie told me. "She doesn't talk to any of them."

"None of them?"

"Not a one," she said. "Not anymore."

"That's very strange."

"You'll have to be nice to her," Julie says.

"Me?"

"Now that you're her neighbor and all.," Julie is multi-tasking; I hear the click of the computer keys.

"She's nice," Julie says. "You'll see. It will be fun to have someone like Barbara in the neighborhood."

"It will?" I ask.

"Trust me," Julie promises. She's typing like a mad woman. The keys click away. "You'll see."

I don't gloat, but this is not exactly what happened.

Chapter Three

I grew up in a house with a party line. We shared a phone with people we would never meet, and this sense of anonymity piqued my curiosity. The woman at the other house had several problems, all of which she talked about with her sister. I listened in. She was a great talker, with precise details and a great deal of anger about her lot in life. Her sister was either a good listener or a good sport; she rarely said much. She never told stories, but was there to listen, to ask the right questions, to give sympathy.

Then suddenly in the middle of a good story, the party-line woman would fall silent. She'd stop talking mid-sentence.

"Are you still there?" the sister would ask.

"What? Did you hear that?" the woman would demand and I knew she had heard something in our house.

"Maybe it's the doorbell. Are you expecting a package?" The sister had problems with her ears. She was always asking the woman to repeat herself. She never would have detected me hiding out on the other line.

"Is there someone on this phone? Hello. Hello." She knocked the phone on the counter and I put it away from my ear. "It's those kids," she'd tell her sister.

"What kids?" The sister was always confused. "What are you talking about?"

"On the party line."

"Can't you do something? I think it's against the law to listen to other people's private conversations." The sister did not know the law.

"Do you hear that?" the woman would shout into the phone. "I could get you arrested."

I covered the mouthpiece so the woman wouldn't hear my breathing.

"Get off the phone," she'd yell. She was adept at transferring her anger.

But I was stubborn. The only thing that got me off was my mother, who knew that too much quiet meant I was up to no good.

But my eavesdropping was entertaining and addictive.

I liked the woman's problems. I liked hearing how she discussed them. I liked the way she smoked. The way she exhaled on every other word. I could see the smoke streaming out of her nostrils and mouth like a dragon. I saw the ashes scattered about. She stubbed them out and a few minutes later I would hear the strike of the flint as she lit another one. She cooked while she talked. She chewed on carrots and tasted her stews. She burned her tongue – her speech becoming incomprehensible while she sucked on ice-cubes.

I learned that her son had run away. At first I thought he was a young kid but as I listened more, I came to understand that he was an adult man. He had been married in the Church. His running away was religious and I didn't find that aspect so interesting.

The woman's voice was low, gravelly. She coughed and complained. I liked the way she pitied herself.

"No one deserves these troubles," she would say. "And why He thinks I'm strong enough to handle it, is beyond me." Her voice changed and she addressed God directly. "I hope You're aware of my interest in You. I aim for You to hear my words."

I liked how she felt comfortable enough to speak to Him in such a pointed manner.

"Who can say?" The sister was casually sympathetic. I suspected she wasn't always listening as close as all that.

"I hope He's going to say," my party line woman's tone grew sharp. "I've got quite a number of questions for Him and I aim to get me some good answers." Then the voice inflection grew higher. "Quite a number of questions – things I've been dying to know for years now."

The sister was the dreamy one. "I never thought this would be it," she said. "You ever feel like getting on a bus and just letting it go where it takes you?"

"How could I?" Party-line woman was the realist. "Too many people need me."

"I guess so, but I still think of leaving," the sister said. "All the time."

The woman and her sister said the rosary together on Friday afternoons. It took half an hour and my mother hated when they did this. I thought it was a personal thing – she wasn't one for prayers and organized religion and didn't want it around her. She'd pick up the phone and hear the ritual of prayer. She would cough, then excuse herself. She'd wait three minutes, then pick up the phone again. "Excuse me," she'd say. "I need to make a call. It's not an emergency, but I would appreciate your promptness in allowing me this consideration."

This was how the phone company suggested we deal with a busy phone line. In those days people didn't use the phone very often. We were less busy. Less apt to cancel appointments, less likely to be late for dinner parties – the phone was for emergencies and my mother was a firm believer that one didn't waste one's time talking on it.

"Your kids listen to my conversations."

"Excuse me?" my mother said.

"They do," the woman bellowed. "I hear them. They're sneaky. Very sly. But I know what I hear. They're like mice in the wires."

"I'm sure they have better things to do with their time."

My brother lived outdoors. He hung around with a group of hoodlums who lived on our block – a posse of five bad boys.

They didn't waste their time with the telephone. When one of them wanted to talk to another of their friends, he walked to their house, banged open the mail slot in the front door and shouted the kid's name into the house. In those days, only grown ups used doorbells and phones to communicate.

If the woman was right, and someone was listening, it had to be me. My mother was aware that I was not exactly a truthful child; I lied when it suited me.

"Don't listen to other people's conversations," my mother scolded.

"Why would I do that?"

"I hope you wouldn't," she would warn. "It's not polite. People have a right to their privacy. Besides, why would you want to listen? That crazy woman goes on and on. You don't know her. Why would you care about her troubles?"

"I don't," I promised. I looked at her with my jaw hanging open in disgust as if what she was suggesting was impossible.

"I wouldn't think so," my mother said. She was testing me.

"I have better things to do with my time," I said. These were her words. I was just repeating them back. She recognized her own speech patterns and smiled.

"You have your own problems," my mother said.

"What problems?" I wasn't aware that I had problems.

"The ones right here in front of you," she snapped. "The ones in your own house." She didn't elaborate, but if she had I would have told her that the fights she and my father had were dull as watching the dishes dry. No one would care to listen to them. They argued money – real dollars and cents and future. It even bored them. Later when they divorced my brother and I did not have to ask why.

Gradually the party lines went away and there was only the dial tone when I picked up the phone. We had our own line.

One of my Allan fantasies involves a party line. I pick up my phone and he's on the line. He's talking. Talking in that deep, rich, heavy accent. It takes my breath away and he pauses. "Hello. Who's there?"

He's talking to his friend, a university friend, who often comes to the States on business. They're having a manly conversation, talking about sports and politics. There is a sexual subtext to their entire conversation – lots of jokes and laughs. And then Allan says something about me.

"Caroline?" the friend asks. "Is that the neighbor you're always talking about?"

"Lovely," Allan says. "She's just lovely. Funny and witty. Quick with a joke and an opinion. Always something interesting. You have to meet her. I hate to say it, but I think I'm in love."

Bliss. I sigh.

He stops. "Is someone there?" he asks, but I've had practice at this. I clam up and breathe through my nose away from the phone.

"One of these days you're going to have to do something," the friend instructs Allan.

"But what?" And then like the party-line woman, his voice becomes different. "Tell me what I should do," he pleads. "Help me. I'm hopelessly in love!"

I'm here, I want to tell him. I'm here for you. I have been for some time. Open your eyes. Don't ignore me. Don't waste this time. Here I am.

Allan was born and raised in the Kingdom of Fife in Scotland. I've read everything the Scottish Tourist Board has to say about the region. Since the night of the barbecue I've collected a shoebox of information on Scotland, on civil engineers, and on men named Allan.

I ordered a calendar that highlights a different photograph of Scotland every month. I put it in the kitchen. Now

I look at landscapes of rolling hills and charming cobblestone streets and think of Allan being there. These photographs play a role in my daydreams. I see the two of us picnicking on the hillside. I see us having dinner at the quaint restaurant on a corner in Edinburgh.

I also ordered a tablecloth. Lace. It was delicate, unlike anything else I own. It looked more Irish than Scottish, not that I'm an expert, but I sent it back. They gave me a credit for another purchase with the company. I'm still contemplating my next procurement.

I say his name.

I make dinner reservations in his name, then call back later to cancel.

At the drug store the other day, I turned to the woman, who was also buying shaving cream and said, "Allan is always running out of this stuff."

I misjudged her age. She was a teenager and not overly interested in my imaginary lover's medicine cabinet. I smiled and put the shaving cream in my little red basket. I had the good sense to ditch it in the next aisle. I tucked it behind a gigantic box of envelopes and left the store without buying a thing.

The things that I now know! The Internet is a wonderful tool. I spent an enormous amount of time googling and searching and finding articles that relate to the ones I'm reading. I've collected dozens of facts and figures in my pursuit of Allan.

According to the Oxford University's Human Reproduction magazine, Scottish men are the most sexually potent men in the entire world. They've tested and discovered that men from Edinburgh have incredibly mobile sperm.

I don't yet know how I will share this information with Allan. Or even if I should.

It's not the end to my knowledge. I know for instance that Scots were the tallest race in Europe around the turn of 20th century, but that the devastating loss of lives in World War 1 changed that statistic. The average height of men is nine inches less than it was a century ago.

I know that James Watt invented the steam engine, John Boyd Dunlop the bicycle tire, and Alexander Fleming penicillin. I know the history of the country – the ferociously complicated story of Mary Queen of Scots who was beheaded while hiding her Scottish terrier under her skirts. I know about Braveheart William Wallace. I know what haggis is. I'm aware that Robert Burns drank too much and died at the age of thirty-seven. I know that other famous Scotsmen include Alexander Graham Bell, who invented the telephone, Sir Arthur Conan Doyle who invented Sherlock Holmes, Kirkpatrick Macmillan who invented the bicycle, and Andrew Carnegie who invented Pittsburgh.

In the days of Pangaea, Scotland was a separate landmass from England. They collided millions of years ago and have been together ever since.

I like this as a metaphor.

Allan and I could collide – a simple act of fate.

There must be ginkgo trees in Scotland, but I've found no data to support my supposition and yet don't hesitate on this belief. I subscribe to a ginkgo newsletter service. Chat rooms with people interested in the ginkgo trees. Their primary focus is art – paintings and such – but they concern themselves with other aspects of the trees. I sign up to receive weekly E-mails updating me on any newsworthy item that may come across their desk. I wait anxiously. And remind myself to ask about ginkgo trees in northern Europe.

Despite my misgivings about her rather flighty personality and her wicked witch laugh, Barbara moved into the neighborhood. It was July and had rained every day for more than a week. There was a general restlessness as everyone waited for the weather to break. Jane was stubborn. She was up in her tree every day, seemingly unaware or unconcerned about getting wet. I was too – stubborn in my own way. My obsession with

Allan was new and therefore full of possibilities. I was in my giddy stage, not yet sick of my own longings.

A gigantic moving van came and unloaded all morning – it seemed a lot of furniture for a single woman. I counted at least three couches. How much lying around could one woman do?

Two days later, she came over carrying a huge garbage bag. She thrust it into my hand and told me that my boys could have these things.

"What are they?" It was heavy.

"Things I'm sure they can use."

I looked inside and smelled wet wool.

"No thanks," I tried.

"I insist," she said.

"Why?" I asked. I set it down.

Then she told me she was going to a have a get-together at her place. "I want the chance to meet everyone," she said.

"Great," I said, not meaning a thing I said. She asked me to call some people and invite them. "You're in charge of the guest list. Okay Caroline?" She had a bossy way of doing things like she had been a supervisor too long. I used to work with a woman who started every sentence with, "would you mind doing me a favor?" Except they weren't favors. They were work she wanted done. She was hated by all and we imitated her and mocked her incessantly. She moved up in the city offices and now works for a huge law firm in Washington D.C. that specializes in big business policies. I'm sure her rhetoric hasn't changed.

Barbara reminded me of this woman.

I frowned. "I don't know your friends, do I?"

"I'll make friends with whomever you invite," she said. "Invite lots of men."

I sat at the doorway reconsidering the idea of a party. I was a month into my fascination with Allan and a party was just what I needed. We had met at a neighbor function, why not organize another for us to continue our relationship?

"Okay," I said. "No problem." I would have to wear something nice. Not fancy. That would be out of place, but something that looked good on me. My mind raced. We were so strong at the barbecue, but the summer seemed to be slipping by without us getting together as often as I liked.

"They don't all have to be neighbors," Barbara said. "You can call your other friends – people who live on other streets."

"We'll start with the neighbors," I said. "It'll be great."

Barbara was thinking of a Sunday afternoon get-together, but I said early evening was better. "You don't want to interfere with the golf games."

"Do people play golf in Pittsburgh?"

"Oh yes," I said. "All the good guys golf."

Calling people was better than the job Barbara gave Maggie – Maggie was in charge of the food.

"The food?" I asked her. "What does that mean?"

"She wants me to cook," Maggie said. She was not in the least upset by Barbara's boldness.

"Everything?" I asked.

"I guess so," Maggie said. "Barbara's a little pressed for time that day."

"Then change the day of the party," I suggested, but didn't want that. Allan was coming to the party. He had told me himself that he was free that night. If we changed the date, I might lose him to other commitments. "Or call a caterer. Pittsburgh does have catering services."

"Barbara's new to the area," Maggie said. "Maybe we should have thought to give her a party. It's nice to feel welcomed."

"Don't tell me you're feeling guilty," I said.

"I am, just a bit," Maggie admitted.

"You're too nice," I said. "Way, way too nice." I told her she was going to get in trouble one of these days.

51

"That's what Allan says," she nodded.

Passionate minds belong together. But see what I mean about Maggie? How could you hurt her? She was cooking food for someone else's party. For all I knew, she was probably going to tidy up Barbara's apartment beforehand. It would be cruel to disturb Maggie's life.

Karen was in charge of the wine. I gave Barbara credit for that. She knew what her neighbors did best and wasn't afraid to get an expert. It would be a good party.

Barbara's apartment was tastefully decorated. A sort of American southwest theme going with muted colors and coyotes. She had books and prints. Lots of black and white photographs of cacti and thin leafless trees. There were no family photographs or any evidence of a family, though I knew she had family nearby. Someone had said that her parents lived in Meadville, only 90 miles north, so maybe she didn't feel the need to show them in her apartment. There were also no pictures of old friends or siblings. Her dining room was done in all white. White slipcovers, white tablecloths, white wallpaper, white curtains. It looked like some movie set that would be used to show that the tenants were out of town. Barbara instructed us to stay out of this room. "Not in use today," she said and cackled.

That was not a joke. But she continued to hoot at her words as she gave mini-tours of the apartment. I opted out. I would snoop on my own when I felt the urge.

Maggie's trays were artistically crafted, like miniature sculptures. Some of the guests applauded when she carried them to the table.

"You really should open up a restaurant," Greg told her.

"No she shouldn't." Here was Allan carrying up the extra food. "Don't give her any ideas."

Allan went into the kitchen. I followed. He set the trays down, then went out for more.

I followed. "Need some help?"

"You've got a free hand?" he asked.

"Two," I said, and showed him.

"Brilliant." He flashed me a big smile – all white teeth – his tongue coming over them quickly, then once again. I swooned.

I loved this party.

Karen overdid it with the wine. She bought way too much. I applauded the excess. She had made a special trip to the state store in Aspinwall that sells very good American Zinfandels. Allan complimented her on the selection.

"Exceptional," Allan told her. "Finally something good produced in the United States." He had wine glasses on a tray. I had an excuse to go over to him.

"The Californias have been terrific the last decade," Karen said.

"I still hesitate to spend much on something from California," Allan said.

"You're drowning yourself in old prejudices," Karen said.

"Granted," Allan laughed. "Still, habits are hard to break."

He filled my glass. I wanted to talk metaphors with him, but knew that was overstepping.

"Though I'm not sure what we're celebrating," Karen said, swilling the wine in her glass.

I could think of a few things – Allan. We could start there.

"What's got you so pessimistic?" Allan asked her.

"Are you kidding?" she asked. "You ever look out your window?"

"Not often," Allan said.

There went any hope that he was staring up the street looking for me.

"You see how they're raping the empty lot?"

"You lost that battle," Allan agreed. "Big time."

53

"That's an understatement," Karen said. "Those people are criminals. They're going to ruin the integrity and beauty of the neighborhood. Everything we were afraid of."

I didn't want to talk about the empty lot. Allan was wearing jeans and a black t-shirt that wasn't tucked in. His hair was wet at the ends and maybe because of the shirt, maybe because of his tanned face, it looked even more romantically dark – if that's possible. I was going to tell him how good he looked just as soon as I could think of a way to do to it without him thinking me insane.

Barbara, perhaps sensing that we were going to talk food and drink all night, clapped her hands and told us that the party was a theme party.

Everyone groaned.

"No. No. No. It's going to be fun," Barbara told us. "Look at me. Do I look like the kind of woman who would throw a boring party?"

She was wearing a light blue shirt with khaki-colored Capri's. She did look a bit dull, like a private school kid dressed in the uniforms everyone wears these days.

Five-year olds needed planned entertainment. Adults were happy with food and wine and gossip. I hoped we weren't going to play games. I checked under my appetizer plate. I didn't see any special numbers or color codes.

"This party is about love," Barbara said. "We're going to tell the story of how we met our husbands or if you have no husband, and some of us don't, than we'll tell about the first time we fell in love."

I wasn't the only one who groaned, but Barbara would hear none of our protests. She clapped her hands some more and told us that it was going to be fun.

Joe's cell phone rang. He excused himself, then came back into the room and gave me some sort of hand signal. "I'll be back," he promised.

"No rush," I said. "Do what you have to do." I felt better that he was leaving. It left me without a witness to my lust.

Barbara asked Karen to go first.

"How I met Greg?" Karen said.

"Tell us how you fell in love with him."

"It was years ago," Karen said. "I don't remember."

Maggie encouraged her. "Of course you do. You're just being shy. Everyone remembers the first kiss of love."

She's right about that – an early summer barbecue, fireflies in the evening light, two lawn chairs set off to one corner, the hush of concerned neighbors trying to save an empty lot. A man, wet from a dip in the pool. Wine. Absent husband. Who could ever forget?

"I'm not shy," Karen said. She had obviously sampled her product before bringing it over. Her teeth were stained. Maybe it was a permanent thing. She did drink a lot.

She went ahead in great detail, but I didn't think I had to hear this. I leaned forward and busied myself with the appetizer tray. Maggie had stuffed olives with anchovies and bits of red pepper, some with feta cheese.

I looked around the room counting how many times we would have to hear these stories, trying to think how long it would all take. Maggie was sitting off to the side, looking distracted and I realized that I wanted to hear how she and Allan had met. I knew I couldn't change history, but I was curious how the two of them had gotten together. A quick fantasy – me as a time traveler, moving back over the years to their first encounter. Me replacing Maggie. Me now with Allan. Me with him always.

"Maggie's next," I called out.

"I'm not finished," Karen said. "He drove me down this dirt road. My parents would have killed me had they known where I was. I mean this man worked for my father. But I was a flirt. Even then. At sixteen."

"I think we can figure out where this ends up," I said. "Let Maggie talk."

For once Barbara agreed with me.

"Next," she said. Again with the clapping. "Maggie, you go."

"I don't think it's as exciting as Karen's story," Maggie protested.

I hadn't realized that Karen's tale had been captivating or even the least bit interesting.

"Maybe you should let Allan tell the story," Barbara said. She was a flirt. She was perched on the ottoman, doing something strange with her hands. I guess she was being coy or cute, deliberately upbeat. The neighbors were polite, but I don't think anyone would have rated the party as a good time.

"That's a great idea," Maggie said. "Why don't you tell everyone how we met?"

"Fine," Allan said. He was patting his stomach, hand under the shirt and he lifted the material just a bit and I saw the dark hairs on his stomach.

"Go ahead," Barbara said.

"All right," Allan said. He dropped his hand from his stomach. His shirt fell back into place, hiding the dark tangles. I closed my eyes and sipped my wine. He paused and sipped his wine. Both of us drinking at exactly the same time; this must have meant something in the world of karmic collisions. "I haven't a clue," he said. "I haven't the foggiest notion of how I met Maggie."

"You don't remember?" Barbara asked as if shocked. "Of course you do. How could you forget meeting someone as wonderful as Maggie?"

"I'll tell the story," Maggie said. "I remember it very clearly. Very clearly. Almost as if it happened yesterday."

As Maggie talked, I tried to plant myself into her story; I was thinking Scotland, but she was half a world away.

"I was selling flowers," she said. "In Thailand." Everything Maggie did was intriguing – I should have known she hadn't met Allan in a bar. Maybe I wasn't so gung-ho to hear this.

"We were in a small village. By the seaside. I had gone to the Far East with my flakey boyfriend who immediately left me for a very young, very sexy Australian." Maggie laughed at her own story. "I was dripping with self-pity and an inability to decide what I should do next. I was pathetic."

It was hard to imagine Maggie as pathetic.

"And then Allan came in and swept you off your feet?" Karen asked. "How romantic."

Maggie smiled. Even now she radiated beauty. "I loved Thailand. It's a beautiful mysterious place. I didn't think I had to leave just because I was heartbroken. So I stayed on. Alone. I lived in a hut twenty yards from the ocean. I surfed. I had friends. Half the world was traveling then. All of them seemed to stop in Thailand."

"Half the world was smoking pot back then," Allan said. "They stopped in Thailand for their supplies."

"No fair," Maggie shook her head. "You don't remember this.

"We fished, we swam, we ate like natives living off the land and occasionally when I needed money, I worked for the local flower vendors. They liked the foreign girls to sell flowers. I called out to the British tourists who thought it strange and exotic for an American to be working in a seaside village in the middle of nowhere."

I could see it; a younger Maggie, all those blond curls, her pug nose, and her sky blue eyes. At twenty, I'm sure her skin must have been golden brown. She was probably wearing something flowing, a white dress down to her ankles, something that clung to her slim figure.

"Allan was buying flowers?" I asked. I turned to Allan who was standing up near the bookcase scanning the books as if

57

looking for something to read. He turned when he heard his name and looked over at me. He raised his eyebrows, and then shook his head. "Hardly."

"Let her tell the story." Barbara told me to be quiet. She was not exactly a polite hostess. Guests are allowed to interact at social functions.

"Allan was on the beach," Maggie said. "Picking up girls. He was good at that back then."

"It's good to know that not everything changes," I said. My comment was horribly inappropriate. Barbara thought me funny. She laughed for three minutes at my comment. I kicked myself mentally. Watch what you say, I scolded my tongue.

"Was she beautiful?" Karen asked Allan.

Allan had finished perusing the books. "She was young," he said. If he weren't Scottish, you might have thought he needed to be reprimanded, but people seemed to find everything he said humorous. Everyone that is, except Maggie, who looked at her shoes.

I felt a flicker of tension cross the room – a glint of hostility passing between the two of them.

I can't say I was disappointed.

But Allan must have heard his tone and he seemed to reconsider his statement and added more. This time he went for humor. "I married Maggie because she appreciates whisky and has a strong aversion to golf. I knew I could have some time away from her."

Maggie placed an olive pit into a cocktail napkin, carefully folding it into smaller and smaller pieces. When she spoke, it was quietly as if it wasn't intended for the entire party. "That's right," she said. "That's why he married me. Because I love whisky and hate golf. It's a tough combination to find in a woman." She got up and took the trays into the kitchen.

I was thrown – at Karen and Greg's barbecue, Allan had made it sound like I was special for not liking golf – now his wife also didn't like golf. My special status melted.

"Anyone for dominoes?" I said. I saw a box on the bookshelf – an odd game – at least, in my mind, for a single woman. Did she set them up at night, making intricate patterns only to knock them down, watching them collapse one by one?

To my surprise everyone wanted to continue with the stories. They were having fun. It threw me for a minute – I was sure everyone was just being polite. I was startled to see that they were actually enjoying themselves.

"What about you Caroline?" Karen asked. "Why don't you tell us how you met Joe?"

I didn't want to talk about Joe, not with Allan in the room. He had refilled his wine glass and gone back to the bookcase. I hoped he was looking at me. I had dressed carefully for the party. I had a tube of lipstick in my pocket – I would reapply it when I thought I needed more color in my cheeks.

"It wasn't very interesting," I said. But even my cynical self had to admit that no matter how mundane our initial meeting had been – we were set up by friends who thought we would be perfect together – it had been romantic. In a Pittsburgh sort of way. Shortly after we met, Joe had informed me that I was exactly the kind of woman he wanted to marry. He called me perfect. "You've got everything." And that's how I felt about him.

"I'm sure it was thrilling," Allan said. "Joe doesn't seem like the sort for a boring love story." Scottish accents do sound sarcastic.

"We didn't meet in Thailand," I said. "There wasn't a beach and no one was selling flowers."

"I can't see Joe selling flowers in his bathing trunks," Karen said.

I wanted the party to break up into groups. This one big discussion thing was wearying. I wanted to go over and be sarcastic with Allan, even if it was at my expense.

But Barbara had had enough of listening to these tales of love. "It's my turn," she announced.

It was her party so no one pointed out that it might be difficult to tell how she met her husband when she didn't have one.

"I once put an ad in a personals column," she announced. "In Boston."

"A classified?" someone asked at the same time Karen was asking "You did what?"

"I put an ad in the personals," Barbara explained. "So I could meet a man. Boston was a friendly town. Lots of nice men walking around. I was going to meet a good man. Instead let me tell you about the men I did meet."

She paused. "The one who was most in love with me wore green lederhosen." She put up her two fingers and nodded her head several times. "I swear – " She laughed at her own story. "I never felt them, but I think they were made of rubber. It wasn't cultural. He was from Worcester. He didn't speak any foreign languages. This was a fashion decision on his part. He wore them everywhere. To the symphony, to the opera. He wasn't afraid to wear them to a fancy restaurant. I wanted to know, but was afraid to ask if he wore them to work."

She was laughing so hard, she had to stop talking.

"He was a judge," she screeched. "So he might have worn them under his robes."

"Oh my," Karen said. "That's so funny."

There were more stories about horribly inappropriate men. Men who wore toupees, men who were accompanied by their mothers, men who cried in the subway, men who borrowed money, men who sang to her in public restaurants. All of them had been madly in love with Barbara. All of them had been disappointed when she told them there would be no more dates.

I wasn't fooled. She had been planning to tell us this tale of her personal ad. It had the feel of a practiced story.

It was funny. If you like that 'miserable men, poor me' sort of saga. My neighbors did. They were wildly entertained.

I finished my wine and stood up. Allan motioned me over.

I scurried.

"I'm going for a cigarette," he said. "You want to come?"

"Sure," I said.

We went down the steps.

I had taken up smoking – a habit I had never really had, but I had dabbled in when I was in college. It was a way to be with Allan. He offered me a cigarette and I put it to my mouth and waited for him to light it.

"Sorry," he said, when he realized that I was waiting. He had lit his. He handed me the pack of matches, which became a missed opportunity for him to put his head and hands near my face.

We walked down the street together. There was something pleasant about the smell of the cigarette in the summer air. It reminded me of campfires. I liked the smell better than smoking, but had no choice. Joe was surprised by my new habit. "It's not healthy," he said.

"You're kidding?" I asked. "I hadn't heard that before."

"Visit the VA one afternoon," he advised. "Those guys will make you quit."

"I don't smoke that often," I said.

"Then why bother doing it at all?" he asked.

The reason seemed perfectly clear to me. Allan and I got to the end of the block and turned up towards the women's college on the hill.

"What happened to Joe?" Allan asked.

I'm not sure why he was so steadfast on talking about Joe.

"It must have been an emergency over at the hospital," I said. "Either that or he didn't want to reveal how he lost his virginity to a roomful of strangers."

Allan kind of snorted.

I jumped right in. "She's awful isn't she?"

"Who?"

"Barbara." I stated what I assumed to be the obvious.

"She's not so bad."

"She's not?" In my fantasy world, he always agrees with me. It took me a moment to adjust to reality.

"She's kooky, but it's kind of refreshing," he said.

I didn't like this attention he was giving to Barbara. "Refreshing?"

"I don't think Barbara is worried about what others think of her," Allan said. "Not many women, especially women her age, are like that."

I looked at him. He had his head back blowing smoke out of his mouth like a dragon might. Had he meant that for me? Did he think I cared what people thought?

At that moment, I saw Joe, coming down the street with our dog Spot, who was sniffing the ground furiously as if she had been trained for hunting, straining the leash. I vowed to get rid of that dog.

"So is this the emergency?" Allan asked

Joe laughed.

"Did you go to the hospital?" I asked. "Did someone really call?"

"Just my muse," he said.

"Your muse?" Allan asked.

The warmth of the last few minutes was fleeting. I wished I could make Joe my brother – just for the rest of that day.

"That's right," Joe said.

"You are so bad." He made up the phone call. It wasn't the first time. The book had consumed him.

He looked down at the dog. Spot looked up at him, her tail wagging happily.

"Guilty," Joe confessed. "I'm guilty of being a bad neighbor. I hope Barbara wasn't offended. There's absolutely no time in the day. The weekend is so short. It's the only time that I have to work. I'm sorry I left," Joe said, but he wasn't. Ever since he started writing his book, he didn't care about being social. He read, he wrote, he made all kinds of notes for his book. We only went to movies because he thought I wanted to go. I only went because I thought it was good for us to get out together every once in a while. It also gave the boys a chance to be alone in the house – something they had hinted to us that they valued. Maybe even more than money.

"So tell me what was revealed," Joe said.

I didn't want to talk about love with my husband and my fantasy lover. It wasn't a comfortable situation.

"We didn't make it all the way around the room," Allan said. "Some of us were forced to abstain." He paused. "From storytelling, that is."

"Next time," Joe promised. "Next time I won't leave so early."

"I hope there's not a next time," I said. "I think that's enough of first love stories."

Allan was interested in Joe's novel. "What's this about a book?" he asked. I noticed he had put out the cigarette. Most people find it extremely uncomfortable to smoke in front of physicians.

Joe nodded. "I'm writing a book, if you can believe it."

"Is that right?" Allan asked. "Literary genius and a doctor? Quite a combination."

"He's writing a mystery novel," I say. I realize my tone was a bit disparaging. I'm not sure mystery writers are in the same category as literary geniuses.

Allan was enthusiastic. "That's fantastic. Who gets killed?"

"The wife," Joe said. The two of them thought this was very funny.

"Is there a butler?" Allan asked.

"No butlers, no maids, no chauffeurs. There's not a servant in sight."

"How do you get rid of her?" Allan asked.

"I strangle her. In the garage while she is putting away the lawn chairs. A rainstorm comes, which is why the husband doesn't realize she's missing right away."

This was a new detail. I hadn't read the part about the rainstorm. I wasn't sure why rain would delay a husband realizing his wife had gone missing, but I'm sure he had his reasons.

"I'm intrigued with books where the wives get themselves killed," Allan said.

"It's like making a jigsaw puzzle," Joe explained. "You have to have all the pieces laid out before you can go forward. It's incredibly difficult."

The two of them talked police procedures for several minutes. I hung around, feeling left out, but hoping perhaps that Joe would get a real call on his beeper.

Instead the three of us walked back. Joe was animated and excited that someone was interested in his novel.

I would not have ended that evening with the three of us walking down the street, but that's what happened.

Maggie came by the next day with Tupperware containers full of leftovers. "My girls are vegans now. They won't eat any of this," she explained, setting it all out on the counter. "I thought your boys would like the corned beef and chicken legs. They're fresh – everything from Whole Foods."

"They'll eat anything," I said. "Plastic included."

Even her leftovers were stylishly decorated.

"You did too much," I told her. I offered her iced tea and invited her to sit on the back porch. I thought it would be great if we could sit down and talk about her marriage. I wasn't wishing her ill will; I couldn't, but it would have been nice to hear that there were problems, things I should have known about. I wanted to hear more about the tension that at least to me had been so obvious at Barbara's. But she steered clear of her marital woes and talked about the party.

"It was nice, wasn't it?"

"If it was, it was thanks to you," I said. "You did everything."

"I don't mind doing parties," she said and shrugged as if all that work had been easy.

"That story she told was so crazy, wasn't it?" Maggie asked.

Say what you want about Barbara, the story she told was awful.

"It wasn't fun. Not at all," I said. "It was long and boring and really awkward. It was like a lecture on Barbara's life."

I chomped on my ice. It hit a cavity and I felt the shock follow the nerve up my face.

"I think she's funny."

I could easily alienate all my friends with my bold, negative opinions. I didn't want to lose Maggie. She was the one person I knew who could actually carry on a conversation. I'm sure we could have been much better friends if only I wasn't lusting after her husband.

"I guess she's okay," I relented. "If you like that sort of thing."

We could hear the neighborhood dogs barking. Spot went to the front door, her dog tags jingling against her collar. A minute later she joined in the chorus.

"Your problem is that you're too nice," I said.

"I'm not nice," Maggie said. "I'm tolerant. I have patience. In fact maybe that's my problem. I should learn to be intolerant."

"That would be interesting to see," I said. "Who would you attack first?"

Maybe this was her way of talking about the problems in her marriage. Yesterday's display wasn't just jovial banter. He

65

had not waited for her to clean up, nor had he offered to help her carry the trays and leftovers home.

Maggie picked up a sponge and wiped down the end table between our two chairs. Her gesture wasn't a reprimand or a critique and I didn't interpret it as such.

"I feel sorry for her," Maggie said. We were back to talking about Barbara.

"Why?"

"I'm not sure," Maggie shrugged.

"Because she once dated a guy who wore lederhosen?" I didn't even know what lederhosen were. I guessed it was leather. Leather shorts, leather overalls? Maybe they had been cute. Maybe they were even green. I'm sure I dated men who wore worse.

"Because she obviously felt the need to tell us that she had dated a lot."

"Isn't that bragging?" I asked. I couldn't feel sorry for Barbara. She didn't inspire this emotion at all.

"She wanted us to know that men had once loved her."

"Would that change our opinion of her?" I asked. It hadn't changed mine.

"People want others to know that they're loved," Maggie said. "Life is lonely. A single woman, someone with Barbara's personality, has it tough. I don't think marriage is in her future."

Leave it to Maggie to interpret the wacky conversation with some deep understanding of another's pathos.

"You think she's lonely?" I asked.

"I'm sure she is," Maggie said. "Wouldn't you be?"

I considered the question. "I might be. But there are days when I'd like a break from all this."

"You wouldn't want to be alone all the time," Maggie tells me. "That would be dreadful."

"She could get a dog."

"That never really helps, does it?" Maggie said.

"People swear by it," I said.

"But honestly. How could a pet help a lonely heart?"

Maggie carried our ice tea glasses into the kitchen and rinsed them in the sink.

Barbara didn't want a dog. She wanted a man. And she had this crazy notion that I could help her.

"You're from this city," she told me. I've told her a zillion times that Joe and I are both from New York, but she forgot this fact. Her attitude on the greatness of Pittsburgh was waning. You could hear it in her voice. "You must know lots of men."

I considered the people I knew. At least half of them were male.

"You worked in city government. Isn't that all men?"

"There were a lot of men," I said. And then I defined for her the word – yinzer. Yinzers as in steak-fed, Steelers-loving home boys who consider crossing a bridge out of their neighborhood world travel.

I worked with a lot of yinzers. They wouldn't like Barbara. She's too skinny. She doesn't watch football. She's not local. She's not their type. I tried to tell her that this was a good thing. "Yinzer. A form of 'you guys' as in *yinz want to go drink a beer with me?*" This was the local offering in males. It wasn't what she was looking for. You had to be from here to want that.

She got Joe to set her up with one of the emergency room residents. They appear from far and wide every July so he didn't know any of them that well. The one he brought to dinner was polite and good-looking. He played basketball with the boys, then Joe went out and said something to him. He went into the living room and sat across from Barbara.

When I went in a few minutes later, Barbara was talking about the years she had spent as a stand-up comedian.

"I was the victim of the writer's strike," she told him.

I had heard this story before so I planted myself in the kitchen and gave way too much care to the rosemary and thyme-roasted potatoes. Joe, I noticed, was overly attentive to the fish he was grilling.

"Do you need any help out there?" I came to the back door.

"I'm fine." He had been standing with his back to the grill.

The grill was hot; I could see the red heat from the window. The boys were still playing basketball.

From the dining room, it was still possible to hear Barbara telling her story of a failed comic career.

She had worked in a comedy club in Cambridge doing opening acts for Tracey Ullman. It was the best time in her life, the most exciting, the most thrilling, the closest she ever came to fame. Three weeks later, the Writers' Guild of America went on strike.

"It was a living nightmare," she explained. Her descriptions of the event were exactly as they were the first two times I heard this story. Her words are very practiced, bordering on memorized. I had this image of Barbara practicing her lines in front of her bedroom mirror. She had very strong diction; she enunciated her words, stressing each syllable.

"Anyone in comedy would have been insanely jealous of my gig. Then boom." She smacks her hands together. "Like that, it was all over."

In solidarity for the writers in Hollywood, comedians across the country supported the strike and they refused to go on stage.

"Three weeks was the extent of my career. Three weeks of bliss and then nothing." She flipped her hands over and held them out flat. "No more comedy. No more funny girl."

There were some holes in that story. I couldn't believe that a Hollywood writer's strike would have any influence over a comedy club in Boston. Especially for someone of Barbara's stature. Who would have cared if she performed?

"Tracey Ullman was so nice," Barbara said. "She invited us to her house in London where she thought we could find work. Some of the comedians went over, but I had other commitments."

"What did you do?" the resident asked.

"What could I do?" Barbara lamented. "I had no choice, but to quit. It was a very short career."

"How long was the strike?"

"Endless," she sighed. "Don't you remember it?"

I didn't. Neither did the resident. Barbara seemed surprised. "I find that hard to believe," she said. "Television was nearly blacked out. All they had were bad reruns. Old episodes of everything."

I could see Barbara on stage. I could see her laughing at her own jokes. She probably talked about the lederhosen date.

The resident was polite and cute enough. He seemed too young for Barbara. Too young and too involved in his work. He talked to Joe, asking him a dozen questions, telling him stories of the patients that had come into the emergency room the night before.

The guy left before I served coffee. He said he was beeped by the hospital, but later when I asked Joe if he believed the emergency call, he shrugged.

"It's possible," he told me.

"Do you believe him?"

"But it's also possible that he made it up."

"I don't think he enjoyed himself."

"Barbara's a tough one," he said. "She's the kind of woman who looks better on paper."

"I'd like her on paper too," I said. Joe was the only one who felt my apprehension about Barbara. I appreciated his negative feelings on her.

Joe had some papers on his lap. He looked drained, but he had his pencil out ready to read what he had written that afternoon. I felt another wave of guilt for my thoughts about Allan. I feigned interest in the book.

"Do they have any more suspects?"

"I'm not sure," he said. "I'm adding all these plot lines and I'm making all these changes. It's difficult to keep track of everything. This is harder than I thought. Much harder."

"I bet," I said.

"I have a confession to make," Joe said.

"You do?" For a few seconds I had this unbelievable fright that he was going to tell me he was having an affair. That certainly would have complicated things. "What is it?"

"The resident," he said. "He's married. His wife is doing a residency in Baltimore. I invited him to dinner and then asked if he was with someone. He seemed so happy to have a dinner invitation that I couldn't take it back. I told him to come and just go along with everything. I told him he could leave right after dinner." Joe's chair creaked as he swung back and forth in it. "Are you mad?" Joe asked.

I wasn't invested in Barbara's matchmaking and didn't really care about the fake blind date. "Not at all." I got into bed.

"Really?" he asked.

"Really," I replied. He had lied to me. I didn't have any reason to feel guilty. We all make mistakes. Little errors in judgment.

"Is everything okay, Caroline?"

I turned over to face my nightstand. "Why?"

The sheets had just been washed and the smell of detergent was strong.

"You don't seem happy,"

Joe and I have known each other so long and have talked about so many things. So many emotions have passed between us that I almost told him the reason for my melancholy.

"You know you don't have to work."

"Financially, you mean?" I sat up.

"I know you want to work, of course," he said. "But not having a job shouldn't make you this unhappy."

"I don't want a new job," I said. Like most people I hadn't been hysterically happy in my job, but I hadn't planned on losing it. I had always wanted to work for local government. I had thought we were doing good things for the city. I was an idealist – I thought our decisions mattered and though I knew people mocked us, I thought they also respected us. "I wish I had never lost mine."

"I understand that," he says.

"You don't know what it feels like," I told him, but I wasn't sure what I was talking about.

"I know," he said. "I don't."

I had to stop talking about my lost job. It wasn't the reason for my funk and I couldn't let him think it was. That wasn't fair. I was having fantasies about a man who lived four doors down. But I couldn't sabotage my marriage simply because I spent so much of my free time in dreamland.

"I'm fine," I said.

He followed me into the bathroom. He picked up his toothbrush the same time I picked up mine. I handed him the toothpaste.

"Do you want to go away?" he asked.

Going away was the last thing I wanted to do. "I don't know."

"Maybe you're bored," he said. "Going away might help."

Frustration isn't boredom, I wanted to argue, but couldn't. Joe wasn't my target. He was being so nice it made me ache. I physically felt awful.

"Where would we go?" I asked.

"We could go anywhere," he said. "As long as I can get the time off work."

"Like where?" I concentrated on rational thoughts – maybe it was smart to go somewhere. Maybe somewhere else I wouldn't be so madly in love with my married neighbor. Maybe somewhere else I would forget my crush. Maybe these feelings of utter frustration would disappear once I was somewhere else.

"Aren't you always talking about going to Ireland?"

Ireland, Scotland. Close enough.

"We've never been," he said. "We should travel. We have the money now."

"With the boys?" We brushed our teeth, both of us standing in front of the mirror.

"I don't think we'll bring them." He spoke with a mouth full of toothpaste.

"They'll be furious," I said.

He waited for me to spit, then he spit into the sink.

"We'll leave them here. My mother can come watch them. They'll love it. She'll let them get away with murder."

He rinsed his mouth, then handed me the little blue cup and waited for me to rinse before turning off the bathroom light.

"I'll look into some cheap flights," he said. "Maybe we can go in November."

November seemed a long way away. If only I could have turned off the thoughts about Allan. An on-off switch.

"That sounds good," I said.

He followed me back into the bedroom. I got into bed and sat back against the pillows.

In my bones I could feel my self-pity and I hated the strain of that tired and narcissistic emotion.

Joe took his laptop to the desk. He typed, the keys striking over and over, lulling me to sleep.

Barbara called the next morning.

"What time is it?" I asked. I knew exactly. The digital clock is right next to the phone, but I wanted her to say it. It's not polite to call anyone before nine am.

"So?" she asked. She was calling me on her cell phone. I could hear the static and the noise of the rush hour traffic.

"So? What does that mean?" I asked. I had no clue why Barbara, who I just said goodbye to eight hours ago, would now be calling me.

"Did he say anything?"

"Who?"

"That guy. From last night. Did he say anything about me?"

"He left before you did," I reminded her. "When would he have said anything?"

"I thought he might have come back."

"He didn't," I said.

There was a spastic blast of car horns. I wondered if she were involved in a near miss.

She carried on. "Do you think he liked me?"

"You were funny," I told her truthfully. Just because I'm not a fan doesn't mean that I don't recognize that her stories are humorous. I can see her being a stand-up comedian. She probably told that story of the lederhosen guy and had single women rolling in the aisles thinking about how lucky they were not to be Barbara.

"If he calls, you'll let me know." She told me.

"Absolutely," I promised.

I was sure she phoned Joe at the hospital and left him the same sort of message.

I thought we'd be setting her up all year, playing matchmaker, pouncing on single men, searching for potential partners for Barbara, but sometime after that night she changed her mind about a man.

Now she wants a baby.

Chapter Four

Some people think that cockroaches also date back to the time of the dinosaurs, but they are actually a much more recent creature. What they do have in common with the ginkgo tree is their ability to survive radiation. This isn't guesswork. After the atom bombs had been dropped in Japan, teams of scientists and medical people went in looking for survivors. The only living thing were thousands and thousands of stunned cockroaches and the ginkgo trees that seemed not to have suffered at all. It was the same after the Chernobyl disaster. Cockroaches and ginkgo trees. Hardly harmed at all.

The ginkgo tree is also resistant to insect pests and to fungal, viral and bacterial diseases as well as to ozone and sulfur dioxide pollution, and even fire. The ginkgo tree can tolerate snow and ice storms. Research shows that the ginkgo tree has no trouble adapting to greenhouse-effect conditions with elevated CO_2.

It is the most popular choice for city trees. They're planted all over the globe and survive no matter the conditions.

Barbara is going to name her new baby Lily.

"She's a Chinese girl and you're calling her Lily?" I ask.

"Is there something wrong with that?" Barbara asks. She's had cards made announcing the baby's arrival. On the front is a fuzzy stork carrying a white bundle with a pink bow wrapped around his beak. *"Please Welcome Lily to the Neighborhood,"* on the inside. I didn't realize storks were hairy.

It's August. Barbara has lived on the street less than a month. I'm sure some of the neighbors don't have a clue who she is. But she has a stack of cards she's passing around.

"Isn't that a little obvious?" I ask.

"Obvious?" Barbara echoes. She's defensive about a child she hasn't even seen.

"Cliché," I translate.

"It's beautiful," Barbara informs me. "It's very in to call Chinese girls by the names of flowers." Which is my point exactly, but Barbara is stubborn. She goes off to ring doorbells and drops off notes announcing her newest endeavor.

She goes up the walk to the sculptor's house. He lives directly next door to me. I haven't seen him in three years. I wouldn't bet on him for a baby gift. Barbara tucks the yellow envelope inside his door.

Barbara doesn't have a photograph yet though the agency, who she has already paid gobs of money to, has promised that she will get one before she leaves the country.

The agency has given Barbara lots of information – Lily is eighteen months old, black hair, black eyes, and a little button nose. She's very friendly. She's warm and tender. She likes trees, playing with blocks, and has just learned to walk. She spends her days toddling around. Her parents were madly in love but because of cultural and religious differences in their two families, they were kept apart and not allowed to marry.

Barbara loves this detail. "Like Romeo and Juliet," she sighs and smiles proudly.

I nod as if I'm thinking about all the information she's giving.

"The families are bitter enemies," Barbara explains. "But their love was pure."

And that makes this baby, this Lily, a very special child. Barbara glows with anticipation and excitement. I don't think she remembers the end of that play. There was not a lot of happiness in that one.

I have no opinions on single motherhood. At least I don't think I do. Like most people, I think it's great that the babies are being adopted. Anything is better than living in an orphanage, but there seems something foolish about what Barbara's doing.

She has no idea how tired she's going to be. A vial of poison or a sharp-edged knife, either one, will seem like a welcome relief after two weeks with a screaming child. And for a moment, albeit a very quick moment, I empathize with her. A baby alone is going to be a very tough road. I know what it is to want children. At one time, I'm sure I wanted mine, but that was more than a decade ago and they've changed so much from when we first met. I have a vague memory of incredible maternal desire at one time in my life.

But desire is one thing – the reality of children has nothing to do with desire. Everything about them is overwhelming. And to do it without a husband, even if he's a workaholic, or no good, you still need someone to blame when things are going horribly wrong and they go horribly wrong almost thirteen times a day. I used to feel crazy all the time – when the boys wouldn't eat, when they wouldn't go to sleep, when they cried for hours on end.

Parents with young kids are zombies. Visit a playground and you'll see sleepwalkers chasing and screaming after their kids.

Barbara is off her rocker, but no one has solicited my advice these last few months. I keep my opinions to myself – neatly tucked away so that no one recognizes that I have this terrifically negative attitude.

I would like to ask her if she really knows what she's getting into but for some reason, most likely my sardonic attitude, Barbara and I aren't the kind of friends who commiserate with one another. It's easier for me to carp about the baby's name.

Barbara is flying to China the first week in September. Maggie, it seems, is going with her.

"You're kidding?" I confront Maggie. I had no idea her translation skills were still being used. I'm impressed, but hesitant. I want to make sure that I'm understanding this situation.

"She needs help," Maggie said. "She can't go all that way alone."

"She'll have baby Lily," I point out.

"It's such a long flight. So much could happen. We didn't have our babies alone."

I had my mother-in-law and my mother with me. They both came in – to stay indefinitely. It was a terrible combination; they didn't get along and I spent most of my energy trying to keep them away from each other.

I'm surprised but not disappointed by her willingness to help others. "You really do have a big heart," I tell her.

"I don't mind," Maggie says. "I like to travel. I like babies."

"You're very brave," I tell her.

"China's a fabulous country," Maggie says. "It's been years since I've been there."

"To travel with Barbara," I clarify.

"It's a long trip," is what she says, but in there I think is some doubt about the journey. I already predict that it will be much less than fabulous.

"I just hope I'm up for it," Maggie says.

I don't think that's possible. "Valium," I suggest.

"Really?"

"Tons," I recommend. "As much as you can get your hands on legally. And then I'd turn criminal to make sure you have enough."

Maggie has other concerns. "I just hope nothing goes wrong here," she says.

"I'll take care of things at this end," I say.

"You promise?" Maggie lifts her head and smiles broadly.

How can I say no to that? "Of course. I'd be more than happy to look after things here." I will be happy to look after your garden, your mail, your daughters, and much more than that, I would be very happy to look after your husband.

I hate to see Maggie's act of charity as a self-serving window of opportunity, but I can't help myself. The thought of Allan without a wife for ten whole days thrills me.

Everything seems set for something special to happen. Everything except this one particular complication. Maybe complication isn't the right word. It's more like a nagging feeling that something isn't exactly right. Perhaps I am simply imagining this, but my relationship with Allan seems to be going into a standstill. There hasn't been much recent growth – it hasn't exactly progressed as I had hoped. His lack of enthusiasm puts a damper on my fantasy life. It urges me to consider that these entertaining fantasies of the last few months might have been in vain, a total waste of time, but I can't allow that. They have to mean something.

But now I have these days. These Maggie-less, wife-free days. It's time for optimism.

Chapter Five

The Scots have over fifty words to express fatigue. This according to Allan, who has told me that they are an exhausted people, a condition some people blame on the weather, others on the alcohol. I blame Allan's aloofness on his nationality – a part of his cultural identity. I'm not fond of overly enthusiastic people and this makes his reserve part of why I am so infatuated with him and not some other man.

He gives me examples – shattered, tattered, smashed, drummed, crushed.

"Sounds like you're describing the intake of too much alcohol."

"Is there such a thing?" he asks. "Too much alcohol brings to mind words like joy, pleasure, bliss, ecstasy, heaven."

We have this conversation a few days before Barbara and Maggie's anticipated departure day. I'm walking Spot; he's getting out of the car complaining about his day.

He has more words to describe his condition. "Bushed, drained, drowsy, weary, fucked, flattened, puffed."

"Puffed?"

"Puffed," he nods.

It's not a particularly interesting conversation. Talking about one's physical fatigue is not in the least bit flirtatious.

I vow to take advantage of the China excursion to get Allan and me back on track.

I'm not delusional. I don't foresee us sleeping together. That wouldn't be fair to Joe, especially now that he's so worried about my well-being. But I see nothing wrong in trying to get back to that flirty, giggling, I-find-you-so-fascinating-stage that we had both enjoyed last June.

I make plans. Ten days is a long time. There are complications and concerns, of course. It isn't going to be easy. But I ask myself what it is that I really want. I want the fantasy, but know that that's impossible. I am determined to be more realistic. And this is what I come up with:

I want him to admire me in the same way that I admire him.

That's all. Admiration doesn't equal infidelity.

It's a start. That's my goal. For now. I'll settle for this. Everything else can stay in my head – a part of my daydreams, a part of what entertains the dull moments of my life.

Friday, Maggie and Barbara leave for China. I'm in my spot – perched at my bedroom window, spying on their house. I have to make sure there are no snafus. I do not want to be caught off guard.

Finally around 10:00 I see Allan come out of the house. He loads a slim black bag into the trunk. Maggie is next; she's dressed in an ankle-length black dress looking sophisticated and calm. They get in the car.

I switch windows, running across the hall, to Josh's bedroom. Allan parks in front of Barbara's building. He runs in. Moments later, he's back. A few more minutes pass. He honks. More minutes. Then Maggie runs in. Ten more minutes and Barbara comes down. She's got an enormous suitcase that Allan struggles to lift into the trunk. Barbara is wearing a tracksuit and tennis shoes. She looks ready for a long jog. She's talking – moving her hands all about. I can't hear what she's saying, but Allan cuts this short and gets her into the car.

They drive away.

The neighborhood sighs, or at least I sigh. No Barbara. No Maggie. Fifteen days – maybe longer if there are complications.

I am thrilled. Almost giddy with the possibility of having Allan to myself.

I wait 24 hours. Just to be on the safe side. I don't want to go over with my invitation for romance in my hand only to have Maggie answer, informing me of a missed connection or changed itinerary. I am cautious. I watch his house like a hawk. Seeing nothing that would make me suspect fouled up travel plans, I make my move.

Jane answers my knock at the side door.

I act neighborly. "How's the global ignorance going?" I ask.

"Not even worth talking about," she says. "It hurts just to think how ridiculously stupid everyone is." I've noticed that Jane has started to use a slight Scottish accent. I agree with her decision. She sounds much more intelligent with an accent.

"You've given up the tree?"

"For now." She explains that she's taking a much more active approach. "Any lame-ass can protest. That's the easy part."

"I thought it looked difficult, your position up there always seemed precarious."

"Now's the time for action. No more talk. It's time to put meaning to my diatribes."

I worry about pipe bombs exploding in the back yard. I sense darkly dressed anarchists arriving *en masse,* upsetting the tranquility of the neighborhood.

"Anarchy is a dangerous thing," I warn.

"But in terms of peril, absolutely necessary," Jane says. She's been coloring her hair. It's now a very bleached blond, not exactly the color of the revolutionaries, who in my mind were always cropped brunettes with strong Russian accents and thin pursed lips. I smile and ask if Allan is around.

"Not home," she says. "*Comme d'habitude.*"

"Which means?"

"That he's never here."

"Working hard?" I ask.

"You can call it that," she sighs. "If that's what you want to call it." She's got all that teenage attitude and aloofness that I don't want to penetrate. I guess it is worse in girls. She doesn't offer anything.

I can't exactly leave a message so I tell her that I'll stop down later to see if he's returned.

"He won't be home until late," she says and smirks. Lipsticked lips pouting as if she has something over me. But as I've been so discreet, even casual about my feelings for her father, I don't think it's possible that she suspects something and yet here it is, this smirk.

"Oh," I say.

"If it's an emergency you can call his cell," she says. It's a number I don't have, but one I'm not sure that I want.

"But only call if it's an emergency. Otherwise he'll go ballistic."

"That's nice to know," I say. I certainly don't want anyone to go ballistic on me.

She writes it down on a piece of paper and hands it out the door to me.

"Thanks, Jane," I say. I can't call. What if he's in a meeting? What if I say my name and he says Caroline who? It would be too nervy of me and once I called, I would have to explain myself. I can't do it.

"Hey where are the guys?" Jane asks.

"The guys?"

She sticks out her hip and puts her hand to her face. "Your sons? You still have them, don't you?"

She even jokes like her father.

"As far as I know they haven't gone anywhere," I say. "Wait, listen."

Four houses over you can hear the sound of a basketball hitting the pavement. "I think that's them," I tell her.

"Tell them to come over. My sister and I are here. We can play ping-pong if we bore each other with our conversation."

I look at her blankly.

Josh is thirteen going on ten. Max is twelve going on five. Jane is sixteen going on forty and her sister Katie is thirteen going on indecent exposure. She wears these string bikini bathing suits without t-shirts as she cuts across the front yard from Karen and Greg's pool back home.

"I'm cooking dinner," Jane says. "It's ravioli. Guys like ravioli, don't they?"

"Guys?" I ask.

"In general," she nods.

"I guess they do," I answer. My boys like sports. They like to act like animals and make burping sounds. They still watch the Cartoon Network and play Nintendo. I don't think they'd have a lot in common with Allan's girls, but I tell Jane I'll give them the message.

I'm not surprised when they shrug and continue playing ball. I'm a bit taken aback when ten minutes later, they come tromping in the house and announce that they've decided to go over and see what Jane's talking about. I'm bowled over when they change their t-shirts before leaving the house.

I don't see Allan that night even though I watch for his car. But the next morning I'm up and walking the dog to catch him pulling out the drive at 7am.

The window is open. He sticks out his head and gives me a short flat wave of his hand. "You're up early," he comments – there's a distinct note of disapproval in his voice as if there's something wrong with being up. Obviously not a morning person.

"So are you," I state the obvious.

"I haven't got a choice."

I'm not in the mood to talk the benefits of not having a job. I blurt out my invitation. "I was wondering if you want to have dinner some night," I offer. "Seeing that Maggie's away and all."

"This week isn't good," he shakes his head.

But this is the week Maggie's not here. I stare at him trying to give him a hint that this is a fantastic week for dinner at my house.

"It's a beautiful day, isn't it?" he says.

I'm not in the mood for pleasantries. "You sound like an old man always talking about the weather."

"I'm Scottish," he says. "It's what we do to pass the time."

I'm pissed that he's refused so capriciously; doesn't he realize what's at stake here? I'm rude. It's the only defense I have. "It's boring," I say. "Even with that accent, it's dull."

"I'll have to remember that," he says and winks at me. I don't get that gesture. But I guess he finds my bad manners humorous.

"See you," I say to his car as it drives down the block.

I take several breaths as if reaching a calm state of mind will help erase the scene that's just taken place. Our relationship isn't supposed to be like this. We have much more to discuss than the weather. Being treated like a neighbor is not what I want from this relationship.

I've got to stop wanting him. The unfulfilled desire is wearing me down.

The ginkgo tree is considered to be a phenomenon, an object of veneration, a sacred tree of the East, a symbol of unity of opposites, seen by some as a symbol of changelessness, possessing miraculous power, bearer of hope and the immeasurable past, a symbol of love. Because of its strength and history, the ginkgo tree is associated with longevity. The ginkgo tree is thought to protect against fire and is planted near temples.

One of the problems I've noticed with getting older is that there isn't anything to do with the extra hours in the day. I tell myself I'm wasting time with all these romantic scenarios starring Allan and me. When you're young, you have the future, the promise that things will change dramatically every three or four years, and it keeps the present from appearing dull. When you're working, you have the concerns of the job – the petty, back-stabbing, repetitive squabbles that take up so much of a working day. But take that away, take away any major life changes, and what's left is the day. I'm afraid to say that there are a lot of minutes in the day. I know I'll come out of this. I know I'll look back on these months and chastise myself for the pure waste of what I'm doing. But actually I can't think of how else to fill the day. The boredom and the frustration of not getting what I want infuriates me. I walk around the neighborhood with Spot, cursing Allan. What does he mean this isn't a good week? How can he not see that it's the only week?

I try to come up with another plan of attack. But I am stumped. I used to be such a good problem-solver when I had a job. Now unemployed, I grab at straws. I consider fainting, but that brings up issues of health and therefore weakness. The direct approach is sensible, but the truth doesn't form into comprehensible sentences. I walk in front of his house – back and forth – boldly as if I don't care what he thinks. Isn't that what he said he admired? Women who don't care what others think?

I need to confide my obsession with Allan to someone. I want to talk about him. I want to force the fantasies into some other shape and even to mention him to another feels dangerous and somehow exotic.

I pick Julie, because she's normally so busy with work and with lamenting the loss of her youthful figure that I know she won't be too judgmental or overly concerned with my business.

"I think I've gone overboard with a crush I've been having," I say.

She laughs. "You've got a crush on someone?"

"My neighbor," I say. "A man who lives on my street. Isn't that weird?" I am not expecting the rush of excitement in talking about it. But I'm excited and flush with the relief of putting these feelings into words.

"Why?"

"I'm not sure," I answer. "I just do."

"That's so high school," she tells me.

"I guess it is," I agree. But I don't feel high school. High school I had crushes every other week. I barely had to know the guy's name to have a crush. I just saw him, loved him, knew nothing would happen, and went on my way. They were never specific and didn't live in my head, the way thoughts of Allan do.

Julie gets right to the point. "I'm assuming he's married."

"Yes. He's got a wife."

"And do we know if there are problems in the marriage?"

"Not exactly.

"But we're hoping there are."

"You, too?" I ask.

"There should be if you're going to have an affair with him. Happily married men are hard to distract."

Does she know this from experience? Was she skinnier when she tried to attract a married man?

"Have you slept with him?"

"No."

She's a nosy one. "But you've come close?"

That doesn't sound right. I want to give value to my fantasies. I think they mean something, but I can't negotiate them into the conversation. "I haven't even kissed him," I say truthfully.

"You're just contemplating an affair?"

"I've thought about it," I say. "Once or twice." Seven hundred, eight hundred times.

"I don't believe it," she says. "You should see your face. You're guilty about something."

She's wrong. I don't feel guilt. I feel frustrated and disappointed. I feel desperate. I feel overwhelmed with the continued futility of my dreams. This has nothing to do with guilt.

"What's wrong with Joe? Is he having an affair too?" she probes. Why did I think I could tell a reporter something? They are so nosy.

"Joe and I are fine." We're fine except that I'm obsessed with another man. Otherwise things are good. "He's writing a book."

"He is?"

"It's a mystery," I say.

"He's very literary," she says. "It should be good."

"He thinks it's going to be great," I tell her.

"Does Joe know anything?"

"He was an English major in college. He can write," I say.

"I meant does he know that you're head over heels in love with your next-door neighbor?"

"He doesn't live that close," I clarify. "I don't stare into his window or anything creepy like that."

"But you walk by his house?"

"Every chance I get," I say. "All hours of the night and day. The dog's so tired, she cringes when she sees the leash."

I go ahead and tell her about the fantasies.

"Every day?" she asks.

"I think about him all the time," I say. "Every minute of the day. I can name the moments I'm not thinking of him."

She shakes her head. She's giving this way more attention than I bargained on.

"You're delusional," she determines.

"Bordering on it." I'll give her that.

"Totally," she judges. I should have remembered she was a psychology major in college and that one of her dreams is to quit writing for the stupid newspaper and go into private practice.

"You need a job." This is her advice. The first time I've indulged my fantasies to a friend and she brings up the status of my employment. I suddenly wish I could take back my words. I should have known I couldn't confide in Julie. She doesn't care about other people. She's a woman of the '90's – self-centered and self-serving – someone who never looks outside of her own life.

Julie has ordered a salad with dressing on the side. It comes; it's iceberg lettuce with tomatoes and red onions. Not at all appealing. I order a hamburger and fries, but can't eat. I push it to the center of the table. She pushes it back towards me, but keeps picking from it.

"You need a job to get your mind off this guy. If you had a job, you wouldn't have time to think. And I do think you should stop thinking about him. He's going to ruin your marriage."

"It didn't ruin Jimmy Carter's," I say.

"Do you think you and Jimmy are anything alike?"

"I've never considered it," I say honestly. "I haven't thought of him in years."

"Get a job," Julie says. She finishes what's left of my hamburger, but like me, she doesn't seem to care for it. It was my choice to eat here – I don't think I'll do it again.

She doesn't understand, but I no longer want to share it with anyone. It's mine. I don't need any more discussion on it.

But Julie gives me more counsel. "Whatever you do, you have to stop thinking of him."

Confiding in Julie was not a productive move; it did not get me anywhere.

It's not exactly the right weather for a casserole dish, but it's impossible to drop off grilled salmon or a poached pear salad.

I grate three different kinds of cheese, and simmer onions in thyme-flavored oil for real tomato sauce. I make several layers that you can see through the glass casserole dish, and bring it over to Allan's.

I ring the bell. The noise sets off Cinnamon. She barks like I'm dragging costly items out of the house. The dish is covered in tin foil and I decide that I'll leave it on the back steps with a note, *Thought you'd enjoy, Caroline.* That seems a bit personal so I go back a minute later and tag on Caroline & Co. so it seems like it came from the whole family.

I made a second one for Joe and the boys. They tell me it's great, the best I've ever made. Actually it's the first I've made in a long time. They eat the entire thing, micro-waving their second and third helpings.

We eat in the backyard. I listen for the slamming of car doors, the sound of voices, people coming home, but as far as I can tell, the McIver's house remains quiet.

Tuesday night, Joe and I go out. Movies and dinner. We go out with another couple – friends from years ago who are visiting relatives in town. Their kids are older and live in exotic and dangerous places – Israel, Bali, Costa Rica – we hear travel stories that make our lives seem provincial and secluded in comparison.

"I went to Cleveland," I tell them. "Just before I was fired. We went to see what we could learn from that city."

"We went to Erie in June," Joe says. "We took the boys windsurfing."

"It was actually quite perilous," I jump in. "The waves and the sand were incredibly hazardous."

"Next week we're thinking of driving to the West Virginia border. Just because we can."

They like to hear us tell them that their lives are glamorous and exhilarating. They continue with more stories and it's midnight before we get home.

Waiting for us on the front porch is my dirty, but empty casserole dish. Inside is a note.

"Squirrels or raccoons had a feast. Next time call and we'll come over for dinner. Just call u.s Love, Jane and Katie. They've drawn X's and O's along the bottom.

I thought anarchists were more into anonymous letters.

Wednesday I go over *au natural*. No props – no covered dish, no excuse, just me ringing a neighbor's doorbell, curious if he'd like to sip wine with me in some dark bar in the neighborhood. I dress in a black sleeveless dress and sandals.

To no avail, the house is empty. Either that or the three of them are hiding in the basement playing some sort of perverted joke on me.

I've run out of ideas and plans.

The next evening, I'm sitting on the front porch with the day's newspaper, rethinking Julie's advice. I've read every story including all the ones in the sports section. People have a lot of opinions on the current baseball season, and there are huge predictions for change in the hockey franchise in Pittsburgh. The boys are just home, back from a late pick-up basketball game at Whitman School. Joe is working late. He won't be home before 10pm.

Max grabs the newspaper and reads the box scores aloud to his brother. They talk baseball for a minute.

"Can we order pizza?" Josh asks.

"Sure. Why not?" It's that kind of night. Easy. They hang with me for a minute, the laziness of doing nothing matches the weather which feels more like June than September.

"Can we call for it ourselves?" They have a menu and want to order the things that they like. I spent years cooking for them, trying to find things that they would like. I used to decorate a scoop of cottage cheese with cherry tomatoes and grated carrots with rows of raisins – little faces that they loved. Now what makes them the most happy is to have control in the kitchen. They want to order exactly what they want to eat.

"That's a good idea," I say.

They'll order extra things. Bread sticks and garlic butter, extra marinara sauce. But they'll scarf it all, the empty boxes stacked on top of the garbage can. Dinner's done. I, like most mothers, am eternally grateful for the invention of the to-go pizza parlor. I like everything about them – the convenience, the price, the amount of food, the carbohydrates, and especially the speed. I even like the taste. I think the concept of pizza delivery should be nominated for one of the highest prizes of our times. I can't imagine my life without it.

"You look happy." Allan's walking up the drive.

"Hey," I say and catch my breath. I'm not expecting him.

"It's so warm," I say. "I feel like we've moved to a tropical island."

"I thought we weren't allowed to talk weather," Allan says. "I thought we were making an effort to stop sounding like the aged."

I'm surprised he remembers. "Guilty of a double standard," I admit.

He's smoking a cigarette. "Are the boys home?" he asks cautiously.

"They're ordering dinner," I tell him. "Pizza."

"That's what my girls are having. We should get them together. It might be cheaper."

I don't think he knows about the other night. The boys got home after midnight, but when I asked them what they had done, they couldn't tell me. "Hung out," was as far as their description of the night went. It makes me curious – if Allan doesn't know the boys were there, what time did he come home? Maybe he came home and went straight to bed. Stop, I force myself. It doesn't matter.

91

"You busy?"

I'm not sure I've heard him right. I shrug as I try to replay what he's just said. Busy? Is that what he asked me?

"Do you fancy a walk?" he asks. I've been waiting so long for this invitation that when it finally comes I'm a momentary mess.

I stand. "Should I get the dog?"

"God, no," he says. "I'm in need of some company, not some yappy little shit," he pauses. "I'm sorry. I hope you don't take offense."

"Not at all," I say. "You're right. She does yap."

I'm wearing a pair of khaki shorts. They're not flattering. "Give me a minute?" I ask.

He nods.

I go in. Josh and Max are in the kitchen, poring over the pizza place menu. "I'll be back in a bit," I tell them.

"What kind of pizza do you want?" Josh asks.

"Whatever you're having," I say.

"Whatever I'm having or whatever Josh is having?" Max asks.

"Whatever," I say.

"How about an extra large anchovy and red onion?"

"Great," I say, and nod towards my purse on the kitchen counter. "There's plenty of cash in my wallet."

The boys look at each other. I don't usually give them free reign with my wallet. But why shouldn't everyone be happy tonight? I'm nervous; my palms sweat. I wipe them on a towel, but smell the onions from the night before. I wash them. Hurry.

My jean skirt is in the laundry room. I change quickly, then brush my hair. I take my lipstick but don't apply it in front of the boys. I don't want them to look out the window, see Allan and think that I'm doing all this for him. They're not stupid. They've been known to put two and two together.

Allan is on down the sidewalk. I can smell the cigarette he's just put out. "All set?" he asks. If he notices the change of clothes, he doesn't say anything.

We walk down the street, heading towards the shopping area in Shadyside.

I get the wife question over as fast as I can. "How's Maggie doing in China?"

He makes this odd noise in his throat. I wouldn't call it a snort, not exactly, but it's very close.

"I got one call when they arrived, but haven't heard anything else," he says.

"Is it hard to call the States from there?"

"I'm not sure where they are," Allan says. "You would think in an international hotel it would be simple. They should be in Guangzhou in a five star hotel called the White Swan. It's where everyone adopting has to stay. I think that's where the U.S. embassy is."

Barbara gave me her entire itinerary and I saw the White Swan listed there for days three and four. I had no idea it was a five star hotel. I imagined it to be a like a baby crib, a white beacon in the lush jungles of the Chinese countryside. The image that comes to mind is of a gigantic white swan cradle.

"Hmm," I nod.

"How hard can it be to dial a phone in a five star hotel?"

"I don't know," I say. "I've never stayed in one."

"You haven't?"

"I don't think so."

"You should travel more."

"I'm not sure more travel would guarantee me a stay in a five star hotel."

"Adopt a baby," Allan suggests.

"I think I'd rather slum it for the rest of my life."

He gives me a laugh. Okay, a snort.

I don't ask anymore about the trip. I think that's enough talk about his wife.

I wait for him to say something, but we walk in silence. A few neighbors pass by. I say hello. Allan ignores them. The girls who work at the dry cleaners on the corner of Walnut and Shady are outside smoking. They spend half their shifts out there. Allan knows them. He nods. "Hi girls."

"Hey Allan," they say in unison.

"They're a good source for a fag when you need to bum them," he says when we've gone half a block past them. "The problem is they smoke menthols."

"I'll remember that," I say.

Then there's silence. We pass the Banana Republic, the coffee shop that's changed names and owners several times in the past few years, the Rite-Aid, and the hair salon that just opened up. It's called HAIR.

Allan is distracted, almost moody. I'm not sure what to do with this moodiness. In my fantasies he's extremely attentive and always engaged with the matter at hand. I choose to ignore it. I walk beside him enjoying the moment. It's not bad.

We're almost to the end of the shopping area when Allan motions to a bar. It's the kind of place with three or four giant screen TVs, and a few card game machines that as far as I know are illegal. There are baskets of peanuts scattered about, and you toss the shells onto the floor.

"Should we go in for a drink?" he asks.

The average age of the place is around 20, most likely younger if you eliminated the fake ID's. I've never been in, never had a desire to drink there. But I guess in some respects it is our neighborhood bar. But this change of attitude is positive. "Sure," I say. "A drink sounds great."

Allan laughs and I nod and again tell him what a wonderful idea a drink is.

"You need to get out more," Allan advises.

"I'd love to," I say. "Invite me anytime."

He looks at me but doesn't say anything.

They have a patio upstairs and we sit in the back. We don't know anyone. At least I don't know anyone. The waitress comes over and lights the candle. The wick is low and it takes her a couple of tries to even catch it. Allan offers to do it.

"What will you drink?" he says, then offers a suggestion. "You can't drink wine. Not in this kind of place."

"We've got wine," the girls says. She is suddenly defensive as if Allan is disparaging her place of employment. "We've got Chablis and Zinfandel."

"Let me guess," Allan says. "The Zinfandel is pink?"

"That's right," she says. She has a bellybutton piercing. A gold ring hangs over the buckle on her jeans.

Allan orders a beer and I say I'll have the same. The girl brings our beer and our very own basket of peanuts. Allan warns me to be careful. "Some of these peanuts may be over 100 years old."

"I'll stay away," I say.

But Allan reaches for one. He cracks one open and tosses the shells onto the floor.

I'm not making up the next part.

He drinks, then kind of laughs, but as there's nothing funny, I assume I'm supposed to ask him what he's thinking about, so I do.

"I don't know," he says.

And I'm not sure how to respond to this, so I shrug and drink my beer. I haven't had beer in so long that I feel like I'm drinking a memory.

Allan wants to say something. I can see him struggling to clarify his thoughts. I close my eyes, worried that he's going to tell me that he realizes that I'm infatuated. I'm nervous that he's going to tell me to stop the craziness.

"Caroline," he says. "Do you ever think about changing your life?"

I take a huge breath. I'm actually about to faint, but I hold onto the beer and concentrate on the physical coldness of the glass so I don't scare him away. "Yes," I manage.

"You do?"

"I do," I say, carefully pronouncing each of my words. "Often. Very often."

"Really?" I don't know why that should surprise him.

"Losing my job kind of changed it for me."

"Right," Allan says. "But do you ever think about changing the rest?"

I can't speak. The bar is nothing like my fantasy, but the conversation follows the course almost word for word.

"It is hard to imagine, isn't it?" he says. He leans forward.

I don't think he's going to declare his undying love for me, but it is an eerie conversation. It's almost as if he's following one of my dream scripts line for line like an actor.

"What's making you so unhappy?" I lean forward and try to neutralize my tone.

Allan's neck is only a few inches from my lips. I wonder what would happened if I just brushed his skin. I wouldn't want anything else. Just a moment to pull him into me.

"I can't keep on like this," he says. "I have to do something."

The conversation is charged with a sexual energy. The electricity is coming from both of us. I lean even closer. An inch or two further and I will be in his lap.

Someone approaches the table. I assume it's the waitress asking us if we want another round. I still have half a glass. Allan's is empty. I want him to drink more.

"He'll have another," I tell the figure.

But it is not the waitress. It's Jane, Allan's daughter. She's come to ruin my night.

"What are you doing here?" Allan asks.

"I saw you come in," she says. She's chewing bubble gum. It's fluorescent green.

"Are you following me again?" Allan asks. "I thought we had agreed that you weren't going to do that."

"I was outside the Gap," she says. "We're protesting their use of sweat shops in Honduras. Didn't you see us?"

Allan shakes his head. I know she senses our guilt. I am hugely disappointed to see her standing there. I blink, hoping she'll go away of her own free will.

"I thought they didn't use sweat shops in third world countries," Allan says. "I thought the Gap was better than that."

I hope he'll tell her to run along and play with her little band of protest warriors. I'm sure there's something else they should be attending to – these are dire times. No use hanging out in bars –not when you're not wanted.

"Dad. Don't tell me you're shopping there again," Jane wails. She has a huge set of lungs on her and the other patrons look over. I would have thought the bouncer would have barred her from entering. Her presence is a clear violation of some law.

I want to go back in time. Five minutes. I want the bartender to lock the door. I would like him to start a new rule barring all sixteen-year-old girls from entering adult establishments. How are you supposed to carry on illicit affairs when children are walking around messing up deep and sexually exciting grown-up conversations?

Allan's forgotten his wallet and I don't have any money; we have to borrow $4.00 from Jane.

"God Dad," she says and pulls out a ten dollar bill from her back pocket. "This is so typical of you – to leave the house without your wallet."

"Yes it is," Allan says.

"Don't talk like that," she commands. "I wasn't paying you a compliment. I think it's embarrassing and immature that you do things like forget your wallet."

"I'm not sure there's anything immature about forgetting one's wallet," Allan says. "Embarrassing, yes, but maybe in the end it's just forgetful."

She looks at me. I'm guessing I'm embarrassing and immature too.

"You're lucky I came in," she says and snaps her gum. This she addresses to me. "Otherwise the two of you would be doing dishes. Four bucks might take you all night in a place that serves their food in plastic baskets."

I am not feeling lucky.

We go home. It's too hard to walk three abreast on the narrow sidewalks, so I drop back and let the two of them go on ahead.

The ginkgo berries cover one large patch of sidewalk. They've been smashed over and over as people couldn't avoid them. Allan swears and we walk in the street. I plan to ask him in for a drink. The boys don't usually linger long at meals. My guess is that they've wolfed down their pizzas and are upstairs watching a movie. The backyard can be ours.

Jane grabs hold of Allan's hand. He's mine, I want to tell her. I feel protective and possessive, not to mention put out. I practice my casual invitation into the house for a nightcap sans Jane.

Jane explains the protest in front of the Gap. "The manager almost flipped out. It was her third day on the job and she told her staff she didn't know the protocol for sweatshop protesters."

"It's probably rare in the provinces."

"I think it's reprehensible not to know the politics of the place where you work," Jane says.

"Maybe she knows them," I say. "Maybe she knows them and doesn't see anything particularly wrong with providing employment in third-world countries."

"It's called exploitation." Jane is seething.

"But do you really know that?" I don't. I haven't the slightest idea what I'm talking about. I can't even remember the country where the Gap gets their clothes made. It's not my issue, not my concern. I don't shop there, but I'm antagonistic. It's time for Jane to go home. Maybe she can write the company president a letter voicing her concerns.

"Thanks for the walk," Allan says.

"You sure you don't want to come in."

He lifts his hand – the one attached to his daughter and shakes his head. "I should do something about dinner."

"It's too late for dinner," Jane says.

And I agree, but they walk ahead and I have no choice but to go inside. Alone.

Jane *is* his daughter, I reason as I sit in the dark house, cursing her. I'm being unfair, but it feels good to pout a bit. We were so close. My mind reels with the possibility of everything that might have happened.

Joe gets home a few minutes after I do. I don't tell him that I've been out, though he does ask if everything's okay.

"Why shouldn't it be?" I ask. I am too agitated to hide my fragile aggravation.

"Just asking," he says.

It's not fair to punish him for something he doesn't understand so I tell him that everything is fine. "I'm okay. I really am. Just moody," I say.

"But I was wondering why?" he asks.

Joe and I have been married for fifteen years. I know him better than I know anyone. I don't like it when women call their husbands their best friends because I think husband is a sufficient term. I've told Joe everything and am close to telling him how I feel about Allan. I'm this close to just admitting my condition. He knows everything else about me. It feels natural to confide in him, but I realize the nature of my complaint might just alienate him. As much as I'd like to, I can't get his advice or his help this time.

We take the boys' leftover pizza out to the back yard. It's 10pm, but the night is too warm to waste inside. The boys come out and eat what Joe and I don't. They drink another carton of orange juice, then find a bag of Oreos and eat those. Then a half gallon of milk. I've heard it gets worse. I don't see how that's possible.

Joe wants to rewrite the latest chapter before letting me read it. I get in bed, still dressed in my jean skirt and t-shirt, and turn out the light.

"You're wearing that to bed?" he asks.

"I'm not going to sleep," I say.

He looks surprised.

"Actually, I'm doing a bit of revision." Again, I think how easy it would be to just spill my guts. I could tell him everything. He's very good with frustrating situations and interpersonal communications. I always liked discussing my problems at work with Joe. He didn't automatically take my side – he listened, asked good questions, and then offered advice, which I usually took. I realize the absurdity of confiding in him about my Allan problem, though I think he'd point me in the right direction.

"Without pen or paper?" he asks.

"I'm just thinking of a new ending," I say.

"Are you writing a book now?"

"I might start," I tell him.

"Will it be a mystery?" he asks. "One piece of advice – I'd read some before I started writing. They're much more difficult than they seem."

"Absolutely not," I say. "No one will be killed in my story."

I'm going to rewrite the end of the scene at the bar. I'm going to leave out the part with Jane and get to the heart of Allan's unhappiness. I want to know exactly what he's thinking about changing. I cut out the candles on the tables and put up Tiki torches. I change my dress. I'm wearing something long

100

and clingy, sandals, and an interesting above-the-elbow bracelet. I've never owned an above-the-elbow bracelet, but have always found them commanding – full of sophistication and sexual savvy. My hair is shorter.

In my revision, Allan looks exactly the same. I see no reason to change his perfection. I do edit out Jane. I remove all thoughts of any other family members. There is no guilt or rush. We're content to just be. In my made-up world, it's just Allan and me talking about our problems. He tells me what's troubling him.

He is, of course, unhappy in love.

I sigh and offer to help.

Why is it that Europe is considered the perfect place for romance? Is it the presence of the past everywhere – the old buildings, the cobblestone streets, the sense that things have been the same for years? Maybe it's the pace of life? The wine at lunch, the attention to meals, the absence of car travel replaced instead by the romantic and comfortable train travel. Is this just for Americans? Do Europeans have fantasies about illicit affairs taking place in the United States? Is Niagara Falls a popular choice? Or do Europeans fantasize about a great apartment on the Upper East Side? Is a bungalow in Key West a place that comes to mind when a European contemplates adultery?

I move us to a coastal village in Scotland. We're walking hand in hand on the beach, navigating our way around the rocks. The wind is fierce, but it's not cold. We start talking love. My bracelet looks great.

I've got us where I want us. I take off my clothes and slip into bed.

"Finished? Already?" Joe asks.

"Just about," I say. I conjure up the image one more time, and feel sleep taking over.

Joe's keys hit faster and faster. If nothing else comes of the book, he is getting to be a much faster typist.

The fall is a lovely time to be in love, even if you live in Pittsburgh. I'd like to convince Allan of this. And yet I worry about Maggie, Joe. My kids, his kids. My age, my weight, the black hairs on my chin.

Chapter Six

For a long time, scientists believed that the ginkgo tree had become extinct. Like the dinosaur the ginkgo tree was gone. Then in 1691 it was rediscovered in Japan. They also survived in China. They were found in monasteries in the mountains and in palace temple gardens where for several generations Buddhist monks cultivated the ginkgo berries for medicinal purposes.

Barbara is back from China. She calls from the airport and asks me for a lift.

"You're here?" I ask. "Here in Pittsburgh?"

She doesn't answer my question, but the twing-twing of the bells coming over the loudspeaker warning the pedestrians that the moving sidewalk is coming to an end tells me that she's most likely at the airport.

It is impossible to believe that fifteen days have passed since they left. For a moment I consider the possibility that someone is playing a joke on me. Barbara isn't the type. Humor is not her strong suit even after those short months as a stand-up comedian.

"Did you get the baby?" Maybe there were complications and they'll have to go back. Maybe things went horribly wrong and they're only returning for a change of clothes.

Things were definitely progressing between Allan and me. I felt like this time was the prelude to something very special. Our drink, his attempt to confess something intimate about his troubled personal life. Give me another ten days and this time I won't waste a minute.

Barbara is tense. "Can we save the details for later?" she asks. "I'm exhausted and dehydrated."

"You're what?"

"Unbelievably dehydrated. Bring water." Barbara is very bossy for someone in need of a favor.

Pittsburgh's International Airport boasts the best shops and restaurants in the country. Maggie's a world-class traveler; certainly they can navigate a bottle of water or a drinking fountain. Between the two of them they should figure out how to obtain some liquids.

"We'll be at baggage claim." She raises her voice to a yell and then the line goes quiet. She didn't exactly give me a choice or a chance to say no, so I'm forced to go out there, but I do wonder if she'll be this casual with her plans now that she has an eighteen month-old baby on her hip.

I pull up to the signs marked baggage claim. I don't see them. I don't see anyone. The place is quiet. But still, the cop won't let me wait; I drive the loop again. Pittsburgh's not a busy airport and the police patrolling the empty lanes are looking for something to occupy their day. I come back again and the cop walks over to the car. He motions for me to unroll the window. "You can't be here."

Just then Barbara comes rushing out of the terminal. She's got the baby in her arms and is dragging or trying to drag that mammoth suitcase. It's so heavy and awkward that even with the wheels she can't navigate it to follow her. For a minute I watch her. She looks like Olive Oyl, those long arms and legs, this ridiculous situation – baby and enormous suitcase – she really could have been a good stage comedian. But the cop is there. He's watching too – obviously entertained by a situation I no longer find funny. I go over and help her.

He, on the other hand, continues to be amused by our struggle to get the suitcase into the trunk, which we do, mostly because I'm so determined not to let the situation get the best of us.

Mission accomplished and I stop and catch my breath.

I look around. "Where's Maggie?"

"China," Barbara says.

"What did you just say?" I demand to know. "What happened to Maggie?"

"China." Barbara points up to the sky, which I guess is her way of giving me a geography lesson. Then she holds out the baby. My attention is momentarily distracted.

The baby is wrapped in a bright yellow outfit, the hood pulled over the face as if in anticipation of cold weather.

"She's not here?" I ask. A tiny sliver of hope rises in my chest.

"That's why I needed the ride," she explains. "Otherwise Allan would have come."

She opens the back door and lets out a sigh. "You don't have a car seat?"

"You're kidding?" I ask. "I certainly did."

"You did?"

"Ten years ago. I had two. I've been robbed. Officer." I put my fingers to my mouth as if to whistle for the policeman's attention.

Barbara doesn't think I'm amusing. She tells me that car seats are the law. "All kids under the age of five have to use them."

Because I know she's traveled halfway around the world, I'm going to give her the benefit of the doubt. I know how tired one gets on those long international flights where they keep passing around hot towels even though what you'd really like them to do is to bring down the plane. She's also got the baby. I will tolerate her wacky behavior because of her newly adopted little girl. My patience will be generous, but short-lived.

"If we're stopped, we'll tell the cop that we're headed directly to the car seat store."

Barbara puts Lily on the back seat, then gets in beside me.

"I'm not sure I'd leave her alone back there," I say. "She might roll forward."

Barbara gets in the back seat. She holds Lily in her lap.

"She doesn't move much," Barbara says. "She's awfully docile." She sighs. "That's what everyone's been saying. She's so quiet. She's so peaceful, so calm. I guess I'm lucky, huh?'

To me the baby simply looks tired – tired, but mildly curious. She's awake, but straining to stay alert.

Barbara also looks exhausted. Her skin looks like its stretched across her face. Maybe she did get dehydrated over there. Her ability to care for the baby is suddenly a concern of mine.

"Hey Barbara, is your family coming to help you?"

"My family?" she gasps. "They better not be."

"Oh no?"

"God, no. They're incapable of helping anyone."

"But don't you need someone?" I ask. "Especially at first as you get used to having Lily?"

I don't know any of her other friends, but maybe someone's coming from another city, maybe one of her comedian pals.

"They better not be," Barbara says.

"But you've got someone to help you?"

"I think I can manage," Barbara says. "Now that we're done traveling. I miss Maggie. She was a great help."

"I'm sure," I say. It's exactly the kind of thing Maggie would be good with. I'm sure she did everything when they were together. Which makes it a real mystery why she's not in the car with us.

"So?" Barbara asks as she resettles into the passenger seat.

"So," I return the volley.

"So what do you think?"

"I'm not sure I understand why she didn't come back," I say. I could speculate of course. She might have been devastated by the country and decided that her life's vocation was to work on a farm in rural China. Maybe she decided that she should devote her life to the underprivileged in Beijing? Allan might soon be getting a divorce. I think of a thousand possibilities, my mind moving into fantasy mode.

"I'm talking about Lily," she says. "What do you think of her?"

I haven't really given Barbara or the new baby much attention so I say the first thing that comes to my mind. "She looks like you."

Barbara stares at me. "Caroline, sometimes I just don't get you. You are so inappropriate."

"I'm being serious," I say and when I turn to look at Lily I can see that I'm not pulling this observation out of thin air. It's true; the baby does look like Barbara. Not exactly, of course, but a relationship of some sort doesn't seem out of the question.

Barbara smiles. "Do you really think so?"

"Yes," I say. "Absolutely."

I didn't mean it as a compliment, but Barbara preens. And suddenly I realize that it is the truth. Since she's moved in, her looks have changed. She plucks her eyebrows very thin, so thin that they almost look painted on. Her hair is over-dyed. It's jet black, which I took to be a solution to the gray, but with the lighter base and the red lips, I realize it is a deliberate attempt to look like someone she is not – Lily's mother.

I'm actually touched by her effort. It shows that she's doing something to connect with the baby.

I want to talk about Maggie, but Barbara puts up her hands to fend off my curiosity. "I'm too tired to talk," she says. She shuts her eyes and a few minutes later, she begins to snore. Lily, unlike her mother, is now awake. I watch her in the rear view mirror. She's alert, seemingly happy. She watches the passing cars as we head into the Fort Pitt tunnels. I talk to her just in case she's nervous about the sudden darkness.

"It doesn't last long," I assure her. "It's about a mile. Maybe a little more."

We come out onto the bridge that spans the Monongahela River and the point of Pittsburgh and the best view of the city.

"Welcome to Pittsburgh," I say. "I hope you'll be happy here. Most people are."

Then I reconsider what I've just said. "That's not quite true. Though the unhappy ones leave as soon as they can. The ones who stay are genuinely happy. Good-natured and glad to be here."

She seems to like the cars and keeps a careful eye on each one that passes.

We drive through the neighborhoods near the universities and I show Lily the Cathedral of Learning, the largest academic structure in the world when it was built as a tribute to the steel industry. It is forty-two stories tall with no real viewing area at the top. We pass the Carnegie Museum with the gigantic dinosaur in front. Andrew Carnegie supported archeological digs and this dinosaur is named after him. Carnegieosaurus or something like that. Lily doesn't express her initial reactions to her new place of residence, but I think she's impressed.

Barbara's apartment is spotless. Not just clean, but extremely orderly. Lily is exploring. She grabs for things on the coffee table, Barbara says no and moves them away. "You need to child-proof the place," I say, and want to tell her that it's the last time the place will be this neat.

"I think I'll just encourage her not to touch," she tells me as if this is an option. There are different approaches to mothering. I think of the broken vases, the smashed candlesticks, the glass in the picture frames. That covers the toddler years before they could throw things. Once that started, I lost everything I ever treasured. Soccer is not a contact sport, but played indoors it does wreak havoc.

"So when do you think Maggie will be back?" I ask.

"Who knows?" Barbara shrugs it off. But if anyone would know, it would be Barbara.

"Look at all these souvenirs I bought," Barbara says. She's dumped out the suitcase on the floor and a dozen packages tumble out.

"The hotel was a mile from this wonderful jade market," Barbara says. She unwraps one of the red wrapped packages and shows me the pieces of jade. They're so green they look fake. "Everything was dirt cheap."

She holds the jade piece to her ear and admires herself in the mirror. "I bought so much, I was nervous they were going to stop me going through customs."

"Is this illegal?" I ask.

"I thought it might be a way to make a bit of cash," Barbara says. "You can't believe how expensive everything was in that godforsaken country."

She is doing something illegal. "I thought it was cheap?" I asked.

"The jade was cheap. Everything else cost an arm and leg," she explains. "I was dying for a Diet Coke and told the bell-hop that I'd pay anything if he could find me one. He charged me nine dollars."

Lily starts to fuss and I bounce her for a bit. She gets fussier. I hold her out for Barbara to take, but she shakes her head. "Would you mind holding her?" she asks. "I'm so exhausted I can feel my eyelids when they go up and down. Lily and I had to share a seat. My legs will never recover."

I remember I was the only one who could calm the boys. My husband would find me and beg me to take them. "I can't get them to stop crying," he'd complain. I liked being the one who could do something. It gave me a special feeling, a sense that I was doing the right thing in the way that I was mothering them. I guess Barbara hasn't gotten to that point yet with Lily.

The bell rings and Barbara looks at me. "Who can that be?" she asks. "Who would come here at this time?"

"Why don't you open the door and find out," I advise. "That's usually how other people handle things when the doorbell rings."

She hesitates. "There's no one I want to see," she says. "Absolutely no one. I just got home from a horribly long trip."

I go. There's no one I want to see either, but it's rude to leave someone standing on the front stoop.

I can't hear who it is through the intercom, but I press the buzzer, allowing them entry into the building, which ticks off Barbara.

She scowls at me. "You didn't even ask them to identify themselves."

"There are two of us," I say. "If it's trouble, we can fight them off."

"I'm tired," she whines. "I can't fight off anything."

It's Allan. Allan coming up the steps two at a time.

I don't need Barbara to help me with this.

"Hey, Allan," I say.

He comes up the last flight and nods when he sees me standing in the doorframe.

"I'm so glad you're here," I say because suddenly the trip to the airport wasn't a total waste of my time. I grin. It's hard to turn down.

"Hey, Caroline," he says. He's in his work clothes – light blue button down, the shirtsleeves pushed up. He looks very good. Handsome, tanned, and white teeth. I look at his neck and wish for privacy. It would feel so good to be sexual with him at this moment.

Barbara is repacking the suitcase. I guess her jade purchases are obviously not to be shared with the entire neighborhood.

Barbara takes Lily from me and carries her into the front bedroom. Allan looks at me, and then follows Barbara into the bedroom.

I don't wait for an invitation. I'm in the room two steps behind Allan. I stand as close as I think is acceptable without getting Barbara suspicious.

Barbara is busy cooing over Lily, giving her lots of attention as a way to avoid Allan. This evasion tactic is interesting.

Allan isn't so much curious as he is angry. His lips are tight and he talks quickly, almost harshly. "I'd like some clarification," Allan says. "I want to know what happened."

"I already told you," Barbara says.

"What did you tell me?"

"I called you from New York," Barbara reminds him.

Allan sighs. He's frustrated – not in his usually sarcastic mood.

Lily's crib is painted pink and black – like an off-colored zebra. The room is packed with baby things. Everything smells new as if it's just been unwrapped and still needs time and space to air. Lily is asleep.

"Pretend I'm really stupid," Allan says. "Tell me again."

Barbara covers Lily with a thick blanket that goes along with the zoo theme.

"We got separated," Barbara whispers. "It's a huge country. There are so many people it almost makes you insane. Really. I don't know how people live like that. Bodies, and cars, and bicycles, and noise. It was exhausting."

"You got separated?" Allan asks. "And you never hooked up again?"

"That's right," Barbara whispers. "She got on the wrong bus back from the orphanage. It wasn't anyone's fault. Just a mix-up in communication."

"And that's it?" Allan asks. "You left her in Guanzhou?"

"That's the last time I saw her," Barbara says.

Allan wants this spelled out. "Is she still there? In Guanzhou?"

"I think so," Barbara says.

He waits for her to say something more, but Barbara simply shrugs.

"Does she have her airplane ticket?" Allan asks. "Does she have a way home?"

"She's got credit cards," Barbara says.

"And her plane ticket?"

"As far as I know," Barbara says.

"But you're not certain?"

"Can we talk about this later?" Barbara asks. "I want Lily to get some sleep. She's exhausted. The plane trip was awful. They showed this lousy movie with a dozen car chase scenes. All that noise was really frightening."

"Do you have any idea when she'll be home?" he asks. I'd like to know too.

"I don't," Barbara says. "I really don't."

Allan looks at her carefully and it's obvious that he doesn't believe her.

"Will you call me if she gets in touch with you?" he asks.

"Why would she call me?" Barbara asks. "You're her husband."

Allan shakes his head. It's not my place, but I could offer him a drink. Barbara's opened some windows and the apartment no longer feels so stuffy. "Just let me know if she calls you," he insists and then leaves.

He doesn't say anything to me when he leaves, but I understand this isn't the best moment to concentrate on us. But that's no longer a concern. With Maggie still in China, we have been given a reprieve.

"I don't know why he's mad at me," Barbara says. She walks in a circle, her heels pounding on the wood floor. So much for Lily's nap. "It wasn't my fault."

"Is that right?" I ask. "Are you keeping something from him?" I ask.

"From Allan?" she asks. "Of course not."

"You seemed a bit reticent to share information with him. I think he was just trying to make sure that Maggie wasn't in trouble. You two did go to China. It's a bit different than going to Cincinnati."

I'd bet money that whatever happened was Barbara's fault. That's the kind of person she is – one who causes trouble.

"Maggie's a very headstrong person," Barbara says. "She's extremely independent and doesn't like to follow directions or take advice from anyone. Even the Chinese and it's their country."

"Did you two get in a fight?" I ask. "Is that what happened?"

Maggie is not the type to lose her temper, but then Barbara isn't your average traveling companion. Difficult is a word I might choose to describe her.

"It was nothing." Barbara shakes her head. "God, you and Allan are pests. Nothing happened. Maggie decided to stay behind. That's it. That's the end of the story."

"She wanted to stay in China?"

Barbara puts her hands on her hips. She's very thin –the image of a stick figure comes to mind. "Let me just say that Maggie didn't seem particularly interested in hurrying home. That was my impression."

"What does that mean?" I ask.

But she cuts me off. "Enough about Maggie. She'll be home in a day or two or whenever she feels like it and then the two of you can question her until your heads fly off. But I'm tired of talking about her."

I must talk to Allan – his visit and obvious frustration with Barbara gives me the perfect excuse. I can be a shoulder to cry on – a sympathetic ear. I'll ask if he wants to walk up and have a drink. He can tell me why he's so upset about Maggie's prolonged Chinese stay and maybe we can get back to that confession he was lingering near the other day.

"Where are you going?" Barbara asks when I walk towards the door, keys in hand.

"Home." I turn back.

"I was hoping you could stay for a little bit," Barbara says. The front of her shirt is stained with something dark – it could be red wine, but my guess is that it's grape juice. Soon all her clothes will acquire that need for stain removal.

"You don't mind staying, do you?" she asks. "I have a few errands to run."

I think I've done enough for one day. I have limits.

She senses my hesitation. "It won't be for long."

"I'd be happy to go to the grocery store for you," I offer.

Barbara's insistent even when she's not answering my question. "Lily's easy," Barbara says. "You'll see. She never cries."

Barbara leaves with a promise that she'll be back soon.

I read a magazine and then, bored and anxious to get over to Allan's before he leaves, go and look in on Lily. She's awake and looking out the window across the room where a tree branch moves in the afternoon wind. She stares, not turning her head when I walk over to the crib.

I used to worry constantly about the boys. Especially when they were infants. It helped that Joe was a doctor, but I still worried. I would go in when they were napping and check to make sure that they were still breathing. I wasn't satisfied to see their chests moving up and down – I had to hear their breaths. I never felt like I was overreacting. Even now sometimes, I get nervous. They sleep so long that sometimes I go in and check just to make sure they haven't died in the night.

The trees near the window fascinate Lily. She watches the leaves as they press against the windowpanes.

It's been a long time since I've babysat someone who wasn't taller than me. Lily is still in diapers. At least she should be. I don't see any on the changing table. I open a drawer, then finally find some in this giraffe- shaped cloth bag hanging on the doorknob.

Barbara's right; Lily is a peaceful baby.

My boys, even at this age, were rarely quiet. I remember how I would beg them to sleep. I hated when they gave up their morning naps. I missed their afternoon naps. I mourned when they were no longer my little babies.

They grew bold, loud and rambunctious very quickly and everyone told me I must have had my hands full with two boys so close in age and I agreed with frustration and despair.

When they were toddlers, I used to cry in the car on the way home from the playground. I cried because they wouldn't mind, because I was always on the verge of losing track of them, because I couldn't keep up with them. I cried because they told me that they hated me and I knew they didn't mean it, but my head would be aching and my arms tired and I wanted someone to be nice.

I wanted them to go back to when they were sweet, when they were cuddly. I loved them, but they were hard to care for. Joe had an easier time. But I still wanted babies even as they were growing up into boys.

I loved them when they were sick, when their energy was deflated, when they crawled into bed with me and complained of sore throats. I loved the red flush of their soft faces, the way they didn't want me to leave the room. The way they asked for things. Small things. More toast, something more to drink. Popsicles. How they wanted me to watch television with them. How they wanted me to hold them until they fell asleep again.

I don't get much of that anymore and watching Lily who is watching the trees reminds me of that time.

Now as young teenagers their arrogance is hard to love. But there are moments when I still feel their need for me. The other day Josh asked me to take him to the pharmacy. He wouldn't tell me what he wanted, just that he needed something. I shopped one aisle, he went to the back of the store and then he brought up a few tubes of acne cream to the counter. I tried not to make a big deal about his desired purchases but told him quietly that his choice might be better for a girl. "It's got a lot of perfume in it."

He snarled and I started to apologize.

"Can you show me which one I should get?" Josh asked. We went back up the aisle to look for a cleanser that was more suitable for a teenage boy. I gave him a couple of options and he picked out one. He was obviously embarrassed and I offered to take it up to the cash register.

Halfway to the car, Josh thanked me. "Was it expensive?" he asked.

"Not if you're going use it." That sounded snooty, so I shook my head. "Don't worry about cost. Buy what you need. Whenever you need it."

"Do I look bad?" he said. He turned to face me. He doesn't usually confide in me. My heart surged. He had acne, it was particularly bad around his jaw line.

"Try not to pick at it," I said. "It makes it redder."

"Tell me about it," he said.

"The cream will help," I told him.

"Will it really?" he asked. "Or is that just the advertisers doing their job?"

We both laughed.

"Whenever your skin feels greasy, you should wash," I told him. "Keeping your face clean will help."

"I'd be at the sink all day long," he laughed at himself.

"It will go away," I said. "I promise." He let me put my arm around his shoulder. I didn't keep it there for long.

Max was waiting for us in the car. He wanted to know what was in the bag and surprisingly enough Josh showed him. "You're lucky, you dog. You don't have them yet."

Max didn't make fun of his brother – he sensed that he was next in line for acne. He sat in the back, hunched forward, listening to his brother and I discuss acne.

"Everyone gets it," I told him.

"Did you have it?" Josh asked.

"Oh God yes," I said. "Tons."

"That's good to know," he said, studying my face.

These are moments when I feel needed and when I am glad to be a mother. That afternoon I wanted to hold the moment. But knew I couldn't. The future was inevitable. I wanted to be with them. Just the three of us, talking and hanging out. I didn't want there to be any balls or bats about. I didn't want there to be any fighting between the two of them, or any television, or phone calls. They're too old for ice-cream, or cookies at Prantls Bakery. I wished they were old enough to drink. "How about a quick beer?" I wanted to say just so I could prolong the time together and good will. I might have suggested pizza, but Josh had sworn off pizza until his face cleared.

I'm not done being a mother, but as the boys get older, I feel less like one and more like I'm simply something they have to put up with. I've heard daughters are different, but I won't ever know if that's true.

"Is that right, Lily?" I ask her. "Are you going to take care of Barbara? Will you be kind to her when she's old and needs her diaper changed?"

But that's a long way away and now it's Barbara who has all this work and worry in front of her.

Parenting is something to share. Joe and I discussed every one of their three-year old utterances. The way Max would grab hold of the dog and smother his face into his fur. "I just love my dog," he'd tell me. "Can we keep him forever?" Not just once, but several times a day. "I just love my dog," he'd tell strangers on the street.

I look at Lily and feel sorry for her. It will be hard and perhaps lonely growing up with just Barbara. But maybe this is better than where she came from. I hope that's true.

"I'll be here," I whisper in her ear and again suddenly I'm weepy. I pick up Lily and cry. She doesn't protest, but lets me have my tears. Motherhood is such an emotional time. The memory of the highs and lows is both comforting and overwhelming.

Barbara apologizes for being late. And for once I don't give her grief; she'll have enough to do now that her mother adventure is underway. Lily's really asleep. She's settled into the crib and had a bottle and a half of formula. She'll sleep for awhile.

"Do you have everything you need?" I ask, but I'm ready to go.

"How do I know?" Barbara asks. She's nervous and I understand because I used to panic when I was first left alone with Josh. The trip is over. There is no more paperwork, no more bureaucratic nonsense, no more lines or plane trips. There's nothing else she has to take care of. Except Lily. Lily's here in Pittsburgh and it's time for Barbara to start being a mother.

I'd be scared too.

Regardless of how I look, which isn't my best after all those tears, I go directly to Allan's.

The side door is open. He's on the phone; I hear his one-sided conversation. "Allan." I say his name through the screen door.

He continues talking so I knock. "Anyone home?" I call as if I can't hear him in there.

He walks into view, but doesn't come down the steps. "Just a minute," he says to me, then talks into the phone. "It's just my neighbor," he says.

I am going to ignore that comment.

"I'll call you right back. Fifteen minutes. I promise."

I think I deserve more than a quarter of an hour.

He puts down the phone. "Be right there, Caroline. I have to change." He's not wearing a shirt. I see the flash of skin, then he's gone. I'm standing there on his back steps feeling awkward, but I rehearse what I'll say to him.

Just checking. That will be my lead-in. Just being neighborly, checking on you and seeing if Maggie's all right. I'll vilify Barbara. Easy enough for a line of attack.

Unfortunately I don't get the chance.

There's some commotion from inside the house, a door slamming, voices.

"Mom. Mom." It's Jane. She and Katie are home from school.

There's pounding on the steps, then Allan says something. I'm not comfortable standing here. Like most things that happen these days – this is not how I imagined it would be.

I am just about to give up. I can admit defeat and retreat. Our feelings for one another have always been precarious. I understand their fragility.

Allan comes down. He's dressed. Jeans, dark-blue top. No shoes. The barefoot look is very sexy. I notice it all.

"Caroline," Allan says.

I'm smart. I realize this isn't the right time for confession or cocktails.

"You were upset so I just wanted to come over and see if I could do anything."

He nods. "What did Barbara tell you about Maggie not coming back from China?"

"That it wasn't her fault."

"That's how she explained it to me," Allan snorts.

The girls come downstairs and crowd to the back door. "Can we still go out to dinner?" Jane asks.

Allan turns to them. "Sure, that sounds like a good idea," he says.

"Just the three of us," Jane clarifies.

If it's possible, I feel even more foolish.

"Sure, sure," Allan says. "Just give me a minute here."

Now I only have a minute?

"We always do," Katie says.

He pushes the screen door open and leads me down the walk. He obviously doesn't want the girls to hear this part of our conversation. "I just hope Maggie's not doing something foolish," Allan says.

"Do you think China is dangerous?" I ask, not understanding what he meant. "Are you worried for her safety?"

"Not that," he says. "She's a very competent traveler."

"Then what?" I ask.

"I just wonder..." He hesitates and looks at me with a sheepish grin. "If she's being deliberately reckless," he says.

"That doesn't sound like Maggie," I say.

"She might have reason to be now," Allan says. He's barefoot. He kicks up a stone with his toes and balances it carefully just below his ankle. He waits a minute, struggling for more balance, then kicks it up and catches it with the top of his other foot.

"She does?" I don't know what we're talking about. My attention is on the stone, which he flips up again, only this time he misses. It rolls off the drive onto the grass.

"But I hope that's not the case."

"I'm sure it's not," I say

"You are?" Allan asks.

"Of course," I assure him. I want to be on firmer ground. "I'm sure Barbara's to blame," I say.

"Yeah," Allan says. He puts his head back and howls at the sky. The muscles in his neck are tense as the strange noise strains out of his throat. Karen and Greg's dog starts barking furiously. That sets off Spot, who's in the backyard now going crazy.

"Dad. Stop it," Katie yells from the house. "You're being weird again."

"I'm embarrassing my kids," he says. "Best to go and see if I can't make amends."

I nod; the howling is a bit strange.

I'm halfway home when it comes to me. He doesn't trust Maggie. That's what he was telling me, but I was too clueless to grab the bait. I replay our conversation – word by word – carefully weighing every nuance of what he told me. He's worried about what she's doing over there – nervous what her actions mean to him. He must have reason to be suspicious. He's not worried about China or about travel, but about his wife. He believes she's cheating on him. He was accusing her of infidelity.

It is such an odd thought that I stop mid-step to think this through. He called her deliberately reckless. That certainly has sexual implications.

This is an avenue that I have never explored. Maggie's cheating offers me a whole new world. I put my hands together in sheer happiness. What a turn of events, something I would never have predicted. I applaud – madly applaud – this sudden turn of events.

This is bliss.

The fantasies come immediately. I imagine Maggie in China with a man – he looks nothing like Allan. They're madly in love and she's trying to explain her commitments, but he doesn't want to hear them. I see her flying home and telling Allan that their marriage is over. They're in the Pittsburgh airport just outside the Clinique Shop where the sales help wear way too much of their own products. Perfume and foundation

121

galore. Maggie's impatient; she still cares for Allan and doesn't want to hurt his feelings by dragging out their break-up.

"I've fallen in love," she says.

Allan is calm. "I guessed as much," he says.

I imagine Maggie telling Allan that she loved him once, but that like all things in life, it's time to move on. They talk about their time in Thailand and vow to remember those happy days. That's how they'll remember one another. Maggie turns around and boards the plane back to China. Allan comes home. Back to the neighborhood—back where someone loves him ferociously.

I, too, could howl at the sky.

Chapter Seven

Bliss, as it turns out, is not at all romantic. Not in the world where I reside. Oddly enough, bliss on my block resembles motherhood.

A few days after her return from China, Barbara comes over with Lily and asks me to lend her a hand.

"I've only got two," I say, and hold them up. My nails look awful. I should take care of them, even if I don't have anywhere special to go. Make a manicure appointment; I mentally type this into my empty schedule.

"I was hoping you could watch Lily for a while," she says and then scrunches up her face. "Please." She draws out the word into several syllables as if she's a teenager begging to borrow the car. Politeness is out of character and it strains her physically.

Watching Lily doesn't seem too difficult. It's a neighborly request – one I'm sure I made of my neighbors when my kids were young. Barbara is a single mother – newly adjusting to a child and all the fears and uncertainties that come with a new baby. I'm not cold. Opinionated, but not unreasonable.

"Sure," I say.

She pushes Lily towards me. Lily's head is down. She's not looking at either me or at Barbara. Her lack of curiosity pinches my heart. I squat and hold out my hand.

"We'll have some fun here, won't we, Lily?" I smile. She looks at me, but doesn't react. She probably doesn't understand a word I'm saying.

It's then I notice that Barbara is dressed in a suit. "Where are you off to?" I say, standing.

She shoots me this look like I've been lobotomized and in need of special help. "Where do you think I'm going?" The teenager has been replaced by a snippy, stressed-out working woman, the kind who uses the word *busy* as a mantra under the false belief that people find her overt display of nervous tension fascinating. My working world had been filled with women who shared this strategy; they were all incredibly dull, incredibly self-centered.

I don't need or want to play guessing games with Barbara. "I haven't the slightest idea," I tell her honestly.

"Work," she says in that tone that I don't deserve. "I'm going to work," she says, then she pauses before saying. "Some of us still have jobs."

My jaw tenses. She's bad for my blood pressure. I don't think bringing up my employment status when she's asking for a favor is a particularly good move.

"Lucky you," I say, lowering my voice like I'm wounded. This is my martyr act, something I don't pull often even though I'd like to. "You're fortunate. Employment isn't an easy thing to hold onto these days."

"I'm sorry," she rushes ahead. She's not dumb – she is asking me to help her; she doesn't want to make me mad. "I didn't mean anything by that."

"Then you shouldn't have said anything," I tell her. I'm not patient with people's imperfections. Ask Joe. He walks on eggshells, though I'm trying to correct this, seeing as I'm engaging in an extramarital, albeit imaginary, affair with Allan.

"How long?" I ask. It's been a while since I've babysat. I'm not sure I remember how to do it. Lily carries a miniature backpack. It doesn't look like it will hold more than ten minutes worth of toys.

I imagine Barbara is going to run to the office, check her voice mail and email, maybe catch up on a few odds and ends. I used to love breaks from the kids. Sometimes I wouldn't go anywhere specific. I would simply drive down by the river by myself and play the radio, glad not to have any fights or sticky hands, or demands that we go toy shopping.

"Until five," she says, and then under her breath adds, "or so."

She wears too much foundation. It accents the crow's feet around her eyes. Women often make this mistake; they continue with the same make-up routine, the same one they had in their twenties.

"You're kidding, aren't you?"

"Do I sound like I'm trying to be funny?" she says.

"You're trying my patience," I tell her.

She rushes on ahead. "I'm back at work. And I have to work all day. We're swamped down there."

She really does ride on my nerves. She's extraordinarily presumptuous – first the ride from the airport and now watching her daughter. I do think that motherhood underscores her quirkiness. Did she think she could just stop by and ask me to watch Lily all day long? Not even a call the night before. And what if I said no? Does she have other options? I don't think she's friendly with a lot of the neighbors, but I'm sure I wasn't her first choice. She doesn't like me enough to make me her first choice. But I'm not thinking fast enough to refuse her a favor.

"What about maternity leave?" I ask.

"I didn't get any."

"None?"

"Just what I took to go to China," she says.

"That's a terrible policy," I tell her. "You should check that out. It doesn't sound right. It doesn't sound legal."

"But that's how it is," she protests.

It does sound wrong. I know from Joe that the hospital has a very generous leave policy. It's required, like health care – the Family Medical Leave Act. Benefits are benefits. But maybe Barbara is too new to qualify. I'll have to look into this.

I have more sympathy for her than I should, especially after that crack about my not having a job. She is new at being a mother and her world has just been turned around. So, thinking this is an emergency and just a temporary situation, until Barbara can find Lily a spot in a local day care, I agree to baby-sit Lily. Besides tracking down Allan and that manicure appointment that I'll never make, I have nothing else on my calendar today, after all.

My babysitting duties continue the rest of the week. Barbara drops off Lily, we have our day together. She picks her up. They go home. She comes back the next day. I don't have a logical explanation for why I'm letting Barbara take advantage of me except for some reason I can't say no. Maybe there is nothing wrong with Barbara. Maybe I am the one with the problem.

I make plans to fire up my relationship with Allan, but by then it's dinner time and I'm exhausted and thinking of what Lily and I can do the next day.

I have to say it's not a bad way to spend the day. Lily is a dream.

Lily is nothing like my boys. She's light, easy to carry, even when she's asleep. Her nose doesn't drip; she likes to keep her clothes clean. She doesn't squirm when I wipe her face with a wet-nap. She likes me to brush her hair and even when I tangle the ponytail holders, she doesn't cry.

She likes the swings at the Blue Slide Park, likes the painting station at the Children's museum. She especially likes the butterflies in Phipps Conservatory and shudders in excitement when one lands on her shoulder or outstretched arm. She falls asleep, her head in my lap, in the Orchid Room; the sound of the waterfall is like a lullaby and she sleeps for an hour. Everyone tiptoes past us, all smiles and nods. "Isn't that adorable!" "She's precious!"

And she is. Even when she's awake.

She's timid around strangers and when we're out and about, she sticks close to me. She likes to watch the other children play, likes to hear them shout and yell at each other, but she won't participate. She stays with me on the bench, her arms entwined in my legs, eyes focused on the other kids. Only when they've gone and the swing set is completely empty will she let me push her. She smiles and when she goes higher she laughs.

Josh and Max were never still. They'd run from me. They'd hit and scream and call me stupid. When I wouldn't buy them a treat, they called me a baby and told me I was grounded. "You have to move out of the house," they'd yell at the top of their lungs. When tired, they were rude and out of control.

Max went through a stage when he was 2½ when he would scream. High-pitched, full force, no particular reason screams. It was a long stage. Little things would set him off; the sun in his face, too many crackers in his baggie, gum stuck to the sidewalk, the wind. He'd start and then wouldn't stop. It made Josh berserk and then finally it would drive him to tears. Max screaming, Josh crying, we'd be in the middle of traffic and I'd have real doubts if we were all going to make it home alive.

Neither of them would tolerate strollers. They'd undo the seat belts keeping them in their car seats. They'd climb into the front seat and pull on the steering wheel.

I dreaded taking them places, not because I didn't want to get out of the house. I did. I longed to be around people, to be out doing things, but I wasn't sure I could control them. I lost Joshua in the bookstore one afternoon. He thought we were playing hide-n-go-seek, and ran. The store manager came to help and they actually locked the front door. A male customer found him. "I think your son might be in the bathroom," he said. I rushed up the escalator, dragging Max who also thought we were playing a game. "I want to be *it*. Why does Josh always get to be *it*?" he said, pulling my arm out of its socket.

Josh was also screaming. "Wipe my bum. Wipe my bum." Four years old, toilet trained more than a year except that he refused to use toilet paper.

Lily folds hers into tiny squares and then flips down the lid, without any prompting on my behalf.

She likes dolls and will sit on my bed and dress and redress her baby-doll. "Yes. Yes. Yes," she coos.

Max and Josh are also charmed by Lily. They treat her like a toy and take her out in the backyard and play ball with her. They laugh at her every utterance, her every change of expression. She was shy with them, but they wouldn't stand to be ignored. Now they volunteer to take her for walks. She goes, something I tell them they would never have done. "You didn't know how to walk in a straight line."

They bring her up to the shopping area in Shadyside and buy her ice cream. They take her into the toy store and show her how to turn on the trains, the 'load-em-up' trucks, and the batting machine. They let her dress up in the Snow White costume. They pool their money together and buy her a tiara and princess dress with tiny rosebud buttons in the back. She changes in the store and wears her costume on the walk home. She comes running in the front door eager to show me her new outfit.

Josh and Max are beaming. They are silly; acting like medieval court announcers with fake horns. "Presenting Princess Lily."

Lily curtsies coyly then crawls under the table in a fit of giggles and blushes, overwhelmed by all the attention.

"You should have had more kids, Mom," I'm told.

"Really?" I ask.

"Big families are great," they tell me. "We always wanted a little sister."

"Maybe it's not too late," I say and pat my stomach as if I'm considering pregnancy. "Lots of women have babies in their forties."

They think this is hysterical. They laugh at the thought of me having another child and Lily giggles because they're happy.

"I have time to have two or three little sisters," I announce.

The laughter grows louder. No one can speak.

"I'm not being funny," I protest.

Lily points her finger at my face. "Yes. Yes. Yes."

Joe calls Lily his Little Princess. He comes home from work, his pockets filled with candy from the vending machine in the waiting room. Lily giggles though she's cautious about approaching Joe or even looking at him. She hides behind my legs and squeals. Joe tosses the packages in the air. "It's raining candy. Look. Look." Lily rushes out and tires to grab the candy before it falls on the ground. She is shy about it and hides it in the bookcase in the living room. She pulls out a book and applauds herself for finding it.

"You never bought the boys candy," I tell Joe.

"They didn't need it. You bribed them enough," he reminds me.

"I had to," I say in my defense. This is one of our old arguments. We used to fight about food and the boys all the time. Joe thought I fed them junk. I told him I was just doing what I could to get by. They behaved better when motivated with candy.

"They were wild," he agrees.

I remember the treats I bought them. The back of the car was littered with candy wrappers and Popsicle sticks. I never left the house without at least two different kinds of goodies. It was the only way I could possibly get them home eventually.

My babysitting of Lily is an odd situation. Barbara doesn't make plans with me. She seems to assume that I'm free and willing to watch her daughter. She's incredibly arrogant in this respect, but I don't press her on it. I've grown quite attached to Lily. I like her shy, careful personality. I like the way she seems to like me. She's one of the more interesting souls I've met this past year.

I attempt one conversation where I ask Barbara about the search for a daycare.

"I don't believe in day care, Caroline."

"Oh come on," I demand. She floors me. She really does.

She straightens up as if proud of the stance she has taken on child rearing. It's a great belief as long as it's practical. Having a neighbor babysit for free is probably much more financially appealing than daycare.

"You do believe they exist, don't you?"

"It's not my concern," is how she puts it.

"You read about the ones where the owners lock their children in the basement, or feed them horse meat? The caretakers leave them in hot cars with the windows rolled up in the middle of the summer? Or they let the kids play with knives? Daycare. You're heard of them, haven't you?" I ask.

"Which is why I don't believe in sending my daughter to one. It wouldn't be right."

"Right for what?"

"With how I want to raise my daughter."

"I don't mean to be dim, Barbara," I say.

"Of course you're not," she said.

"But if you don't believe in daycare then who's going to watch Lily?"

"That's the big question, isn't it?" she asks.

"Didn't you think about this before you adopted Lily?" I knew women who had every intention of working after they had their babies, but changed their minds after the birth. I don't know how women work after having kids. How do you shower and get dressed, get them bathed and dressed and then give everyone breakfast before noon? In my house, there were days when we didn't change out of our pajamas until dinnertime.

But most parents consider what they'll do with their kids before the kids come into their lives.

Barbara buttons her suit coat, and then thrusts her hands into the pockets. It's a male gesture – one of power and assurance. She speaks in a voice that matches her gesture. "Life hasn't exactly proceeded as I planned it. I had planned to be madly in love, to be married, to have children naturally. I never planned to be a single woman in her forties raising a child from China. Things turned out a great deal differently than I imagined. You can't plan for life, Caroline. Sometimes it just happens. And you accept it. Take it as it's dealt."

She has read way too many self-help books. I've read one; *Women Are From Venus, Men are from Mars.* It had nothing to do with space.

"You don't like me, do you?" Barbara asks.

I don't know how to answer this, which hardly matters, as she doesn't give me the time to answer.

"See?" she sneers.

"See what?" I ask.

"The truth is unsettling, isn't it?"

"What truth?"

"That you don't like me," she says. She seems happy with her little discovery, happy that she's steered the conversation this way.

I finally think of a word. "You're entertaining," I tell her.

"That's not the same thing as liking me."

"No. It's not."

"See?" she asks again. But I'm not sure what I'm supposed to be looking at.

"I admire what you've done," I say. Adopting Lily is a huge undertaking and I actually have a high regard for adoption. I wouldn't have thought she was the type. I'd like to move away from Barbara as subject – it doesn't make much sense to discuss my feelings for her. I don't think she's overly fond of me, either.

"I'm glad that you've brought Lily to the neighborhood," I add.

It's strange but she rarely talks about Lily. Unlike every other mother I know, she doesn't go on and on about Lily's slightest movement or deviation in schedule. When I ask how Lily slept the night, Barbara looks at me like I've asked her to leap off Niagara Falls.

"I mean how has she been sleeping?" I clarify. "Does she sleep through the night?"

"Why?" she asks. Her arms akimbo – she becomes stressed-out working woman suddenly.

"Because that's what mothers talk about," I inform her. She has to have learned this by now.

She looks at me, puzzled.

I remember being pregnant and listening to other young mothers going on and on about the littlest details of their kids' lives. And then I had Josh and I talked the same way. I talked about their nap schedules, their poops, their ability or willingness to eat green beans. Joe and I talked about it. I talked about it with the neighborhood mothers' group. I talked about it with strangers I encountered at the grocery store. It was the same with Max. I talked so much I even annoyed myself, but I couldn't do anything about it. It was a need and I'm thrown off by Barbara's silence on the personal aspects of Lily's life. Particularly the details I now know more about than she does.

I notice that Lily fusses when Barbara comes to pick her up. If I'm holding her, she tightens her grip. I notice that Barbara doesn't run up to hug her. In fact they never hug, at least not in front of me. And it's not Lily. Lily hugs the boys, she hugs the dog, she hugs the little blonde whose name I can never remember from the playground.

Barbara doesn't ask about our day. She doesn't ask how we spent the hours between 8am and 5pm. She doesn't ask if

Lily was good, if she napped, what did she eat? She doesn't ask if Lily had fun, if she cried, if she seemed lonely, if she had any problems with the day.

I take it personally, because I'm in that fragile emotional state where I happen to think everything is my fault. I figure she doesn't think I'm capable of caring for her daughter and therefore my opinions on her care are irrelevant and simply not needed.

Barbara doesn't kiss Lily good-bye. She doesn't kiss her when she comes to get her.

And this, I realize, has nothing to do with me.

I sympathize with Lily's point of view – who would want to kiss Barbara? – I know it's not right. I shower Lily with kisses. We kiss in the library when the bears in the book we're reading kiss goodnight. We kiss at the noodle shop when our chins and lips are coated with sesame oil and soy sauce. We kiss in the park when she goes down the blue slide by herself. We kiss when we nap; we kiss when Barney and the Backyard Gang sing that annoying, but surprisingly touching song. And when she's asleep, I kiss her eyelashes when they flutter with dreams.

It is Tony, my unreliable, inefficient housekeeper who confirms that something is fishy with Barbara. Tony has been working for us for so long that I could never fire him, even though he suffers from short-term memory loss and doesn't always clean the house – he forgets what he's doing there. I find him in the second-floor television room, munching on the boys' leftover popcorn. He cooks an egg in the middle of cleaning the stove. He rakes the leaves, piling them up in the backyard even though I've never asked him to help out in the yard.

Until Tony called Barbara a strange bird, I hadn't realized that she and I shared Tony.

"How did that come about?" I ask. I didn't give her Tony's number. He's not someone I'd recommend, even to

Barbara, so I'm a bit surprised to hear that he cleans her apartment.

"Since she moved in," Tony explains. "She saw me loading up the mops and supplies into the trunk of my car and asked me if I'd clean her house too. Good enough for you – good enough for her."

"I guess so," I say, pondering this.

Tony's wife is a Wicca, who runs an online teddy bear business. She sells home-sewn bears to help other witches with their home practices. She used to help Tony – she'd come over and explain her fascination with good magic. Tony's son is incarcerated because he looks identical to a man who recently walked into the Mini-Mart with a sawed-off shotgun and told the cashier to hit the floor, while he cleared the place not of money but of goods – goods he had plans to resell. He took gallons of milk, eggs, bags of Cheese Doodles, magazines, and boxes of Entenmanns's sugar-free cookies. Tony's son is innocent; the cops got it wrong, but he's still doing time. Tony's daughter has a baby with special powers. She's four and can move things with her mind's eye. Physically, that is.

Tony obviously has a very high tolerance for eccentric behavior, which is why I'm curious when he starts gossiping about Barbara. I would have thought her tame compared to what Tony puts up with everyday of his life – not that he can actually remember for too long.

I never used to bother with Tony when I worked. I'd come home, the house would be clean, and there would be no sign of him. Now I spend an inordinate amount of time talking to him. He listens to Dr. Laura and watches Court TV. He's very current on world events and has an opinion on everything, when he remembers.

"What's that?" I ask. I'm used to his opinions and advice about world news. He talked incessantly about the girl who drowned her ageing mother – he sympathized – and about the man who raised horses for personal consumption – this was wrong. Very wrong. We don't usually talk about news so close to home.

"That's Lily, isn't it?" he asks. Tony comes out with a garbage bag and sets it on the curb for trash pick-up.

"It is," I nod.

Late September and the ginkgo leaves have turned a brilliant gold color, the berries have dropped until the sidewalks are completely covered. I am careless where I walk and feel them squash against the sole of my shoes. Lily makes a funny face and bends to find the source. She picks up a berry and holds it to her nose. She recoils and throws it down.

"Nasty, aren't they?" I ask.

"Wash," she says, and holds out her hands. We have spent the afternoon collecting leaves. She has a tiny fistful of red oaks. I have collected every green leaf I could find. We go inside.

"Her mother is one odd duck." Tony sweeps the front walk for the second time that day.

He takes our leaves and stuffs them into the garbage bag. I retrieve them. I have plans to press them into wax paper if I have any – an activity I remember from when the boys were young. This endeavor also requires that I locate the iron, an object I haven't seen in years, though I don't remember throwing it away, either.

We go inside. The kitchen floor is still wet – at least he's washed it. I hope he hasn't used pure bleach. It eats the wood. Lily and I use the little washroom under the stairs. Tony joins us. It's a small space for three people. Lily likes the bar of decorative orange soap. "Pretty," she says and holds her hands under the warm water to rid her skin of the foul smell of the ginkgo berries.

Strange bird, odd duck – I can't argue – but do ask Tony for more details.

"She doesn't seem to like people." Tony has always been a good gossip, but normally he's talking about people I don't know.

He continues. "She hides."

"She hides? What would she hide?" I like this gossip. It supports my harsh judgments of Barbara.

"Well, mainly, she hides herself. I'll go in and she pretends that she's not home. I call out hello. I can hear her breathing. I know she's in there, but she won't come out and say hello. She doesn't say a word." He pauses. "I'm sure if I knocked down the door, she'd be under the bed."

I nod, but realize it's probably not such a great idea to talk about Barbara in front of Lily. Lily seems engrossed in the sink, now filled with water, but kids listen. They repeat things, even without understanding what they're saying.

"And what I'd like to know is why you're watching that little Chinese girl when her mother is home watching television."

I look at him. He nods. "Saw her this morning. Locked herself in the bedroom when I came."

I nod, though I've no idea what he's talking about.

Tony continues. "What's it to me what she does? One less room to clean. That's how I look at it."

"That's right," I say.

Tony packs up his pail and mops, folds his rags, readying to leave, even though he hasn't cleaned the second floor.

I have to be careful when it comes to Tony. As I've said, he's not 100 percent reliable, but he's not totally off base.

I dial Barbara's number. The machine clicks on. "Hey Barbara," I say. "I thought I saw your car. Wanted to see if you were home. Let me know what time you'll be picking up Lily. I've got some things I have to do."

Fifty minutes later, she returns my call.

"Take her with you," she says. "Lily loves errands."

136

"Who said anything about errands?" I ask.

"You did," she responds.

"Where are you?" I ask. I aim for casual, but she detects the accusatory nature of my question. I am not the kind of person who hides their emotions.

"Work. Where else would I be?" she snaps.

"What time are you coming home?" I ask.

"I'll call you the minute I leave here," she says, then before she hangs up. "Have to fly. I'm swamped." She's used those words before to describe her days at the office.

I put down the phone. She certainly sounded like she was calling me from some sort of work environment. I decide to give her the benefit of the doubt, though Tony's story echoes in my mind every time she comes and goes.

Meanwhile, bliss on the Allan front eludes me. Completely.

Since I've become the one-woman, one child daycare, I haven't seen anything of him. Not even his car.

"Maggie's home," Barbara announces after three weeks of my daycare services. She wears the same khaki-colored suit every day to work. She keeps it clean. Her blouse is pressed. She must eat her lunch carefully. My work clothes were stained with coffee and mustard. I was someone who could have benefited from a bib.

"Already?" I ask. I actually knew she was coming home. I had been checking up on Maggie and feared that she was due home.

"You should think about the stage," she says. "You're wasting your talents here."

I wasn't trying for humor. I'm deflated. My hopes for some sort of improvement on the Allan front have blown up in my face. Again.

"She's been gone almost five weeks," Barbara says. "I'm sure her family's going crazy."

"I guess," I say.

Regret sets in immediately. I should have been doing more to advance our relationship. What was I thinking? My reprieve slips away without any progress.

The first thing Maggie does on her return to Pittsburgh is to accuse me of being rude to Barbara.

"I hope you're kidding," I say. Maggie's not a practical joker; she also doesn't criticize or gossip so her comment throws me off-guard. For a few minutes I worry that she knows something. It might be possible that Allan mentioned something. People newly in love have nerve.

She's been back three days. I've yet to ask her about the new man in her life. But I'm dying to know. She looks different. Her face is sunburned. The end of her nose is peeling. Her hair seems lighter as if she's recently bleached it. She glows like a woman who's having an affair. She doesn't seem the least bothered or worried about her husband or children. Some women are ruthless – they only care for their own passions. I wouldn't have pegged Maggie to be that way.

"Barbara said you were grilling her about her work," Maggie says. "I think it bothers her."

"Are you kidding?" I cannot believe Barbara has the audacity to criticize me. Not after everything I've done for her. My jaw opens in pure astonishment.

"I know it's none of my business," Maggie says in her quiet manner.

"She is such a freak," I say.

"New mothers usually are."

"Asking what time she'll be home hardly qualifies as grilling. I am watching her daughter. What time she'll pick up Lily is information that's vital to my daily existence."

"Of course it is," Maggie sighs. "Of course. But you know."

"No. I don't."

138

"How was China?" I deliberately change subjects. Barbara is bothersome on any level.

"It was wonderful," she says.

"Really?" I ask, hoping she'll just come straight out and tell me that she has a lover. I wouldn't have pegged Maggie as the unfaithful type, but the evidence is stacking up against her.

"A wonderful, wonderful country," she gushes. She's definitely in love. "Absolutely thrilling. What a great trip. All those people doing all that good."

"All what good?" I ask.

"Adopting those poor babies. It is so wonderful."

"Is that right?" I ask. I can see Maggie in China. I imagine all those helpless hysterical couples nervous about getting their new babies. They're frantically trying to understand everything and no one seems to be able to help. Then suddenly Maggie comes along. Maggie as guardian angel – Maggie who is patient, kind, and incredibly understanding of their situation. Fortunately for them, she also understands the language.

Then I see her meeting a man. I see a small man with a receding hairline approaching her in a hotel lobby. There is a black and white terrazzo floor, a waterfall that cascades over jade-colored stones, and chandeliers that refract long shadows in the late afternoon.

I'm not sure if it's legal for single men to adopt. I don't see why not. Barbara did it. And if she can do it, anyone can. Maggie's lover, most likely from Southern California where men are more apt to adopt on their own, stops to ask Maggie a translation question. She performs the translation quickly and he falls in love. She is easily seduced, ripe for a new love.

"Will you go back?" I ask. A zillion questions race through my mind: have they made plans for their future? How much of the affair does Allan know about? Is she upset about the girls? Will they move to California? I'm sure he has a large house. I picture a swimming pool and tennis court and a side yard badminton set, which is set up year-round.

"I'd love to," she says. "There's so much to be done." She pauses, and then shakes her head as if she's thinking something. "Next time you should come."

"You'd want me around?" I'm fishing for clues about this new man of hers, but she's keeping things close to her heart. If you didn't know, you wouldn't suspect a thing.

"Why not?"

"I don't speak Mandarin," I remind her.

"I did do a lot of translation but there is so much to do over there. So many people need help. You could find something to do."

"Is that all you did?" I ask. "Help with the babies? Did you have any time to yourself?"

She senses I'm angling for personal information and steers the conversation back to Barbara.

"I think we should be more sympathetic." Maggie continues giving out useless advice.

"You think that would be good?"

"Oh yes. You have to deal with her with compassion," she says. "She's a new mother. She needs all the help she can get."

I've been nothing but compassionate. I think back over these past three weeks. I add the hours I've spent with Lily; subtracting the hours she spends every night sleeping. An average day: Me = 9 hours. Barbara = 2.

Shouldn't I be the one garnering sympathy?

I roll my eyes. "Maggie, have you ever considered how it might look from my point of view?"

"I know," she says. "I know. I shouldn't even be saying anything. I'm sure you've done a wonderful job."

"I have," I say in my own defense.

"Of course you have," Maggie agrees.

But I have to be careful. Maggie is obviously close to Barbara. They must have bonded over there in China. She insists on taking Barbara's side. I know a losing battle when I see it.

"She has to work long hours. She's the primary breadwinner. She's probably frantic about how she's going to care for Lily. Emotionally and financially. It's such a huge undertaking.'

I'm done talking about Barbara. Maggie can talk about her and pretend that she's not crazy. But I can't. I don't have anything else to say about the subject of Barbara or motherhood. It makes me look bad when I stick up for myself so I am finished doing it. "Did you meet people in China?" I ask.

"Unbelievable," she sighs. "Really. It surpassed all of my expectations. I'm so glad I went."

"Anyone in particular?" Admittedly, I'm incorrigible.

"It's such a wonderful place. So interesting. You'll have to go one day." She's starting to repeat herself.

I tell her it's time for Lily's nap.

"Can I help?" she asks. "Would you like me to take her?"

"I'm fine," I say.

Lily and I go upstairs. I put on the Barney tape and the two of us get under the covers. We nap.

I wake up when the tape stops. I get up and straighten the house. We have a toy box in the living room filled with pink and blue costume dresses, crowns and red sparkly shoes.

Lily sleeps until the boys come home from school. They pound up the steps and I hear her footfalls as she gets out of bed. A minute later, she's in a fit of giggles playing hide-n-go-seek with the dog and the boys.

Chapter Eight

My on-line ginkgo club newsletter has recently informed me that Confucius believed in the medicinal and healing power of the ginkgo tree. He called them glorious and thought they deserved to be worshipped. He spent each day reading, meditating, and teaching his pupils under these trees. Many of his followers have reported that he so loved and respected the beauty and serenity of the trees that they felt they were on a higher plane than almost anything else in the world. In his writings he often contemplated their divine nature. In almost every drawing of Confucius, there is also a ginkgo tree.

The ginkgo trees on my street are defective. They're not medicinal or divine. They're not even kind.

I'm replaced. Been made redundant, as they say in Scotland. Two times in one year. My services in caring for Lily are no longer needed. Not that anyone bothered to inform me officially. No one came by with a pink slip or gave me a two-week notice. I had to come to this brilliant conclusion all on my own.

My removal is as odd and as rude as any of the other encounters I've had with Barbara. She simply doesn't show up.

I'm home at eight o'clock, finishing my coffee and waiting for Lily. It's raining and cold so I'm thinking we'll end up down in the Strip District. It's where the wholesale shops are – the cheapest and best produce in Pittsburgh. Lily likes Wholey's, the fish shop with the tanks of lobsters and catfish. They have an electric train that runs overhead; the engine whistle toots every few minutes. Near the fresh vegetables are three singing pigs that animate with a push of the corncob. Lily knows how to work it and we stand near the picket fence listening to the pigs' two-song repertoire.

No one comes. I look out the window. No one is there. I call Barbara's. No answer. I wait until 9:30, thinking that perhaps Lily is sick or that Barbara is. Or maybe they've just slept in. Nothing.

I walk to Barbara's and ring the bell. There's no answer. I go back home and call the apartment again. I try Barbara at her office and on her cell phone. Message machines on both numbers. "Barbara. It's me, Caroline. I'm just wondering if there's a problem or if anything is wrong. Call me as soon as you can."

No response.

I call several more times, ending the day with no idea what happened.

Maggie is the one who informs me that I've been replaced. "I'm going to be taking care of Lily from now on."

"Oh?" I mouth silently because I'm momentarily too angry to speak.

"I'm not busy," Maggie says brightly when she calls. "I'm not doing anything important these days."

"Is that what happened?" I ask. Obviously. Maggie came home and Barbara asked her to watch Lily. I guess I wasn't good enough.

"That should free up your time," Maggie says.

If she knew what I did in my free time she wouldn't encourage me to have more. What am I saying? If she had any idea, she'd consider me a sick and deranged woman without a real sense of purpose in life.

"So now you're the neighborhood daycare?" I ask. I guess she's not making plans to move in with her lover. Fickle is what I'd call her behavior. I wonder if he's heartbroken? Maybe he's got time for me.

"For now," Maggie laughs.

"Fun," I seethe.

"Are you okay?" Maggie finally gets that maybe I'm not exactly thrilled with the new arrangement.

"It might have been nice if someone had bothered to inform me," I say. "I think it's rude to depend on someone for three weeks, then just leave them in the dark about the change in plans. I sat home and waited for Lily all day yesterday.

"I'm sure it just slipped Barbara's mind." Maggie's defense of her friend is incredibly weak.

"Really?" I ask. "Do you really think that?"

"You remember what it was like," she pleads. "I could barely form a sentence when the girls were toddlers."

"I don't think this was caused by Barbara's new state of motherhood," I say. "I think she was waiting for you to come home. I think she was just using me until she could find someone else. Because that's the kind of person Barbara is. She's a user. She talks a good game, all friendly and cheerful, but deep down she doesn't care about anyone else but herself. She didn't even have the decency to thank me for what I've done for her."

I'm steamed. "Maybe I'll charge her. If that's all it was to her – a business agreement. I'll charge her for my daycare services. What's the going rate for one child? Eight-nine hours a day?" I hold up my hands. "Yeah. I'm going to be rich."

Maggie is a good friend. I hope Barbara realizes this. "She's just overwhelmed," Maggie says quietly. "I'm sure she didn't mean anything personal."

"Of course she did," I say.

"I don't think she's like that."

But there is no sense being angry with Maggie. She'll just apologize for things she didn't do.

I cannot be the only one who sees that Barbara is a kook. I really am not that harsh a judge. I used to be kind. I used to have colleagues and friends and people who invited me to dinner. Have I really been reduced to a ball of anger?

Barbara doesn't call, doesn't thank me for the past three weeks. She doesn't have the decency to acknowledge the time I've spent with Lily. I miss Lily. I miss our days and the way we spent our time. She became, in her own way, a part of our family, and it's like someone just yanked her away. I'm resentful and powerless. But this time my feelings feel greatly justified.

I feel like I'm being punished and I'm irritated by the way everything has played out. For all Barbara's strange behavior, I expected some kind of appreciation. A verbal thank you would have sufficed.

"Punished for what?" Joe asks. "And by whom? Who is punishing you?"

"Barbara," I say. I'm so full of anger that after Maggie calls I punch the wall. My fingers immediately swell and I spend the afternoon with a Baggie of ice, trying to bend and straighten them without pain. I tell Joe I slammed it in a drawer. He takes a look at it and determines that nothing is broken.

"Barbara thinks I don't like her," I say. "That's why she treats me like this." I sound as overdramatically fraught and sophomoric as I feel.

"You don't like her," Joe says. "You think she's rude."

"Because she is," I say.

"Then you're being ridiculous," Joe assures me. "This is who she is. This is how she acts."

"I guess I am," I say. My finger throbs. I hold it up, which relieves the pain somewhat.

"Would you want to do daycare-type work?" he asks.

"God no," I say. I like watching Lily, but don't see babysitting as a future employment possibility. Not that I have anything else on the horizon. I walked by a shop up in Shadyside that sells expensive ceramic dishes imported from

Italy. The sign in the window said that they were looking for part-time help and I almost went in to fill out an application, but thought I'd die of boredom and then start breaking those beautiful dishes and water pitchers. I couldn't afford to work there – even on a part-time basis.

"Then this is for the best," Joe says.

"I guess it must be," I say. I feel sorry for myself. I miss little Lily. I miss the days when I had something to do with them.

But no one wants to hear my side, so I vow not to talk about it. "I still say she's just a freak. An ungrateful freak," I complain to Joe.

"I'd be careful," Joe says.

"With Barbara?"

He nods. "I think there's some real pathology there."

"That's what Tony says."

"Tony?"

"Our housekeeper," I explain

"And who would know more about emotional problems?" Joe asks.

He follows me into Max's room where I pull off his dirty sheet and replace it with a new one. Joe pulls the end taut and we head into Josh's rooms. If I were to do it alone, I would be invading, trespassing, snooping, into their private affairs, but with Joe helping me, we're innocently completing a chore that the boys forget to do themselves.

"What kind of pathology?" I ask him. "What exactly do you mean by that?"

"There's something off about her. Not quite right."

"Not right at all," I say. "Have you ever heard her laugh? It would scare you senseless. I worry that she laughs too much in front of Lily. She'll spend her first few years here being frightened of humor." It feels good to talk about Barbara. I want to hear his opinion. Joe doesn't comment frivolously. He doesn't waste time talking about others and he usually doesn't judge others harshly. In fact, in many respects he's the opposite of me.

"I don't know if I'm qualified to judge but from my perspective it doesn't seem like she's connecting to Lily."

Before I had kids I had always read how mothers fell instantly in love with their newborns. I knew that most mothers testified that their lives were instantly changed by the births of their children. There was nothing instant about my experience with motherhood. I was timid and slow and spent a lot of my time staring at the boys wondering what they were doing in the house. I second guessed everything I did. Then eventually I caught on.

Joe checks under the bed for clothes and leftover food. The boys stash dinner plates, soda cans and banana peels under there. Just socks and underwear. He tosses them over to me. "Tell me what you felt when Josh and Max were born," he demands.

"Sore," I say.

"You were only in labor for two hours," he reminds me. "You had the easiest births of any woman in the world."

"I was still sore," I say.

"Besides the physical, what did you feel?" he demands.

"I felt," and then stop, because I want to find the right word to describe the emotions I felt after having Josh and Max.

Joe moves a book on the night table, but then moves it back. We've promised the boys that we wouldn't go through their things. They inspect for the slightest change, especially now that I'm home all day. They accuse me of spying into their affairs.

"Responsible," I finally determine. "That was my strongest emotion. I felt extremely responsible for them."

"Exactly," Joe says. "That's a pretty normal reaction. You were responsible for them. That's one of the emotions I would consider natural for a new mother."

"So?" I ask. "So you think Barbara's not responsible?"

"It doesn't seem to be her guiding emotion right now," he says. "In fact it seems, at least from my limited point of view, to be just the opposite. She seemed determined to shuck her responsibilities onto you, someone she's not even close to."

I can't argue with this.

"Even if she doesn't feel love for Lily, she should feel responsible, which is something I don't see."

"I think you're right," I say.

"Worse, she doesn't seem to be trying," Joe says. "I admit that parenting is hard. But Barbara seems reluctant and that's troublesome."

"It is hard," I say. I would never have wanted to do it alone. Never.

"It is hard, but it's not impossible." If I could do it, anyone could.

"No. It's not impossible."

"And we know that it's not Lily," Joe says. "She even connects with the boys, who aren't exactly motherly."

I push the sheets down the laundry chute.

"It's a problem," I say.

"But it's not yours," Joe says.

But Lily lives in the neighborhood and I've grown enormously fond of her.

Maggie buys a little red wagon – an American Flyer – and gives Lily rides up and down the block. They stop by the house.

"Are you okay?" she asks. They've made strawberry jam and Lily shows me her stained fingers. I kiss them. All ten of them.

"Shouldn't I be?" I ask.

She smiles. "I meant because Lily's with me now. You're okay with that, aren't you?"

I shrug. I can't expect a two-year-old to understand the problems her mother causes. It's not her fault. She's wearing pigtails. I play with her hair and she smiles. "Pretty," I say.

"Yes," Lily agrees with me.

"Barbara thought it might be more of a permanent solution," Maggie explains. I know I can't expect anything from Lily or from Barbara, but I do think Maggie could be more sympathetic. Instead she seems as cruel as Barbara on this issue.

"Is that right?" I ask. My voice drips with sarcasm – something Maggie doesn't catch.

"She doesn't want to put her in a daycare situation and I've got some time. She didn't want to impose on your good will for too long."

I don't believe Barbara said anything of this. I don't think she cares about my will. I don't think she gives me a second thought.

"It's not you," I tell Maggie. "I'm not mad at you."

I would like to tell Maggie about what Joe and I talked about, but I know she'd take it the wrong way. I don't want to fight about Barbara. I don't have the right energy or the right emotional state to deal with Barbara's problems adjusting to motherhood. So for now I'll take Joe's advice and stay away from it.

"Are you sure?" Maggie asks. "I would hate it if you were mad at me."

"I'm fine," I say. "Don't worry about me." My feelings obviously don't mean much on the street. Ridiculous as it may be, I feel sorry for myself and can't shake the hurt.

What is a neighbor anyway? The definition of that word is elusive. It's someone who lives on your street, someone who shares your little corner of the world. You share the same weather, the same garbage day pick-up, the same power outages, though this isn't strictly true. Last year during the huge windstorm the houses across the street were without electricity for two days while we didn't even have a flicker. Like people on a turnpike, the ones you see in the rest areas every forty miles or so. You're all going the same way, but beyond the fact that you're all eating the same crappy food and heading in the same direction, what do you really share?

If we lived on an island in the Caribbean, we'd spent most of our day outdoors in the sunlight. Our homes would probably be much smaller and we would probably be much better acquainted with our neighbors. You'd have all that contact as you walked along the beach, put your feet in the sand, gathered your coconuts and papayas for dinner.

There are good reasons why people have full-time jobs. Otherwise they'd think too much. There isn't a reason in the world to think as much as I do. Analyzing everything in such close detail doesn't get me anywhere. When you're my age, thoughts go nowhere. You just have them. They come into your head, you toss them around, you worry, you fret, and then instead of leaving to be replaced by lofty or ambitious contemplations, they stay, stagnating and clogging your head so that there isn't room for anything worthwhile to get in.

In my inbox today: an answer to my question posted months ago. Ginkgo trees, once widespread in Europe and North American, were destroyed during the last Ice Age. Ginkgo seeds were brought back to Europe in the early 1700's, but oddly enough most of the trees raised in Europe were males. The only female tree was found in a small town outside of Geneva. She was old when they discovered her sex – almost 600 years old. By this time the scientists and horticulturists had named and classified the trees. They were very surprised to find the female of the species and until that moment had assumed that only males existed.

I imagine the sole female Ginkgo standing there – alone, without peers, or colleagues, her foul-smelling berries not making her many friends. Perhaps she was considered a freak. But then I think of the Swiss countryside, the wonderfully bucolic villages outside of Geneva. Lush earth, verdant views, flourishing forests, an abundant world filled with trees and other plant life, and I think that perhaps it wouldn't be so bad. If you were going to be alone somewhere then maybe Switzerland would not be a bad place to be.

Chapter Nine

A recent ecological study has shown that people who live on streets with ginkgo trees fare poorly in love. There's a direct correlation between these ancient trees and the existence of love in the area directly surrounding the trees. Environmental scientists blame the females who they consider to be miserable, needy creatures – the human females, not the trees – which are mixed up souls of enormous desperation desperately searching for something outside their own capabilities to define them.

I made up this last part.

But I do feel like everyone I care for on my block has abandoned me. I feel isolated and shunned. I shut myself in the house and swim in a pity party of ineptitude and unattractiveness. I amuse myself with fantasies of Allan, but even this doesn't cure the boredom of the fall days.

Halloween invades the city in October. Pittsburgh celebrates this pagan holiday like no other place I know. No one abstains. It's as if everyone agrees that this is the big one, this is the important holiday and they go all out. The decorations are everywhere. The streets are covered in orange and black, skeletons and ghosts, vampires and green-faced monsters.

Maggie and her daughters are among those who go overboard. I'm guessing Allan had nothing to do with the gigantic Jack-o'-lantern garbage bags lining the curb in front of the house. I don't think he helped string up the pumpkin shaped lights dangling from the first floor windows and I'm sure he didn't participate with the spiders and their webs hanging from the trees in the front yard.

Maggie sews Lily a pumpkin outfit. It's made of yards of bright orange material with little cutout holes for her legs. She buys green tights and a green beret and sews on a brown stem that sits on top of her head.

They come over to model the outfit for me. Maggie shows me how they're going to stuff the entire thing with newspapers so that she'll be a plump pumpkin.

"It's adorable." I applaud Lily. The sight of her with those skinny legs sticking out of the costume makes me ache and I give her a hug. She hugs back.

She loves the outfit.

"You have to show the boys. They'll love it."

"Me?" She points to her chest.

"Yes. They love you too."

She holds out her hand for me to take her inside. She's too shy to go in alone. I stand, but then see the boys at the window. They've just come home from school and are grazing in the kitchen. They'll eat for forty minutes or so and leave every cupboard and drawer open so that when I go in, the place will look like it's been robbed.

They come outside and make a big deal of Lily. They take her inside to take her picture.

"Don't let her get dirty," I shout after them. "Halloween is still two days away."

Maggie sits beside me on the bench. She's holding a pincushion – a red tomato shaped things with hundreds of pins and needles sticking out.

"Barbara is going to let me take Lily trick-or-treating this year," Maggie says.

I snort. "That's a good one."

"A good what?" Maggie asks.

"Like you think she was going to do it herself?" Isolation is not good for the soul. It's embittering.

Maggie screws up her face. She leans closer to me and speaks in a quiet voice as if she's afraid Lily will hear. "I don't think Barbara feels comfortable going door to door," Maggie says.

"She's an American," I say. "Halloween is a long standing part of our culture."

"She's a bit socially awkward," is how Maggie explains it, but I don't think she really believes this.

"Besides she's not the one who's supposed to go door to door. That's Lily's job," I remind her.

Maggie is wearing a tight blue sweater, with a long dark scarf that she's pulled around her shoulders for warmth. She looks thin. "She's really busy with work," Maggie throws out. "It's a tough time for her."

I'm fed up and still resentful with how things played out with Barbara never once coming over to say something. No-one is that busy. "She's a new mother who, as far as I can see, is avoiding her newly adopted daughter."

Maggie keeps her voice low. She's extremely hesitant. "It does feel a bit strange, doesn't it?"

I have no reason not to be honest. "It's wacko," I judge harshly. "Utterly bizarre."

"I wish you hadn't said that," Maggie says. "I wish you didn't think that."

She speaks in that low voice as if we're conspiring something dishonest instead of talking about something that is really happening.

"Why?" I ask.

"I don't know," she sighs. "Allan thinks I'm being stupid."

Now that's a name we haven't heard in awhile. Allan. I savor it. My latest fantasy – the one that takes place on the boat going down the Nile in Egypt – flashes into my head. Allan and I are tanned and working to uncover some ancient treasure all while we have this incredible sex life. Everyone on the boat calls us the newlyweds and our cabin is incredibly romantic – a 1920s style with lace. Dim lighting pervades.

It's not right to have these thoughts in front of his wife, especially when Lily's with her. I push them to a safe place, where no one can disturb them.

"Allan has accused me of being an ostrich about this." Another sigh. An adulterous wife doesn't usually conjure up images of ostriches hiding their heads in the sands. This is a puzzling comment on Allan's behalf. I'll have to explore it further.

I study Maggie carefully; she's not happy. Maggie usually has this way of being utterly peaceful, of being calm. That quality is lacking now.

"Do you really think there's something wrong with Barbara?"

"Absolutely," I say with real conviction because it feels good to talk about it.

Maggie nods. "Maybe you're right. There might be something wrong, but how do you know it's not some sort of postpartum depression?"

"This wasn't a natural childbirth," I remind her.

"Still," Maggie says. "A new baby is a new baby. There's a certain amount of fear and uncertainty that comes with a new child in the house."

This isn't the first time she's said that thought. The comment sounds tired, and it is. It doesn't begin to explain Barbara's behavior.

"Does it ever hurt, Maggie?" I ask.

"Does what hurt?"

"To have such a big heart?" I ask. "Does it ever get heavy?"

And this time there's nothing calculated about her reply. "You'd be surprised how much it hurts," she says.

She sounds wistful – a woman who has not fared well with love and I speculate that her California paramour has

155

disappointed her. Perhaps she had no choice in the matter. He may have seduced her, lured her into his life with false promises of love, emphasizing his need. Then once she had made promises and compromised her marriage he became distant, finally disappearing all together.

"What is it, Maggie?" I coax her to confide in me. I'm good with other people's problems. I'm sure I can address her concerns fairly and with an open mind for what's best for Allan. "What's wrong?"

"Almost everything," she says. She puts her hand over her mouth, fingers on the top teeth and shakes her head. "Just everything."

She's about to say more when Josh and Max come storming out of the house in marching band formation. Lily is balanced on Josh's shoulders. Her legs kick around his ears. They circle around us playing their imaginary instruments. Josh is on drums. Max plays trombone.

Maggie sits up and begins to clap. She brightens considerably with the noisy interruption. Our confidential talk is over.

"Don't forget about the Halloween party," she tells the boys.

It's the first I've heard anything about a party.

"Just a little fun for the neighborhood," Maggie explains.

"Do we really have to wear costumes?" Max asks.

"Yes. They're mandatory," Maggie says. "Especially for you two."

"We don't have anything," Max says. "I have a vampire cape from when I was six, but I don't think it fits."

The boys haven't said anything to me about getting costumes together. I'm surprised they're even considering it. Our basement is filled with old clothes and things that should have gone to the Goodwill long ago. They could find something if they spent some time down there.

"The girls have been working non-stop on their costumes," Maggie says. "They're quite elaborate even if they are unidentifiable. I'm just glad I can tell what Lily is."

"She's the cutest pumpkin in the world," I say.

Lily kicks her legs when she realizes we're talking about her and Josh yelps.

"We're too old to trick-or-treat," Josh says.

"Nonsense," Maggie says. "I'll need help taking Lily around."

"Lily's going trick-or-treating?" Josh tips her a bit and she screams in delight, but also scared that he might really tip her over.

"Will you share your candy with us?" Max asks.

"Mine," Lily shouts. She learned that word well.

Lily is new to the neighborhood. She has no idea how much candy she'll have by the end of the night.

"The party is just pizza and cider," Maggie says. "I was hoping you and Joe could come, though I realize that one of you has to be here to pass out candy."

She's so organized she's even thought about how we'll handle the trick-or-treaters. "Maybe you could take turns?"

The invitation to the boys was hand-delivered a week ago. Katie brought it over, something Max and Josh forgot to show me.

"I'm very excited for Lily," Maggie says.

The only time it seems that I see Allan is at the neighborhood parties so I'm all in favor of these get-togethers. I wish I could come as someone he would desire. That would be a good reason to dress up.

Daydream scenario #23: I've had this one so many times that I actually now spend time rearranging the décor and furnishing of the pretend apartment I've rented for myself. The place used to be ultra-modern, which seemed cold and a bit off-putting. I've replaced the stark white throw rugs with Orientals and added

157

floor to ceiling bookshelves. Low lighting, and more balconies. The daydream takes place in Edinburgh and was greatly influenced by this BBC America crime program that I watched in September. In my fantasy Allan shares many of the same characteristics of Detective Chief Inspector John Rebus. They're both Scottish, they're both intense, they're both rebels, they're both misunderstood by their bosses, but loved by women. In Allan's case, he's loved by me. Only me. I am a detective who has been brought over from the States to help Allan solve a murder mystery. I rent my fabulous apartment in Edinburgh and Allan and I begin our courtship. He's impressed by me, but resents the fact that I've been brought in to help.

I want him to want me. I want some of this to come true. I spend an overabundance of my day locked in a world that will never happen. In my daydreams I am younger than I am now. No matter what I fantasize about the world at large, I do understand that I will never be twenty-five again and that most of my life is behind me. For years I planned and thought about my future – what would happen, where I would be, what I would have achieved – and then I lived it. And I didn't get to where I thought I'd be. It's much less full, much less enticing or exciting. I've started to count the number of friends and family who will come to my funeral and it's not a full house. Even if all my ex-colleagues were to show up, which they won't because they're not very good with social niceties, there would still be plenty of room.

I drift back to my great apartment in central Edinburgh. Maybe tonight I'll make a pesto pasta for two. Allan has a key. After a day of chasing criminals – murderers and pedophiles – he'll be hungry. And in need of a drink. In desperate need of me.

Halloween boys are in the upstairs bathroom where they've been most of the afternoon. Doors open and close. Drawers slam.

They're experimenting with face paints. Blood, they decide, will be the dominant theme of their costumes.

They rip up t-shirts, put on old jeans, and then decide that they'll be the sloppy vampires. They love their invention and find old hats, a cape, and an overcoat that I think Joe still wears.

I go over to Maggie's with an old witch hat that I find in the turmoil the boys have created in the house. It's a bit tight and I have to hold onto it or fear losing it.

Allan answers the door. He's wearing a Bart Simpson mask. The mouth is shredded as if the dog has been using it as a chew-toy.

"That's not much of a costume, Caroline," he criticizes. His lips are exposed. Soft, pink, luscious. The mask hangs funny and I can't see his eyes.

"I'm a witch," I say and point to the hat, which seems to be slipping sideways.

"Very weak," he continues. The large Bart head bobs up and down. Even masked he has enough charisma to make me forget that I've spent the last week alone and pouting.

"I spent hours on this," I say. I wonder if he knows how many days it's been since we've seen each other. I do. Twenty-three. Our talk in the bar lingers in the arena of things hinted at, but never said. I'm curious if he thinks about his near confession – obviously I know he doesn't think of it as often as I do. Does he still have the same need to tell me about his life? What would he change in his? What about Maggie? Has anything happened there? Somehow I think I would have heard. I'm a nosy neighbor. If they were talking divorce, I would know it.

"I don't think you'll be in the running for any of the prizes tonight."

"I've seen the competition," I tell him. "I think you may be too harsh a critic."

He pours himself a scotch. His eyesight isn't good behind the mask. Amber colored liquor splashes on the wrong side of the glass and he yelps as if wounded. He has to take off the mask to drink. His face is flushed. Flushed and gorgeous. Good-looking men don't change as they age. They just continue to get better looking. He wipes his face with the dishtowel. "It's hot in there."

"I'm sure," I say.

"Will you join me?" he asks.

"Not scotch," I say. "Much too strong for a holiday like Halloween."

"More like something you'd drink on Christmas morning," he asks.

"Exactly," I agree.

"That's too bad because that's all I'm offering," he says.

"You're a charming host," I tell him. This banter feels refreshingly fun.

"It's all I'm offering because it's so good," he says. He holds up the bottle. "Imported from the bonnie land of my birth. Sent to me by my great- auntie who has never stopped loving me."

"Can I get a few ice cubes?"

"Absolutely not," he says. "I won't have you ruining my imported Scotch with that foul Pittsburgh water."

"This is going to be a fun party."

"Drink," he advises. "My advice. And I speak from experience."

We clink glasses. It's the happiest I've been in two weeks. I smile.

"Good isn't it?" he asks. He returns my smile. His is a bit wicked like we're sharing a secret. Maybe he's been thinking about me too.

"Wonderful," I answer though I've yet to sip the scotch. There is something magical and mysterious about Halloween.

Max and Josh are in the living room demonstrating how to bob for apples for Lily's sake. Lily might have reason to learn this rare talent but she dances in front of the full-length mirror on the door in the front hallway and is too busy with her reflection to care about their skill at biting apples without using their hands. They laugh and play with her with real enthusiasm, which tells me that they've missed her as much as I have.

Jane wears little granny glasses and a men's three piece gray suit. "Lenin," she says. She doesn't look anything like John Lennon, and then she starts speaking Russian and I realize she's the dead Soviet Leader.

"He's embalmed in Red Square," I tell her. "Under a glass case."

"I'm dying to see him," she says. "I heard his body is decomposing and they have to keep rebuilding him."

"Sounds attractive," I say.

"Da. Da," she says. The glasses are prescription, but not hers and she trips on the edge of the rug. She lurches towards the bucket.

Josh stops her from falling. "You've got to wait your turn Jane," he scolds.

Her response is in Russian. A long complicated sentence, which no one understands, but which Allan finds amusing. Either that or he's had too many glasses of his great-aunt's scotch.

"Time to go," Maggie calls from the kitchen. She's re-stuffing Lily's pumpkin costume. Some of the newspaper got wet from the apple bobbing game.

I poke my head in.

"Allan and I can take the kids around," I volunteer our services. But Maggie won't hear of missing Lily's first Halloween.

"We'll all go. Come on. It will be great," Maggie says. She stops and motions for everyone to stand together for another photograph. The boys are being good sports. She clicks off a few more – it will be the most documented night on record.

Allan says he'll stay home and pass out candy.

"No more scotch," Maggie tells him.

"What do you mean no more scotch?" Allan asks. "I don't understand that sentence."

"You don't want to wake-up with a hangover."

"I don't?" he asks.

"No. You really don't."

"You sound like my mother," Allan says.

"Which is exactly how I feel," Maggie responds. "Responsible to your irresponsible. Mature to your immature."

"She's been dead for six and half years."

I finish my drink and hand the empty glass to Allan. "Would you like a roadie?" he asks.

"No she doesn't," Maggie answers for me. "This is Halloween. Not some fraternity pledge party."

"You are such a spoilsport," Allan bickers.

"That's okay," I say. I really don't want another drink.

"I'll save you a sip for you to enjoy upon your return," Allan promises.

"I hope to God you save her more than a sip," Maggie says. "There's half a bottle left."

"My mother used to mark the levels with a black pen to keep tabs on my father."

"Go get me a magic marker," she tells him.

Maggie flicks on the porch light, but it's broken and she sends Allan off to find a new bulb.

Katie comes down the steps. She's in a bikini bathing suit top and a very tight very low-slung sarong. Her belly button is pierced; a small silver hoop hangs against her stomach, which is absolutely flat. Nothing pudgy there. If I'm not mistaken, she's drawn in cleavage. That can't be hers. She's too young to have such large breasts. Max and Josh punch each other. I try to get a better look, but the light from where I'm standing isn't good.

"What is that?" Allan asks his youngest daughter.

"Like we saw in Mexico," Katie explains. "I'm a shot girl." In her holster are water guns filled with different liquids.

Katie tells him to open his mouth and she'll give him a drink.

"Your father's had enough to drink," Maggie says.

"Fire me up," Allan says and he opens his mouth. Katie spins out a gun and shoots him with a long steam of Coca-Cola, most of which dribbles onto his chin.

He swallows. "Now go up and change," he tells Katie.

"Change what?"

"Go on," he says pointing to her cleavage. Maybe those are hers. Maybe she's been lying about her age. Maybe she's really twenty-five. I hustle the boys out of the house.

"Are you crazy?" she asks. "Everyone's waiting for me."

"You're not wearing that," he says, sounding so typical and so fatherly that I laugh.

"This is my costume," Katie insists.

"The least you could do is put on a coat." He crosses to the closet and pulls something off a hanger. It's a bright orange rain parka. It's large and would cover her body.

"It's Halloween," Katie argues, which in her world must give license to showing off as much skin as possible.

It's not a strong point. I would have argued that it's hot out or that her torso has been on public display all summer. I've seen more of her bare body than I've seen of my own the last few months.

This is obviously an old argument between the two of them and Katie doesn't take it seriously. She brushes past him and grabs a gigantic pillowcase that's been dyed black and orange. Josh and Max follow her out the door.

It's not dark yet, but Maggie has found several flashlights. She worries about Lily tripping on uneven sidewalks and tree roots. She hands each of us one. Josh and Max don't want them. "Vampires are good negotiating their way in the dark," they tell her.

She should know that male teenagers would rather die than be caught carrying something as plebian as a flashlight, or an umbrella or a bag of any kind.

"How are you going to hold all your candy?" I ask.

"Pockets," Josh tells me.

The night is warm, a real Indian summer Halloween evening. And the change in temperature adds to the festive note of the evening. Everything feels fun. I don't think this is just the Scotch or seeing Allan again. Everyone seems happy. Especially Lily.

Our group, one very small timid child, two adult women, and four adolescents makes for a mini-parade in our neighborhood. Missing, of course, is Barbara.

I deliberately don't bring her up. There is no reason to ruin a perfectly good night with talk of Barbara and her kooky ways.

Joe is on the front porch. He's printed out a draft of his novel and passes out candy as he marks up his manuscript. Lily runs to Joe to show him her pumpkin now overflowing with candy.

"Is this all for me?" he asks.

"Mine," she says.

He adds a fistful to her bag, something she finds incredibly funny.

The neighbors, delighted to see a child at their door, give generously. We don't get very far. Lily stops after every house to show us what she's collected. At first she wants to unwrap and eat each piece of candy, but the boys are experts in the task of candy collection. They advise a quicker pace, the sure fire way to acquire more candy. "Not time for eating," they tell Lily.

She unwraps a lollipop, obviously not heeding their advice. "Halloween only comes around once every year," they continue her education. "There's plenty of time for enjoyment after the trick-or-treating ends."

They hold her hand and help her climb the steps of the next house.

"We love Kit-Kat bars," Katie tells the people on Kentucky Avenue. Josh, Jane, and Max agree on this culinary opinion. They also like Snickers bars and candy corn. They like candy apples, Juicy Fruit gum, and chocolate-covered raisins. Katie squeals when she feels her pillowcase. "It weighs a ton," she says. Lily gets more and more excited. Josh offers to carry it for her and she lets him.

Katie's top seems to be slipping, but it's getting dark. I move everyone along. We walk four blocks and then Lily seems to lose energy. She comes to me and holds up her arms. "Lift."

I hand her bag to Maggie and lift her up. She puts her head on my shoulders. Foot traffic on the street is increasing just as we give up. Maggie suggests that the older kids continue. "There's no reason why you have to come home now."

But Jane tells her they have other plans.

We return to Maggie's. Allan has left the candy bowl on a small chair by the front door. The trick-or-treaters have emptied it clean.

Inside, Allan sits in the dark living room as if in hiding. Maggie flicks on the overhead light. He's in the window seat, drink in hand on the telephone.

"It's Halloween," Maggie says. "You can get off the phone for five minutes and talk to your daughters."

He hangs up immediately, which makes me think he wasn't really talking to anyone.

"I hadn't realized the importance or significance of this pagan holiday," Allan says. "The magnitude of our family traditions has completely escaped me."

"It's supposed to be fun," Maggie snips. "That's what's important about tonight."

"Fun," Allan says. "The concept also escaped my radar."

They snip at each other. Back and forth, inside barbs and digs.

Allan does not fight in my fantasy world, so I'm not comfortable seeing him bicker like this. On the other hand, Maggie is not in my scenarios of make-believe, which I'm guessing is the problem.

"Can you two ever stop fighting?" Jane comes in. "It's Halloween for god's sake."

"Can we watch a movie?" Josh asks me.

Here is my role. I'm the boys' mother.

"It's a school night," I say. It's a knee-jerk response. I really have no opinion on whether they stay or not. But this makes me sound like a protective parent. Allan takes no notice of my excellent parenting skills.

"It's Halloween," Max says. "Please?"

Allan claps his hands. "Now that we've firmly established the rules and rituals of the night, are we proceeding with the festivities or are we just going to continue defining it?"

Jane explains that she's taken out the George Romero film *Night of the Living Dead*. It was filmed just north of Pittsburgh and is a cult classic.

"Was Lenin a fan of the horror genre?" Allan asks.

"Enamored," Jane says. "You should have seen his film collection. Uber-impressive."

"Can we stay, Mom?" Max demands.

"That sounds fine," I say as if maybe I was going to take them home and put them to bed.

Lily sits on the couch; the night's activities have caught up with her. She puts her finger in her mouth and puts her head on the stack of pillows.

"Where's Barbara?" I call into the kitchen where Maggie is opening wine. She's decided that if Allan is going to drink all the whisky, we should have something to go with our pizza.

"She's coming," Maggie calls.

Allan opens his mouth, a perfect O. He turns to me. "That is a lie," he says. "My wife's nose should just have grown a foot."

"It is not a lie. She's coming," she says and then pauses. "Eventually."

"Eventually as in whenever she wants," Allan says.

Lily has fallen asleep.

"Shouldn't she be putting Lily to bed?" I ask. "Look at her. She's exhausted."

Maggie goes over to the couch. "I'll put her in our bed for now."

"Once again," Allan says.

She gathers Lily into her arms and crosses the room, her heels pound against the floor. "What should I do?" Maggie asks. "You tell me if you've got a better solution."

"Grow a backbone."

Maggie has Lily cradled in her arms. She carries her to the bottom of the steps then turns to address her husband. "I don't think a spine of steel would help in this situation."

Allan nods in agreement. "That may be right," he says. "But you shouldn't be the one shouldering the responsibility."

"I'm not," Maggie says as she walks upstairs. "The girls help."

She disappears upstairs.

Allan watches her go. Then he crosses the room and kneels at my feet. "Sweet Caroline," he says. He's a little too close for this to be a casual conversation, especially with Maggie upstairs. He holds my hands. His are dry; mine aren't. Not when they're in his.

"I need to talk to you," he says. He leans forward, his lips are now right at mine. I could simply lean forward and our lips would be touching. He's so close I can see the gradation on his whiskers – black into gray.

"Of course," I say.

"Tonight," he says. And nods towards the front of the house as if to indicate that this future discussion should be kept from Maggie.

"Tonight?" I stare at him in disbelief. I really do have to work on my lines when I'm not in fantasyland. I sound like a complete idiot.

"Ten o'clock. I'll meet you on the corner. Under the lamp post."

Did he say lamp post? I feel like a character in one of my spy fantasies. I relish this part.

The doorbell rings. Allan makes no move to answer it. Someone comes down the steps, but Allan stays at my feet. His lovely eyelashes are a breath from my fingertips.

Maggie carries in the three or four gigantic pizza boxes as if she plans to feed the entire neighborhood. She's got Max and Josh eating, who don't believe in leftovers. They've never seen them therefore have a hard time with the concept that food doesn't have to be eaten immediately.

She glances over at us. "What are you doing over there, Allan?" she scolds. "Stop bothering Caroline."

Guilt is a visible emotion so I get up and go tell the boys that they can stay. "Not too late," I call.

I tell Maggie that I'm going home. She gives me several slices for Joe who won't eat them. He eats enough pizza with the boys.

Allan walks me to the door. He grabs hold of my wrist. "Ten." His breath is all Scotch and nicotine.

"I'll be there." I wouldn't miss it for the world. His asking me is the highlight of my entire autumn. Actually meeting him will send me to the moon.

I have to take the dog. What other excuse do I have?

"You've got a good friend there," Joe comments when I call for the dog.

"What's that?" I ask, trying to sound casual.

"Spot loves you," Joe says. "You pay him so much attention these days."

The dog, that's who he's talking about. "Why not?" I ask. "I have the time."

Joe sits at the computer. It's where he is when he's home now. He stays up past midnight working on his novel. "I just want to finish it," has now become his mantra. He seems preoccupied enough for me to leave without him wondering where I'm going.

It's five minutes after ten. I don't want to be late. Allan might think I've changed by mind and am not coming. I can't give up this opportunity to talk to him. Alone. My heart beats – I'm nervous – I'm so sure Joe picks up on the unnaturalness of my behavior that I can't look at him. I feel reckless.

I'm out of breath when I reach the corner. Allan waits under the street lamp. It's a familiar image, one I've dreamt several times. The rain is missing. In my imagination, we always meet during a thunderstorm.

"Here you are," he says. I like this attitude, as though he's been waiting a long time for me.

"Sorry," I say.

The dog yaps at his ankles and I pull on the leash. He sniffs out some trash in the gutter and is pleased to entertain himself with someone's garbage. The leash tangles around my knees and I have to fiddle with that. Allan looks on. I know he doesn't care for the dog, but she is my only excuse.

"I don't know what Maggie's told you about our current situation," he rushes into his story.

Here comes my future. He's going to tell me that Maggie's in love with another man and that they're about to be divorced. I will pretend to be surprised by his revelations. Surprised but flattered. I think that's the best approach.

"There's something wrong with that woman," he says. He lights a cigarette and puts the pack away. Then he remembers that I'm there. "I'm sorry. Would you like one?"

"What?" I ask. I close my eyes. The darkness, the light breeze of the Indian summer night is incredibly seductive. I feel high.

He's holding out a cigarette. I guess I have to take it. I hold his wrist while he lights it. It's Halloween, a night for boldness.

"Do you agree?"

"I've never disagreed with you, Allan," I say, but I have to ask him to tell me who he's talking about.

"Barbara," Allan breathes out sharply.

I jump to show him my support. "She's a weirdo. She always has been," I say with real conviction.

"She's taking advantage of us," Allan says.

"She's good at that," I say.

"You saw what happened tonight. Where in god's name is that kid's mother?"

"I haven't the slightest idea," I say. "I doubt she's working all this time."

"Of course she's not working," he says. "We've seen her. Both of us. She comes home in the middle of the day. Maggie sees her car. She sneaks into her apartment. Runs upstairs and locks herself in. Then later, she makes a big show of coming over at dinnertime like she's just gotten off work."

So Tony knew what he was talking about.

Allan finishes his cigarette and flicks it into the street. The dog barks though I think it's just a reaction. I don't think the cigarette hit him.

"She even pants."

"She what?" I ask.

"Pants," he says and then demonstrates. He takes in huge gulps of air, his tongue hanging out. The whisky on his breath is soured with the nicotine and he smells a bit like a bar. "She acts like a dog, but it's just a charade."

I laugh.

"It's not funny."

170

"It's not," I agree. "It's pathetic. She's utterly pathetic." People should have listened to me. I didn't like her from the start. Not with that laugh and that rude behavior.

"The worse thing is that some nights she doesn't show up at all," Allan says. I didn't know this part. Maggie's never said anything about Barbara not coming.

"At first Barbara claimed that it was because she needed sleep," Allan explains. "She wasn't sleeping well and then she started taking sleeping pills. She would get so groggy during the day that she would simply forget to pick up Lily."

"Well, that's good," I say.

"How is that good?"

"At least it shows that she didn't want Lily around when she's taking drugs." I see a slight bit of sense here. Maybe Barbara is aware that she's incompetent. Maybe she's aware that Maggie is better for Lily.

Allan puffs on his cigarette. "I'm not sure I can give her any credit. She's just so careless."

It's a good description. Barbara is careless.

"And Maggie's blind to the whole situation. She acts like none of this is a problem," Allan steams. "As if everything is just dandy. No problem. No problem whatsoever."

Maggie's not dumb. She's a mother. She realizes something's not right with Barbara or the situation with Lily. She knows that there's something egregious and wrong with the way Barbara's behaving. She must. But I don't know why she's pretending everything is okay.

"We have a monstrous white elephant sitting in the middle of our living room, but we're not allowed to say anything. You're not even allowed to hint that things aren't peachy keen. That's my wife."

"Maybe she's doing it for Lily. Perhaps the charade is for Lily's sake." Maggie does care for her. I'd be willing to bet that she's that protective. Lily is young. She is impressionable. I can see Maggie going to extremes not to hurt her.

"A mammoth elephant we all dance around and act as if it's just a tiny mouse. Nearly invisible to the naked eye."

"I've never liked her," I say.

"I thought you did," Allan says. "I always thought you two were good friends."

"I'm talking about Barbara."

"I hope you like Maggie," he says. "I hope you'll support her. She's not as strong as she pretends to be."

"She has my support," I say. "I'll help her any way I can."

"I hope that's true. I know she depends on you," Allan says.

Barbara may be careless, but I am reckless. Instead of answering, I lean in and put my arms around him.

He's surprised by my physical gesture, but doesn't back away. "Thanks, Caroline," he says.

I hold onto him a few seconds longer than friends. It's time to show him how I feel.

Someone approaches. I move to give them room to pass beside me on the sidewalk, but the person stops.

"Is this a private meeting?"

It's Joe.

I'm so surprised I don't move. Allan is the one who pushes away from me.

I can tell by the tone of this voice that he's not happy. I step away from Allan, move back into the reality of my marriage and life on Howe Street.

"You've been gone a long time," Joe says. He doesn't acknowledge Allan. "I got worried, thought that maybe something happened, but now I see that you were simply busy."

"Hello, Joe," Allan says.

"Hello Allan," Joe echoes.

It's dark so any guilt we may be expressing is hidden.

The dog barks with the passing of two ghosts who pass. They call out a drunken hello; no one from our group responds.

"We were talking about Barbara," I rush ahead with my own apology.

"You talk about her a lot."

I want to assure him that except for my hug, it was an innocent and important conversation.

"This Lily thing is out of control," Allan explains. "I was seeking out Caroline's advice."

"Yeah, but Caroline is my wife and it's eleven o'clock at night," Joe says simply. I think he's exaggerating the time. It's not that late.

"I'm sorry," Allan says.

"I think you should be home," Joe tells me. "The boys have been back for a half hour."

"Really? Is that right?" I ask. I've never timed my arrivals to coincide with theirs. This is not a typical house rule.

Allan continues to explain his need to talk me. "It's good to hear an outside opinion."

"I told you that if I were in your position, I would call Child Protective Services. They'll tell you what you should do," Joe says. He's curt with Allan who apologizes again.

"I'll see you back at home." *This* he addresses to me. He holds out his hand and I reach for it, misunderstanding that what he wants is not my hand, but the dog leash.

I feel like I'm about to be grounded.

"I didn't mean to get you in trouble," Allan says.

"It's okay," I say. But I can't stay. Our embrace feels lost in Joe's curtness.

Joe is waiting for me on the front steps.

"Was that meeting with Allan prearranged?"

I lie. What choice do I have? "Of course not. Why would you think that?"

173

"Because that's how it looked. Like you had planned to meet him. And if that's the case, I wish you had told me. Otherwise I feel like you're sneaking around and I'm curious as to why?"

"I'm not sneaking around," I say.

"Good," Joe says. "Then let's forget it."

"It was nothing," I continue. "All we did was talk about Barbara."

"I think it's time everyone stopped talking about Barbara and that poor little girl and someone did something."

We walk into the house. He clicks off the porch light. The boys are home. I can hear the television upstairs. They've left their mark of microwave popcorn packages, ice cube trays, and glasses.

I close the cupboards, throw the trash away, and load the dishwasher. It takes two minutes – getting the boys to do the same thing would have taken until midnight.

"And you hugged him?" Joe asks.

"He just seemed so befuddled," I explain.

Joe nods.

"You believe me, don't you?" I plead. Joe has nothing to do with my feelings for Allan. They're two very separate things.

"Enough said," he cuts me off. "I can't remember what we were even talking about."

"Now I feel like I'm talking to Tony," I say.

"You might as well be," he says and smiles at the comparison. True to his word, he's not angry. "Let's stop with the neighbors. Just because we live near them, doesn't mean we have to be involved in their lives."

Easier said than done, of course. At least for me.

I spend the rest of the week feeling vaguely guilty and then oddly pissed that I don't have more to feel guilty about.

Chapter Ten

Joe's hospital's annual party is two weeks after Halloween. It's held in mid-November every year so that it won't be mistaken for an actual religious holiday celebration. The head of the hospital, a painfully shy man, makes a three minute speech in which he mostly names people he'd like to thank and that's the end of the protocol. There's a great deal of dancing and drinking; the food is good. I've always had a good time there – but I'm reluctant to go this year. I blame it on my unemployment, but I'm not sure why I feel prickly and resentful about a party.

Joe refuses to hear my excuses.

"We're going," he tells me. "We'll drink enormous amounts of champagne and then we'll spend the rest of the night dancing."

"I hate champagne and you hate to dance," I remind him.

"See how fun it will be?" he tells me. "You'll be so drunk you won't even remember what you hate."

"I'd hate to embarrass you."

"You won't and if you do you won't remember it."

"Now I feel like Tony."

"Tony is definitely not coming," Joe tells me.

"Tony isn't going anywhere these days."

Tony hasn't been cleaning the house for the past month now – his wife says he's unstable and needs to correct his meds. I'm in favor of med correction and tell her I hope things get better for him.

I go through my closet and cobble together an outfit.

"Are you sure I have to go?" I ask Joe.

"Absolutely," Joe says. He's wearing his tuxedo. It's not been cleaned since last year and there are still some multi-colored toothpick swords in the pocket. I could probably count the number of times we've been out the past ten years by counting the name cards and table numbers he's got stored in his pants' pockets.

We go. We're a bit late and walk into a large room that's filled with people and caterers and energy. We stand looking at everything, then move into the crowd.

"There's the new head of development," Joe says. He smiles and I see where he's cut himself shaving on his jaw-line. He stopped the bleeding with toilet paper and traces of white stick to his skin. "See what I mean? They're trying to change their image."

The woman is quite young and quite attractive, not a combination you see often in Pittsburgh. She stands out. She's stylishly dressed in a way that you know she didn't buy her dress here.

"People are convinced she's going to do a great job."

"You seem like you're quite confident also."

"She is good-looking."

Then I remember something. "Isn't Barbara the head of development?"

"Nope," he says. "Not for a while."

"What do you mean not for a while?" I ask. "Since when?"

"I don't know the full story on that one," Joe says. "But something happened. I told you that."

He didn't. I would have remembered that.

"Where's she working?"

"I assumed she got a new job."

I hadn't heard anything about Barbara's new job.

The party is suddenly very interesting. Even if there are no Scotsmen lurking about, I find myself engaged and dying to know what happened to Barbara. Joe says he really doesn't know.

"Ask Paul," Joe asks.

Paul and I are friends from high school. He was a gossip back then and now that he works public relations for the hospital, he's an expert on the personal relationships of everyone connected to the hospital.

"What's the story on the ex-head of development?" I ask. "Barbara Murdoch? Tall? Bit gangly, huge laugh?" He knows who I mean. "What happened to her?" I ask. "How come she's not working?"

"Because she didn't work out."

"She didn't?"

He wants another drink so we have to go to the bar where he tells me we can't talk about anything except how much weight he's lost.

I make a mistake. "Have you?"

"You're particularly cruel for someone who wants information," he says and grits his teeth. He turns to the side. "Look."

"Oh god, yeah. Now I see what you mean. You're so thin," I rave.

"Really?"

"Really," I say and then, because he actually does look good, "Really thin."

I order a vodka for him and a red wine for me.

The Hotel Southside has a newly opened beer garden that makes me nostalgic for my fantasy of Allan and me in the seaside Scottish resort, but I'm too busy trying to figure out Barbara's deal to linger with thoughts of Allan.

"They never liked her," Paul says.

This kind of retribution is thrilling so I want to get the details right.

"Who didn't?" I ask.

I can tell Paul's not really into our conversation. It must be old gossip. Either that or gossip that never really interested him. He sips his drink. "Wow. This is strong. Did you order me a double?"

"I will if that's what you want," I say, holding my hand out for the glass. He's got information that I want.

"I hate to waste too many calories on alcohol," Paul says.

They're passing hors d'oeuvres – trays of Pan-Asian cuisine, with dips and sauces. I find it hard to maneuver the appetizers with the napkins and drink and just shake my head no. Paul takes one and pops it into his mouth. Obviously much more experience at cocktail parties. I've forgotten the skill.

"Back to Barbara," I direct the conversation.

Paul fans his mouth. "Why the hell do they microwave these things? They're really trying to kill you."

"Who didn't like Barbara?"

"The real story?"

"Why not?" I ask.

"Is she a friend?"

"Just a neighbor," I say as if I lay no claim to those living on my block. If only he knew how much I obsessed about one of the residents.

"She came in. She was supposed to have had all this experience in Philly. She was supposed to help turn this place around. But then isn't everyone? Isn't that why we all live in Pittsburgh? To turn the place around. The Renaissance is just around the corner. Gentrification is just about to happen."

It is the city's theme. I once went to an image meeting and the public relation company had singers dressed in South Beach attire – incredibly tiny bikinis, heels, off the shoulder t-shirts – running up and down the aisle singing Gloria Estefan's song, "Turn the Beat Around." I was in the last row and it was hard to hear. I heard the refrain 'Love to hear Percussion', but didn't get what any of it had to do with the New Pittsburgh Campaign. I voted to turn down the firm, but everyone else was enthusiastic. We hired the overpriced company to give us advice and guidance to turn our beat around. The girls in the skimpy clothes were just hired extras and not part of the transition team. We had tape recordings of that song whenever things stalled out in meetings. It was fun while it lasted but as far as I know, we never turned anything around. Except maybe for the worse.

"Instead she was a total failure," Paul tells me.

More trays are coming around. Paul inspects them carefully, then shakes his head. "I don't want dumplings. Whatever happened to shrimp? Big fat shrimp with cocktail sauce."

"I'll tell you that from the start, it didn't work out with her. They didn't like her from the very beginning. At least that's what I heard."

"What went wrong?" I ask. "Did she steal? Did she kill someone? Did she sleep with someone's husband?"

"Nothing scandalous or salacious, more like just incompetent."

"And do you know when they fired her?"

"Late August?" Paul scrunches up his face. "She really was like the wind. In and out."

"But I don't understand."

"They fired her for medical reasons,"

"What kind of medical reason?"

"Basically her mental state rendered her incompetent."

Paul succeeds at excess so I'm surprised when he shrugs and says, "That's all I know."

"Incompetent?" I say and encourage to repeat what he's told me. Sometimes repetition brings speculations and he might say something worth hearing if he's just thinking aloud.

"It's a hard job." Paul is uncharacteristically sympathetic.

It's odd. The way Barbara never mentioned that she was working somewhere else. There might be a simple explanation for her lapse of information, but I'm guessing it's a lot more complicated.

I do what I think I'm owed; I pounce. I want to hear the truth. From her – from the source. The next day I position myself at my window seat but I focus not on Allan's house, but on Barbara's apartment. I wait. All day.

When I see her blue Honda coming down the street, I run out of the house and cross the street.

"Hey," I say. I'm out of breath and can't say anything right away. She's startled, but acts like my showing up is normal.

I stare at her. She stares back.

"What are you doing here?" she asks.

She looks gray. Hair, face, outfit – lifeless.

"I live here," I explain. "Right up there. One day I'll introduce myself."

"That will be interesting," she comments. Tattered – that's how she looks. This new motherhood thing has really taken a toll on her appearance.

I get my breath and try to think how I'll phrase my question of her employment, but she doesn't give me a chance.

"Excuse me," she says and starts to walk towards the house. "I'm busy right now."

"Are you?" I ask.

"Yes, I am, Caroline. I'm sorry if that offends you, but it happens to be the truth."

She walks up the walk, reaching for her keys.

"Hey, Barbara. There's something I'm curious about," I say.

"Good," she says. "Curiosity is the sign of an active mind." She pulls out the mail from her box. She has several magazines and she can't balance them. The mail spills out onto the sidewalk.

I go over. I kneel in front of her and though she doesn't want my help picking up her mail, I offer it.

She's not wearing an overcoat. The tips of her ears are bright red as if she's been walking outside for a long time.

"I'm curious about where you're working."

She doesn't react. I don't know if she's surprised by my comment or not. Her face registers no emotion, but she doesn't tell me that I'm wrong.

"I know you're not at the hospital. You haven't been there since August, so I'm curious where you go every day. Do you have a new job? Where is it? I'd really like to know."

She stuffs her mail into her leather bag and stands.

"Are you working around here? Downtown? A new hospital? I'm really curious to know."

I've obviously hit a nerve. She turns to look at me and now her face shows emotion – she's furious. "So the little neighborhood gossip has been sticking her nose into other people's business? Well I have some advice for your simple little curious mind. Fuck off."

She's stopped coloring her hair. She no longer looks at all like Lily – someone who I still don't think of as daughter.

She slams the door behind her.

"That doesn't answer my question," I say.

I'm halfway down the block when I spot Allan's car. It's double-parked in front of my driveway. A light snow has started to fall.

He gets out and walks me to the passenger side of the car. "Do you have a few minutes?" he asks. "I'm desperate."

"I've got some news too," I say. I'm sure he'll be interested in what I know about Barbara.

"Get in," he says.

I'm not used to riding in other men's cars, not in the middle of the afternoon and I glance around. I don't see anyone walking their dog. People are peering out their windows, studying the goings-on in the neighborhood, so I act as natural and as innocently as possible.

Then I remember that I have nothing to worry about on the home front. Joe flew to Philadelphia that morning and won't be home until late the next afternoon. The boys are spending the night at the Science Center with the rest of their class. They've taken sleeping bags and pajamas and will sleep in the planetarium with the skylights open as long as it doesn't rain.

We drive down Fifth Avenue to Wilkins to the Inns of Shadyside. "One of the best places for a quiet drink in the middle of the afternoon," Allan tells me.

"Is that right?"

"It's peaceful," he says.

There's a calm about our drive – as if we have all the time in the world, as if we have nothing else to think about except where we'll have a drink.

The present owner of the Inns has renovated his grandparents' turn-of-the-century mansion into a swanky martini bar and upscale bed and breakfast. Fifth Avenue used to be called Millionaires' Row and the homes reflected the gilded age in Pittsburgh. The Inn is reminiscent of that opulent time period. I'd been there once when it first opened. I'm impressed that Allan visits it frequently. I'd like to be a person who has drinks in the middle of the afternoon. I'd like to be a woman who seeks out peaceful drinking establishments. It sounds Parisian and therefore exotic.

A kid in a down-filled blue parka runs out of the Inn. Allan hands him the keys. We go inside. There is a fire, many lamps, a distracted receptionist, and a few people cozily sitting at the tables in the dimly lit bar. Outside the snow is falling more steadily.

"Will you have a drink?" he asks.

I'm dressed in Joe's black turtleneck and my old jeans. My shoes have sleet stains running around them. I might have a trace of my morning make-up, but I usually wear a lot more if I am trying not to frighten people. I'd like to go home and spend the next hour reconfiguring my look.

"They specialize in martinis," he says.

"If that's what you're having," I say. He must be noticing my eagerness to do as he does.

The whole far side of the room is a mirror and when I look at myself I'm surprised by what I see. The turtleneck is actually quite slimming and the jeans make me seem young. My hair, wet from the falling snow, has started to curl around my forehead. I look sporty, extremely relaxed, one might even say pretty.

He brings over two martini glasses; there is something erotic and magical about these clear colored drinks. The olive sits in the center of his glass.

"Let's sit by the fire," he says and guides me into the hallway towards a small library room in the front of the house.

I sit. He pulls his chair close to mine. An inch separates us. We're facing away from the bar and into the orange-red glow of the roaring fire.

We sip. A martini tastes like sin.

Not just the shape of the glass or the way that you have to purse your lips to keep from gulping it down. The olive teases your tongue.

The snow falls faster and more heavily. People come and go, but I don't look up.

"I don't want to think about Barbara," he says.

I agree. What could it possibly matter to me whether or not Barbara is employed – her work at the hospital was never a great concern of mine.

"Agreed?" Allan says.

"Absolutely," I say.

"Now let's talk about you," he says and I feel the magnetic pull into him. It is a magical moment and I have to remind myself to breathe. I don't want to faint and ruin this.

"I'm not that interesting," I say. The martini glass is an extremely sensual object. I hold the stem in my hand and sip slowly.

"I disagree," he says.

He puts out his hand and hands me something.

It's a key. An old-fashioned key that obviously belongs to a room upstairs.

Allan waits for my response. "All right?" he asks.

"Oh yes." I sigh. This is it.

We get up from the table – the two of us together and walk up the stairs together.

But of course this didn't happen.

We're talking about my life – my pathetic state of where I've come to – the place where nothing goes the way I want it to. Nothing at all happens in my life. I think it was Colette who claimed that the best part of a life's journey was the walk up the bedroom stairs, but I don't even get this much.

The truth doesn't exactly measure up to what I can conjure up in my imagination.

Here's what really happened:

Allan drives by just as I leave Barbara's. He waves, but I motion for him to stop. He doesn't pull over, but stops in the middle of the street.

"What's going on, Caroline?" he asks.

"I've got something new to report on the Barbara front," I tell him.

"I can spare five or ten," he says. I guess he's talking minutes.

I guiltily look towards our house. Joe's not home, but his work hours are never steady. The boys are somewhere and they'll be home soon.

There is a huge pile of papers and things on the passenger seat. I wait for him to move them, but he's looking at the garbage truck coming down the street.

It's starting to sleet.

"Careful you don't get that stuff wet," he says as I get in.

"I don't usually smoke in my car, but things have been so miserable these past three months that I'm giving myself a break."

"I understand."

"Where to?" he asks.

"How about the Inns of Shadyside?" I say. I try to pump some enthusiasm into the situation. "They have a nice bar. It's got a great view."

What they have is a garden with a waterfall and a pond that they stock with fish and frogs in the spring. As it's late fall, the garden is certainly closed.

"We won't be able to see a thing in this weather," he says. "Another rotten day in Pittsburgh."

I don't answer. I will not permit weather talk; we're beyond that, whether or not he recognizes it.

The driveway up to the Inns is slippery and he slams the car against the tree in the nearly empty lot. There is a woman vacuuming when we walk in. She doesn't hear us over the roar of her machine. We walk around her, but my foot catches the cord and pulls it from the wall.

She swears. I apologize, but she scowls. She takes the cord and snaps it like a whip as if she means to hit me. "Sorry. Sorry," I say and move past her. She shoulders me and I bump against the wall.

Allan has gone on ahead to the bar, not at all interested in my tiff with the housecleaner.

The bar is just as dimly lit as the foyer. The mood is dreary as if the owner of the place is trying to save money on light bulbs. Two women sit at the table in the center of the bar, the rest of the tables are empty but covered with boxes and papers and cleaning supplies. It looks like we've caught them in the middle of moving, not inviting in the least. The bartender is cleaning the bar with Murphy's Oil Soap.

But the bar is well stocked. There's something reassuring about rows and rows of alcohol bottles. I pretend everything is going along as imagined – as if I've planned it this way – though why I would fight about a vacuum cord is beyond me. And for a few moments, hope continues to surface in the emotional turmoil of my heart.

"They specialize in Martinis,' I tell Allan. A strong martini sounds like an excellent idea on such a horrible afternoon.

"Have you ever been here?" Allan asks. The bartender is a numbskull and hasn't a clue how to pour a good drink."

Hope diminishes, but doesn't disappear, as Allan announces that he will have a beer.

I don't want to have a martini alone, so I ask for a glass of red wine.

We carry our drinks to the only available table near the doorway.

Allan drinks his beer in a hurry. "So what's up?"

I sip my wine trying to slow down our encounter. It's turned and tastes of vinegar. Would a good glass of red wine have been too much to ask for?

"Barbara," I say. "I've got some news on the Barbara front."

"I'm so tired of that frigging woman," Allan says.

At the next table is a bride who wants to have her reception in the Inn. They've been sampling wines all afternoon and are actually quite drunk. Their voices are loud and shrill. They giggle when they're not talking.

"Maggie is extremely protective about Barbara. She shuts down when I tell her we have to do something about this incredible mess that we've suddenly somehow found ourselves right in the middle of. It makes it most inconvenient to talk to her."

"But you have to tell her that Barbara isn't working," I say. "She needs to know that this whole fall has been a farce."

"I don't know if it will make a difference," Allan says.

"You think she won't care that Barbara's a two-faced liar?"

"Not really," Allan says. "The important thing here is that Maggie is not Lily's mother."

I don't think that's as important as learning that Barbara's been conning all of us for the last few months. "She might as well be," I say.

"But she's not." He is forceful as he finishes his beer and motions the bartender for another. The bartender is too busy cleaning to pay attention to his customers. I guess he figures the women have had enough to drink. Allan goes up for a refill.

"She's better than Barbara," I say.

"How do you know that?" Allan asks.

"Because Barbara doesn't want to be a mother," I say. "Maggie does."

"You give that much credit to desire?"

"There is nothing stronger than desire," I say. No matter what I say it comes out sexual. "Desire is one of the most forceful motivating factors we have in our lives." It's a relief to be able to say these things even though I don't think Allan appreciates my comments.

"Then why did she adopt Lily in the first place?"

I'm not sure I'm the right person to speak for Barbara. I don't have anything good to say about her. I shrug.

Allan snorts. "She should have thought this through. She was careless in her desire. I think it's incorrigible."

"Moving to our street is number one on my list of things that Barbara has done wrong."

"This is a disaster," Allan says. "A complete and utter disaster."

He stands signaling what I take to be the end of our rendezvous.

A complete and utter disaster - I couldn't agree more.

He puts on his coat and takes out his car keys. "I'm sorry there," he says. "I think I've forgotten my wallet," he says.

I find this highly suspicious. Once I can understand, but twice seems deliberate. "Just like last time," I comment.

"Have we ever been here before?" he asks.

Would he have forgotten something like that?"

"The other bar," I say.

"You and I have been to a bar together?" he snorts. "That's funny. Not something I remember exactly."

This is getting insulting.

Beer and wine at the Inns of Shadyside do not come cheap and as I don't want the charge on my credit card, I pay in cash. I don't have enough for a tip, not that anyone deserved one.

I go home and think about what might have been. Re-imagining every moment of my life is a pathetic place to live. But I can't think of anywhere else to move.

Chapter Eleven

I am in the Starbuck's buying my ritualistic morning *vente drip with room for cream* when Barbara walks in. She stands two people behind me in line. I turn but she looks past me as if distracted by the offerings on the chalkboard, as if she doesn't know what she's going to order. I continue to look at her, but she never makes eye contact. I take my coffee and pause when I walk by. "Hello Barbara," I say. She doesn't move. She stands as if frozen, not acknowledging that someone has just said her name. "Barbara?" I say again. Absolutely no reaction.

There's a line at the sugar and milk stand-up bar because the half-n-half container is empty. We're forced to wait for the baristas to refill the thermos. Meanwhile Barbara gets her coffee and comes over. She nudges in ahead to pour skim milk into her cup.

"Hey there," I say. There's nothing wrong with her eyes.

She doesn't turn around. Not even when I say her name. There's nothing wrong with her ears. This is a deliberate act of ignoring me.

"Good morning, Barbara," I say. This time I'm loud.

She turns and looks at me. Dead at me. She tilts her head and then as if confronted by a stranger merely shrugs, like she has no idea who I might be.

It really is just one goddamn clown show after another.

I read somewhere that 75% of the people who jump off the Golden Gate bridge do not plan the act beforehand (though how they come up with this number is a bit dodgy.). Their suicides are spontaneous. They're walking across the bridge, looking down at the water and suddenly decide that their lives are not worth living. So they jump. Most of them die, but a few of them hit the water at just the right angle and if they don't drown in the powerful currents of the San Francisco Bay and if the crabs don't eat out their eyeballs (this happens to the ones who don't make it) they are pulled to safety by a Coast Guard boat that patrols the waters 24 hours a day specifically looking for bodies to scoop up.

I decide that I am not a pathetic person. I don't have to live like this. I can do something besides fantasize.

I take my inspiration from the poor souls who if they do live – and there are not many – are fined, which police say is the only way to discourage this kind of impulsive behavior. But I know why they do it. There's an allure to the bridge. I'm sure they feel as if they're called – the sense of flying, of soaring across dangerous waters, those precious moments of absolute freedom must be the happiest and most satisfying moments of their lives. I'm envious of their daring.

I am not a helpless woman. I cannot let my whole year evaporate into a hopeless mass of wishful, wistful thinking. I force myself to take action. I must jump. Metaphorically, of course.

I'm ready to jump. Ready to hit the moving currents.

I walk down to Maggie and Allan's. Early evening – they're home – both their cars are in the drive. They've been fighting, I can hear their disagreement in the silence when I walk into the kitchen.

In the backyard, Katie, Jane, and Lily play in the hammock even though it's cold outside. They rock it back and forth like they're in a swing set. Like it's summer.

"I think I've found a solution," I announce. But it's not as easy as all that. They're dealing with their own problems.

190

Barbara, it seems, has gone missing. "Missing?" I ask. "What does that mean?"

She dropped Lily off Friday morning and hasn't been seen since.

"I just saw her," I say. "At Starbucks. This morning."

Maggie nods. "I knew she didn't go out of town."

"Of course she didn't go anywhere. She's hiding from us," Allan says.

"She ignored me," I say. "Acted as if she had no idea who I was."

Maggie sighs. "It doesn't sound good."

Allan explains the situation. "Four days now and my wife continues to pretend that this was all planned out. She does a wonderful ostrich routine."

"And you, my dear husband," Maggie says, "do a great drunken Scotsman routine."

"This, my dear wife, is no act. I'm Scottish and I'm drunk." Then as if to prove his inebriated state, he drinks what's left in his glass.

Barbara has called. Much to my disappointment. I prefer the intrigue and thought we might be dealing with a missing person or a dead body. But in fact she has left a message and said that something had come up. Some sort of emergency; she would do her best to take care of it and would be over as soon as she could.

The second time she sounded spacey and said that she would come and get Lily as soon as she could but that she couldn't manage. Right then.

Maggie asked her what was wrong. Was she sick? Was she suffering?

I look to Maggie. "Have you called the police?"

"I'm sure there's a reasonable explanation for her absence," Maggie protests, but she doesn't have the energy to offer much of an excuse.

"Nothing with Barbara is ever reasonable." I say. And then say what I think is the understatement of the year. "She's a terrible mother."

"Please don't say that," Maggie says. I'm not used to seeing her so drained of energy and optimism. "She's not that bad," Maggie says.

"She is, Maggie," I argue. "She's a terrible mother."

I am steadfast in my determination that we do something. I have to do something to save myself. This whole year cannot be a gigantic and embarrassing error of judgment on my part. "We can't spend our days just standing around talking about Barbara and her foolish destructive behavior."

It's also out of character – at least where Allan and I are concerned. In my daydreams, we're creatures of great motivation and determination. Not exactly superheroes, but we do take action when there's a problem of such magnitude.

Allan pours another drink. He offers me one but I shake my head. I want my wits about me.

Maggie puts her head on the table. She disturbs a large pile of laundry and the clean clothes tumble to the floor.

"They'll take her away," Maggie says. She speaks into her closed arms. "I know. If we call the police they'll take Lily. They'll call it abandonment and they'll take her from Barbara."

She's right.

"Then it's up to us," I say.

I tell them what I think might solve the problem. "I think we should do something." I am forceful. "For Lily's sake."

"You're going to call Child Protective Services?" Allan asks. Would I call that a sneer? I might, but will not be defeated so early in my rolling out of this new plan.

"Of course not," I say. I had thought of that, but having worked with their Services I know that they're a mess. They mean well but that's as far as that goes. They're disorganized and broke and the people who work full-time for them are overworked, stressed, and unbelievably cynical about every aspect of the process they have to follow.

"Then what's your solution?"

"Her family," I say. I am on a mission. I speak with confidence and assurance – two emotions I haven't felt in ages.

He raises his eyebrows, interested in what I have to say. "Her family?" he asks. "How will that help?"

"We present the problem to her family," I say. "We tell them exactly what's happened and we ask for their help."

"I don't quite follow you." The sneer is gone. I explain with much more confidence than I feel. Allan and I will drive to Meadville, where I've already found the address of Barbara's parents. We will tell Barbara's mother and father everything – her difficulty in adjusting to motherhood, her odd working hours, her general apathy to Lily, who deserves so much more. They will know what to do – after all they are Barbara's parents. And as far as all of us on this street are concerned, the problem will be solved.

Joe doesn't warm to my plan. Not right away.

"Why doesn't Maggie go?" he asks. "With Allan?"

"She doesn't want to," I explain. Maggie doesn't want to make Barbara mad. She doesn't disagree with us going but she doesn't want to be the one causing the trouble.

"I told you what I think you should do," he says. "Call Child Protective Services."

"And I told you why I don't think that's a good option."

"But going to her family for help is?"

"It's the best one I've got," I say. "I actually think it can work or I wouldn't be wasting my time with it." Like I have so much else to do with my time.

"And a phone call won't do?" he asks again.

"No. A phone call doesn't underline the extreme nature of the problem," I say. "It's too easy to ignore. But if we're there confronting them it might motivate them into action."

"Then you should do it," he advises. "Go do it."

I can't believe everyone has agreed to something I created because there are no bridges on my street. I empathize with the jumpers – brashness is a very empowering emotion and I exalt in my own sense of freedom and energy. I haven't felt this good in a long time.

We leave early Thanksgiving morning. It is the only day Allan has off. When I came up with the plan, I assumed that we would spend the night in a hotel room but Meadville is actually only 95 miles north of Pittsburg and doesn't really necessitate an overnight stay. It is still hours alone with Allan in the car though.

A snowstorm is predicted: twenty inches is supposed to fall in a very short time period. The grocery stores go crazy with people buying out milk and batteries and bottles of water, not to mention their turkeys and sweet potatoes.

But Thanksgiving morning comes and the skies remain clear. Not even a flake dancing about. Joe and the boys are going to Maggie's house for turkey. Joe is in charge of the pies, which I've ordered for him and picked up at the bakery. They're sitting on top of the refrigerator, hidden as it were from the dog and the boys. I leave Joe a note to remind him to bring them over.

I imagine us stopping in roadside restaurants. I realize it's only two hours north but I want time to slow down. Allan seems more concerned with getting there. He barrels down the highway, something I put down to habit – men drive fast – and refuse to take personally. He finishes his coffee and I ask him if he wants to stop for more.

"No sense wasting time," he says.

"Are you in a hurry?" I ask.

"I'd just like to get there and get this over with," he comments. It's not the best attitude.

I try and shift his mood. "Sharon Stone's from Meadville," I tell him.

"Who's she?"

"Never mind," I say. I don't know why I'm bringing up a movie star who's shown her private parts to the entire world. I don't know anything else about Meadville except that the zipper was invented there. A century or so ago – the very first zipper was made and changed fashion forever.

We drive north out of the city. The roads are quiet. It's a holiday and most people have already gotten to where they're going.

"Do you like to camp, Caroline?" Allan asks.

"Camp?"

He points to the left of us and tells me there are some great places to camp. "I'll have to remember that," I say.

"People camp more in Europe than they do here," he says.

"Is that right?" I ask. It's 20 degrees outside, colder at night. I don't know what got him started on this line of conversation.

"It's very popular in Europe," he tells me. "People also hike more."

"I guess so," I comment. Boring, I want to scream. I can have this kind of statistical conversation with my sons. They love these kinds of comparisons.

He goes on to tell me that people are more fit in Europe.

"Probably because of all that camping and hiking," I say.

But no. It's not just that. It's their everyday approach to life. "They don't snack either."

"Does Scotland suffer a lack of potato chips?" I ask. "Maybe there's a shortage. Maybe I should start exporting them? Think how welcome they'd be. Then they could be as fat as Americans. What a concept, huh?"

Allan snorts. "People are too indulgent here in the States," he says. "They lack self control."

And maybe to prove his point, to show him that he's right – Americans do lack self-control; or maybe I'm just tired of talking about camping – I dive in to my prepared speech.

"I feel like there's some sort of connection between us," I say. Here's my freefall. I'm on the bridge looking down at the water. It's quite rough. I know it will be cold. I have to aim this carefully.

"What's that?" Allan asks. He fiddles with the radio knob. I want to slap his hand away. I've spent five months of my life thinking about this man. In my head, I've bathed with this man. I've hunted murderers with him, I've drunk and eaten foods from around the globe, we've had incredibly romantic sex, and are so madly in love with each other that people are actually envious when they see us together.

Fueled by the time I've committed to this imaginary relationship, I continue. "I feel like we understand each other," I say. "Like we're more than just neighbors."

It's not a graceful attempt but it's the best I can do on this Thanksgiving morning.

"You're a good person. A very good friend." He looks over at me and smiles. It's not at all what I want.

Allan takes his hands off the steering wheel. "Thank God, we're here."

Up ahead is a sign: *Meadville 10 miles.*

Barbara's mother answers the door in her housecoat. She's suspicious of us – two strangers on a silent, gray Thanksgiving morning. Allan apologizes. "Sorry to bother you," he says.

"What did you say?" she asks.

Allan clears his throat. "I said we're sorry to bother you." The way he's got his hands shoved into his pockets tells me that he thinks the whole trip has been a huge waste of time.

"Are you Scottish?" the woman asks.

"I am," Allan says. He introduces himself and then tries to tell her who I am, but she's got something she wants to tell him.

"I've just been," Barbara's mother says. She's very happy about this fact. Very happy.

I assume she's talking about a trip to the bathroom and groan. She's as batty as her daughter and then some. Allan is all business. He ignores her flighty remark and tells her the reason for our holiday visit.

"We live on the same street as your daughter, Barbara," he explains. "We'd like to talk to you if you wouldn't mind."

"To Scotland!" Barbara's mother beams.

"Excuse me?" Allan asks.

"I've just been to Scotland," she says. "What a spectacular country. What a wonderful, wonderful place. You're a lovely people."

Barbara's mother, it seems, has just returned from a two week tour of Scotland. "The Mature Minglers. That's the name of our group. Retired people, mostly women, though our trip had several men," she explains.

Allan turns to me and under his breath says quite clearly, "Remind me to kill you when we get out of here."

It's cold on the porch and Barbara's mother invites us in. Her husband is watching the Macy's Day parade. Bullwinkle floats by the camera. He mutes the sound and shakes our hand.

"Go upstairs," Barbara's mother says.

"What's this?" he asks, obviously engrossed in the show.

"I want you to change out of your pajamas," she directs him.

"Why?" he asks.

"Because we have guests," she tells him. "They're Scottish. We can't host them sitting around in our pajamas."

"I'm not Scottish," I say. "I'm American. You can stay in your pajamas all day."

"This shouldn't take long," Allan says. "Please be comfortable."

Barbara's mother insists on doing this her way. She and her husband go upstairs.

Allan and I sit side by side on the couch. I inch a bit closer, certain that Allan is too bothered to notice me making a physical move on him.

"Your nationality finally pays off," I comment.

Allan un-mutes the television. A marching band. Cinderella on top of a float, looking like she's about to fall.

We watch in silence for several minutes. Allan closes his eyes.

"We must remember why we're here," I say. I've used this line countless times before in my scenarios. Allan and I are usually doing something more important – saving a country from war, redirecting the bomb, but each mission should be undertaken with loyalty to the cause and a determination to see it to a successful finish.

Barbara's mother comes down first. She's wearing a holiday sweater – green with red berries and brown twigs on it.

"What a coincidence," she tells Allan. "A Scotsman coming to my door on Thanksgiving."

Barbara's father enters. He's not as exuberant as his wife, but he offers us coffee.

"They don't want coffee," Barbara's mother tells him. She goes to the sideboard and takes out a white box where she removes a gigantic bottle of Scotch.

"Are you sure you wouldn't prefer coffee?" he asks.

I don't really care either way. Allan opts for the alcohol so I say a drink sounds like a good idea, though I'm not sure it is.

Everyone is given a glass of Scotch. Barbara's mother makes a toast to *bonny, bonny Scotland*. Things do seem more cheerful after a few sips of scotch.

Allan explains the situation with Lily.

She is not unhelpful, but is not enthusiastic about helping us. She is resigned. Years of tolerating Barbara have obviously worn her down. "Barbara is very strong-minded," she says.

"We know," I say.

"We try to stay out of her business," her father says and I think he's offering us the same advice.

"Your daughter is taking advantage of my wife," Allan says. "We've got two daughters who need her attention. She can't be a full time caregiver to your granddaughter."

Barbara's mother begins to cry.

Allan finishes his scotch.

"We told her how hard it would be to adopt a baby alone," the mother explains her tears. "We offered to help. We told her we'd move to Pittsburgh. We told her we'd do anything she wanted, but she's very independent and busy. We try and see her and Lily but she's a very private person."

Allan looks at me as if to say, *what next?*

I take over and ask them if there's anything they can do to help Barbara, but the mother smiles and shakes her head. "She's very independent. Very stubborn."

The father agrees.

The mother offers us some cheese and crackers and then asks Allan about where he's from. They talk Edinburgh until it's obvious that we've overstayed our welcome. Not the result we were hoping for. I've become very familiar with disappointment.

The accident is Allan's fault. He will blame it on the icy conditions of the road. Black ice is what he tells the policeman, who merely shrugs and says something about drinking and the holidays. Allan isn't drunk. He had a few scotches, but I've seen him drink more than that. He was just driving too fast. Forty-five miles an hour down a side street is reason enough to wrap the front end of a car around a telephone pole.

The weather is brutal now. Cold. Windy. We wait and fill out endless forms and then Allan decides he's going to stay and rent a car. "I've got a meeting in Cleveland tomorrow," he says. "It's just easier if I drive there tonight. Come back tomorrow and get my car."

"What about me?" I ask.

"Can you call Joe?"

Joe's on call. I can't ask him to come get me. I just can't. This was my idea. I have to take responsibility for it.

I explain this to Allan. "I guess I could go to Cleveland with you," I offer.

He vetoes this idea right away.

"I guess I could take a bus home," I offer.

Allan nods his head. "That may be the best solution."

I can't believe this is how this will play out.

I stare at him. He senses something and grimaces. "I'm sorry," he says.

"Yeah?" I ask.

"It was an accident," he says.

I'm not talking about the car. I think he could be better to me.

In the end one of the Meadville police drives me to the bus station where I have a two and a half hour wait for the next bus to Pittsburgh. I have this vain hope that Allan will return and come get me. I stare at the door of the bus station and wait for him to walk through and rescue me from the grim depression of the small bus stop in Meadville, Pennsylvania. I wait in vain.

At nightfall I board the bus. It's surprisingly full, as if everyone had eaten their turkey and then jumped on board to view the country. It's a sleepy crowd. There are only a few seats left – none of them up front.

I am miserable.

According to my web searches: the earliest mention of the ginkgo tree used for medicinal purposes is in the writings of *Pen*

T'sao Ching, published in 2800 B.C. and associated with China's first sage and emperor Shen Nung. At the time certain members of the royal court were becoming senile in their golden years. The emperor looked out of his window, a voice whispered, *"the tree you are now looking at will restore the minds of your relatives and friends."* Not being one to ignore voices in his head, he instructed the staff to pick some leaves and create a brew out of them. The warm tea was served to those afflicted several times a day. Within weeks, the author noted that every one of them had regained much of their lost memories. Ironically, studies of Alzheimer's disease show that Ginkgo biloba shows promise in the alleviation of symptoms.

The bus ambles into every town down I-79. More people get on. The bus swells with snores and sleep. Everyone's breath is foul. The bus driver mutters to himself. We have a rest stop in Slippery Rock where I buy a cup of coffee and a cheese and bologna sandwich from the vending machine in the gas station where there was one working toilet. We sit there waiting for everyone to take a turn.

We reach Pittsburgh sometime after midnight.

I read somewhere that women are more apt to lie to themselves than they are to lie to others. The self-lies stem from the fact that females have incredibly active imaginations. Girls start with Barbies – creating lives and mini-dramas for these dolls. They graduate to high school fantasies, lusting after football players and guys who don't even know they exist. They pass a guy in the hall and fabricate scenarios how they can marry guys with huge problems. These women throw themselves at these men who are serving multiple life sentences and treat them like demi-gods. The Menendez brothers, after shooting both their parents, received hundreds of marriage proposals. Most of the women who wrote them had postgraduate degrees. Most promised to love them forever. Most said they already were in love with the boys. They said they could tell simply by looking at their sweet faces that they were innocent of any real crime. The boys admitted killing their parents. They never claimed to be not guilty. Quite the opposite – they gave flimsy reasons why they did what they did. And though neither of them will ever live a day out of prison, they are both married. Reportedly happy. This is delusional. And I understand it. Perfectly.

Home from Meadville twenty-four hours and I get the flu. Wretched stomach, headache, chills. At first I think it's food poisoning – I got sick on the bologna and cheese sandwich and vow never to eat anything from a machine again. Then the chills and aches start. I sleep. Hours disappear. I have no reason to get out of bed. A few days pass. The boys get sick – they miss a week of school. And though I'm getting better, I'm still too ill to take care of them the way I usually would. They're too sick to notice that I'm not giving them my full attention. Finally Joe gets sick so I have no choice but to get out of bed. Otherwise I'll have to share it with someone who feels worse than I do.

Joe has finished his novel.

He's printed out several copies and has sent them out to friends and colleagues for their opinions. He's anxious to hear what they think.

He won't let me read it.

"You're my wife," he says. "You won't be honest with me."

"I will."

"You say that now but what if you read a part you don't like?" he asks. "What if you don't like the whole thing?"

"I liked the beginning," I remind him.

"That was ages ago," he says. "It's changed."

"But you like it," I point out. "Why wouldn't I?"

"You would say you would, but you might not," Joe says.

"I think you can trust me to give you an honest opinion," I say.

"I'm not sure I want an honest opinion," he says.

"Then I'll lie. I'll tell you that I love it," I promise.

"Then why bother reading it?"

"I thought you like me as a reader."

"I did," he says. "At the beginning. But now I've put too much work into it," he sighs. "It's stupid. I know. But I'm too fragile."

He has a friend who teaches in the English department at the University of Pittsburgh who is going to help him get it published.

I'm cranky and bored and when I think Joe is asleep I try and open up the novel document on his computer, but he's either moved it or hidden it.

Christmas day and we celebrate with the morning in our pajamas. We eat eggs and toast in front of the fireplace, then open presents. The boys, I've noticed, have bought things for Lily. What we think is that Barbara's parents have come down from Meadville. They're with Barbara and Lily.

"We should go down and give them to her," they say. But none of us are dressed and we put them back under the tree. The boys have rented out the ice skating rink for three hours that afternoon. Joe goes down to watch them play hockey. "You want to come?" he asks. The thought of the rink with the smell of old socks and buttered popcorn doesn't appeal to me. I stay home napping in front of the fire.

Lily's presents are still under the tree. I can't help but feel that I've neglected her somehow.

New Year's Day and Karen and Greg invite the neighbors for a glass of bubbly. "Come, let's welcome in the New Year in a grand style," Karen says. "My resolution this year is to be more social."

Oddly enough my resolution is to stop paying so much attention to my neighbors. I'm taking a long hiatus. But Joe says he'd love to watch the football game on Greg's widescreen television. So we go. The four of us trudge over fifteen minutes early. But we're not the first guests. The party seems in full swing as if everyone is like Karen, vowing to be more social, they are so anxious to start partying.

Greg has gone to a wholesaler in the strip where he has purchased 100 oysters to help us ring in the New Year. He rallies Max and Josh to help him shuck them.

"It's a tradition in my family to eat oysters on New Year's," Karen says.

"Twelve of them. One for every month of the year."

"It sounds European," I say.

"Oh it is," Karen says. "It is."

I've got an eye on the front door waiting for Allan. I'm desperate to see him. We haven't talked since Meadville – I don't know what's going on with him or with Maggie or with Lily for that matter.

Karen encourages everyone to eat a dozen oysters. The boys flat out refuse. They won't even try one.

"Is it bad luck not to eat them?" I ask. Maybe it's good luck to eat more, I'll take what the boys didn't want.

"We'll have to see," Karen says. She scoops out a spoonful of horseradish sauce and spreads it over her oyster shell. She's the expert and sucks it down in one long suck and swallow. She finishes it with a long swallow of champagne.

Greg has hamburgers and hotdogs cooking on the grill. Josh and Max go outside to help him bring in everything. Joe is asleep in front of the big screen.

"I invited the McIntyres," Karen says looking out the window into Allan's backyard.

"Are they coming?" I ask. I sip my champagne. It tastes like holidays and weddings. Festive; maybe things will turnaround. I'm hopeful on this first day of the New Year.

"But I guess they've got their own troubles," Karen sighs.

"You mean with Lily?" I ask.

"I think with everything, don't you?" Karen asks. She refreshes her glass and offers some to me. As much as it puts me in a better mood, I remember the hangover – the sharp pain of a heavy head.

It feels like an enormous amount of time has passed since the trip on Thanksgiving Day. But as I haven't heard anything I assume things are better on the Barbara front. Karen is clueless so I leave it like that.

I wait for Allan. It's a new year – a refreshing start – maybe things can get back on track between us. I miss him. Not just what I made up, but the things that were real. I miss the attention he gave me, however stingy it became.

Greg has corralled the troops in for his toast. Everyone gathers around the dining room table while he speaks about all the wonderful things that have happened in the last year. Joe looks tired, but cheerful. The boys have their hamburgers so they're willing to listen to Greg ramble on about all the things he thinks will be important in the coming year.

I don't see much on my horizon.

The doorbell stops Greg just as he is about to tell us his New Year's resolution. Karen crosses to the front hall, champagne glass in hand, but the door opens before she can get to it.

It's Jane. She's frantic.

"My mom's fainted." She stands in the doorway, wearing only a T-shirt. "You have to come over.

"What happened?" I ask.

"Come," Jane demands. "Right now."

I, of course, think she's talking to me. Allan must need me.

But she is addressing Joe. When she senses hesitation on his part, she goes over to him and hangs onto his elbow. She physically pulls him from the room.

"Hurry," she says.

"It's okay, Jane," Joe says. He goes into doctor mode. "Slow down." He's got his glass of champagne in hand and tries to hand it to Karen who doesn't realize what he's doing and the glass smashes on the terrazzo tiles. The glass has splintered and the shards fly everywhere.

"What did she say happened?" Karen asks.

"I'm not sure," I say. "Maggie fainted?"

"That's a horrible thing to happen on a holiday," Karen says. I offer to clean up the broken glass, but Karen tells me not to bother. "We'll get it tomorrow."

"Don't you have cats?" I ask. "Aren't you afraid they'll cut themselves?"

"I hate those cats," Karen says. "If they're stupid enough to eat the glass, let them die."

I hadn't realized it until now, but Karen is extremely tipsy. Still if she wants to kill her cats, who am I to stop her?

Josh, Max, and I leave together. A few snowflakes fall as we cross the street. I look over to the McIntyres'. It looks dark: there are no cars out front. I suggest going over to check on Maggie. The boys are hesitant. "You think it's okay?" Josh asks.

"It's neighborly," I say and they agree that it's a nice thing to do, but they're not enthusiastic about going with me.

The McIntyres' walk hasn't been shoveled and the steps are slippery. The house looks dark and I'm nervous thinking something might really be wrong.

I ring the bell, but no one comes to the door. I ring again.

"I don't think anyone's here," Max determines.

"How can that be?" I ask. "Daddy should be here."

I turn the handle on the front door. It's not locked. I poke my head into the front hall. "Hello? Anyone there?" I ask.

"Don't." The boys are mortified. "You can't do that."

"I'm just looking for Dad," I say. The house is dead quiet.

"You're breaking into their house," Max says.

"Hardly," I say.

But the boys are already walking home. They won't be caught doing anything they've determined isn't right. I hesitate but finally follow. The steps are so icy they're dangerous and that's what I imagine happened to Maggie. She must have fallen and hit her head on the ice.

Joe comes home an hour later.

"Where were you?" I ask. The boys are upstairs – another football game turned on – but they're probably half asleep using it as background noise.

Joe hangs up his coat and sinks into the couch.

"What happened?"

"Maggie fainted," Joe says.

"Is she okay?"

"She was out cold when I got there," Joe says. "I didn't know what it was. The girls said she hadn't hit her head, she hadn't been sick. She was just sitting at the table when her eyes rolled back in her head and she went out."

"Did she go to the hospital?" I ask.

Joe nods. "I drove her myself. I wasn't sure how fast the ambulance could get her there."

"Is she okay?"

"She seems to be," Joe answers. "They're going to keep her in for a while. Run some tests. Keep a check on her heart and blood pressure, but I think it was just a freak thing."

"You think she just fainted?" I ask. "Just like that? For no reason?"

"My real opinion?" Joe asks. "I think it's some sort of reaction to stress. Either that or diet, but I couldn't be sure until we got her to the hospital and started running some tests."

"Stress?"

He stands. "It's just a guess."

He goes into the kitchen saying he didn't get much to eat at the party.

"There wasn't much there," I tell him in case he thinks Karen took a roast out of the oven after he got called away.

I ask about Katie and Jane.

"Hysterical," Joe reports. "Sobbing and crying. They made quite a scene at the hospital. One I'm sure most of the nurses won't soon forget." He describes the half hour when he first got to the house. Maggie was still unconscious and the girls were going crazy. "They acted as if she had died," Joe says. "I thought I was going to have to give both of them sedatives."

"What about Allan?" I ask.

"Allan?" Joe says.

"Wasn't he any help?"

Joe opens up one of the Tupperware containers in the refrigerator. "Allan?" He looks at it – rice from two nights ago – and puts it back.

"Allan usually keeps his wits about him," I comment.

"I think Allan is probably cause number one why Maggie fainted in the first place."

I move away from the sink.

"You're blaming Allan?" I ask.

"I'm sure he's somewhat responsible," Joe says. "And then it's probably her diet. She's probably not eating that well."

He's talking like he knows something I don't. "What's this?" I ask. "Why is Allan responsible?" Why blame Allan for Maggie fainting?

Joe pulls his fingers through his hair and untangles the knots that curl at the ends.

"Allan's gone," Joe says.

"What?" I say. I'm not shouting, but I want clarification – if he's got something to tell me than tell me, but don't dribble out tidbits of information like a leaky faucet.

"I thought you knew."

"Knew what?"

"That Allan left."

No one bothers to tell me anything. "He went back to Scotland?" I ask.

"More like Cranberry," Joe laughs. He names a suburb in the north hills. It's the closest thing Pittsburgh has to urban sprawl – and it's one of the uglier ones. Cheap houses, big box stores – the highway only minutes away from everywhere. I don't see the humor in Cranberry – it's an ugly place, one we never go to. There's no reason to remind yourself that that kind suburban development exists.

"Is that a joke?" I ask.

"No, that's where she lives," Joe answers.

I don't get it. I just don't get what we're talking about.

"Where who lives?" I demand to know.

He shrugs. "I don't like to gossip," he says.

But I press him. "What is it?" I insist. "What are you talking about?"

"Seems like Allan's been sneaking off with one of his co-workers."

The sound of the earth stopping is ear-splitting. It racks the bones, but the worst thing is when the sound stops. I have to struggle to get my breath, then struggle again to make sounds come out of my mouth.

"An affair?" and then several minutes later. "Allan?"

He goes over to the computer and turns it on. As soon as it's booted up, he turns it off. "It's strange, isn't it?" Joe asks.

I make a noise. He interprets this as agreement.

"I wouldn't have said he was the type," Joe comments.

I can't hear anymore. I shut down, but in the end, I can't control the tears.

"You feel sorry for the girls," he says. "It's tough on them."

I sob.

"And Maggie, of course," Joe says. "It's never easy starting over like that, but I think he's going to be good to her financially."

Another sob.

"It's not the end of the world, Caroline," Joe says.

I look up out the window. A squirrel has jumped from the telephone wire to the window ledge. His tail brushes the glass panes, then disappears from sight. I see the telephone wire move, but the squirrel is gone.

"You seem to be taking this hard. It does happen. Men cheat on their wives. Wives cheat on their husbands."

I'm not stupid. The concept of infidelity is one I've heard of. I'm familiar with lusting after someone who's not your spouse. I want to rage against the deception. He had no right to treat me like this. I don't deserve this.

"It's not fair," I say. "It's just not fair."

Joe offers to get me some aspirin and a glass of orange juice. I accept, but I can't swallow.

A few days later I go over to Karen and Greg's, under the pretense of picking up my serving trays from the New Year's party even though we didn't bring anything. She's outside cleaning her front porch with paper towels and kitchen sponges – the wrong tools for such a large task.

I ask her what she knows. "On the Allan front." I aim for casualness, but the desperation in my voice is everywhere apparent.

"He's been having an affair," Karen says. "I thought you knew. You were friends, weren't you?"

"We were really good friends," I say. I'm talking about Allan. He was the one who bewitched and then betrayed me. I feel a fool. A big stupid fool, not a woman desired, but a woman ridiculed and used. Allan knew how I felt about him. He knew I was attracted to him. My behavior wasn't what I would call subtle. He might have been flattered, but most of all he was distracted with his own feelings of lust and desire. I was never the target of his affection. He never had any interest in me.

"You know how it is," Karen says and shrugs. Her big shoulders move back and she goes to the sink and rinses out the sponge of the cobwebs she's collected from the deep corners of the porch.

But I don't know how it is. I was entirely blind on this one. I didn't see a thing.

"Since when?" I ask. I force myself to be calm. I will not show any emotion no matter what I learn.

"Oh God," Karen says. "It's been going on forever."

"How long is that?" I ask. "A month? Two?"

"Oh no. Much longer than that. It's been more like a year," she says. "At least a year."

How can this be true?

"Poor things," Karen says. "I feel sorry for those girls. It's hard on teenage girls when their father starts sleeping with a new woman. The whole concept of sex becomes a little too real. They ask all kinds of questions, most of which they've figured out for themselves and it's their father who's giving them these life lessons. They don't need to grow up that fast."

"How do you know?" I manage. "How do you know this about Allan?"

"I saw them," Karen says. "I saw the two of them together."

I imagine she's talking about a restaurant – Allan and a woman eating together. Perhaps she's mistaken about the nature of their relationship. I've sat next to Allan in a bar. People who saw us together might have assumed something. Maybe everyone is wrong about this. People have been known to make mistakes, but my heart doesn't listen to my line of reasoning. Even it hears the strain of this possibility.

"Our dog got out one night. He's so smart he can push open the back door. So smart," Karen tells me. "I went out searching for him all over the neighborhood and thought I heard him barking."

I nod.

"He was in the McIntyres' backyard. I went over to get him and that's when I caught them. Right smack dab in the middle of things."

'Right smack dab in the middle of things' is an expression I'm familiar with but I'm confused by how Karen is using it in this context.

I deny the obvious.

Karen's on a roll. She snorts. "Right there in his own backyard. Maggie and the girls were on a Girl Scout camping trip, but really they could have come home for any number of reasons. I don't think it's a good idea to do that sort of thing in your own home. There's a reason it's called home. That sort of nonsense only hurts the spouse who most likely doesn't have a clue as to what's going on."

She pauses. "Though in this case, I think Maggie knew something was up. Why else would she have clung to that little Chinese girl like she did?"

I'm still stuck on the 'right smack dab in the middle of things' comment. I need this one spelled out for me.

Karen is happy to comply. "*In flagrante delicto,*" she says. "Out there for all of God and nature to watch."

There's little nuance to this.

I block out all images moving in my mind. I don't need to think so graphically. Not when I 'm in shock like this.

"Two nights after that we had a barbecue – the one to help save the empty lot," Karen says. "Do you remember? Last June?"

I have picture-perfect recollection of that night. The pool, his chest, his crazy attention – it had all been directed at me. I did not make this up. I'm a fool, but I'm not crazy.

"Greg confronted him after the party and Allan confessed," Karen says.

"He confessed?" I've never thought of Greg as the fatherly sort.

"Told him everything," Karen says. "That he was crazy in love, that he and Maggie hadn't been getting along, that they were following different paths in life. That she was more interested in her life than his. All nonsense about him wanting a change. And along comes this woman. His soulmate and best friend. Someone he loves and can make love to. I think he was actually proud of his affair."

I'm not speaking. Vocalizing an emotion is impossible. Karen doesn't need any encouragement. She rambles on, dripping information and details.

"He was like a teenager, wanting to talk about it, giggling and flirting and just so jazzed up. You probably don't remember that night."

It was only the most important night of my life this past year. I am not a woman who misjudges people. I was right about Barbara even though no one would listen to me. Allan flirted with me. I felt it. There was something wonderfully refreshing and engaging about our exchanges. I do not make things up – I construe, yes, but not from nothing. I had reason for these fantasies. I had good reason to carry on as I did.

"A lot of good it did," Karen says. "Look at the lot. A catastrophe. A marriage and our neighborhood green destroyed."

"A tragedy," I say.

"Are you crying?" Karen asks. She puts her hand to my face and the tears increase. "I had no idea you were so sensitive."

She hugs me though I don't have the need or the desire to have anyone touch me right now.

I can't help it. I go to bed. It's not even seven. The dinner dishes are where everyone left them – some in front of the television, others in the hallway, glasses everywhere. The dirty pots are on the stove. Men may register the mess, but they won't do anything. It's not the first time I've had a fit about being the only one to clean the house, but even that seems a redundant argument. I live with three males. That's my lot.

213

Joe walks in. I don't move.

"You asleep?" he asks.

"Kind of," I say. I wish he'd leave. I wish he'd go work-out, run, walk the dog, go talk to the boys. They still need adult supervision every once in awhile.

"Want me to get you something?" Joe asks.

I would love for something. I'm so tired of my thoughts, my stupid thinking patterns. I want to crawl out of my head and visit someone else. A life is a long time to live with the same thoughts. I have grown so weary of mine. They're stale and stagnant – they're middle-aged, saggy, and weighty. I've thought them too many times. I'm exhausted by my own limitations.

I sit up with the desire to get away. "Let's go someplace," I say.

"Now?" he asks.

"Let's get out of here. Let's go. Let's leave Pittsburgh." I kick at the bedcovers which seem dirty and thin as if my toe nails will break through the material. My legs get tangled. "I'm so tired of being here."

"Leave?" he asks, obviously confused by my determination to get out of here. I'd like nothing better than to never see our house or our street again. But it's more than that. I'm tired of myself, tired of my emotions, of the way I've been thinking. My life is such a pattern, but I don't know how people break into a new one.

Joe comes over to my side of the bed. He stands over me, not touching me but staring at me.

"I think you should take it easy," he says. He grabs hold of the sheet and pulls it taut underneath my body. Then he takes the comforter and arranges it neatly over me. "Relax. It's probably just another virus. You must have a lousy immune system."

I have no choice. He goes across the hall and tells the boys that I'm not feeling well.

I get up and go to the window seat. It's freezing cold there, but I sit and stare out into the darkness. I see movement, cars, the trees bending in the wind. Somewhere out there are the lights in other people's houses. But they have nothing to do with me.

Jane makes a huge banner. White with bold red letters, GOODBYE DADDY, that she drapes across the house.

"That's one way to get the news out," Joe says.

Allan moves out of the house. He no longer lives in the neighborhood.

The New Year offers nothing worthwhile. There are no optimistic prospects on my horizon. I stay at my window perch watching, waiting, no longer imagining what might be, simply going over what is. Depressing.

Katie dresses in an off the shoulder, ankle length dress made of some heavy curtain-like material. She wears it every day. To school, at home. She wears it up and down the street. She wears it like she has no other clothes. She claims to be Aragon's lover, Arwen, from the movie *The Lord of the Rings*. I read the books but don't remember the woman's parts. She looks medieval, except for the glitter on her shoulders. Her lips are painted purple to match the lower half of her dress. The top-half is whispery swatches of white cloth. She wears a continual pout – always on the verge of tears, which I gather is in character for this woman. Josh tells me she's half elf.

"I wouldn't have guessed," I say.

I catch Josh and Katie behind the garage one evening. I'm so flabbergasted to see them intertwined that my attitude is casual, bordering on jovial. "What are you two doing back here?"

They look up. Their disappointment in seeing me is palatable, but it also adds to their excitement; both of them blush deep, deep red. Katie's shoulders reveal tiny bite marks, which I refuse to believe came from Josh.

"Up to your room," I say.

"Why?" he asks.

"You're grounded." I say. "Forever."

He gives me a strange look and I'm forced to tell him that it's wrong to make out with a neighborhood girl behind the garage.

"Why?" he asks. "Sex is normal. Dad is always telling us that."

"You weren't having sex," I say. I saw that much.

"You know what I mean," he says. "Sexual feelings are normal for someone my age."

"Katie McIntyre is older than you," I come up with something that sounds good. "I don't think she's a good influence. She and her sister are not the most stable teenagers. Especially now with all the turmoil in her parent's marriage."

"She's fourteen," he says.

"That's right," I say.

"I'm fourteen," he says.

"You can't be," I protest.

"So you're wrong. She's not older than me. We're exactly the same age."

"She's wearing a Halloween costume," I tell him. "In March."

"She has her reasons why."

"I'm sure she does," I say. But if he knows her reasons, he doesn't share them with me.

"It doesn't look bad," he says.

"It doesn't look good."

"She likes to role play," he says. "It's just for fun. She's having fun."

"She's too young to be making out with you behind the garage."

I really would prefer it if Josh would stay away from the entire family. They're not a stable bunch. I'm about to make it a rule – from now on, no messing with the McIntyres – when Josh tells me to stop it.

"Stop what?"

"Don't act like this," he says.

"How am I acting?"

"Like you've lost your mind."

I will ground him for six months. He can come out of his room when he graduates from high school. That should teach him to be more respectful of his elders. That should stop him from making out with the loose girls in the neighborhood. I shudder to think what would have happened if I hadn't seen them kissing. Would they have gone further? Apples don't fall far from the tree – I have reason to believe there might have been no stopping him.

But Josh is not going to his room. He's got more to say to me.

"You act like a crazy person. For months now. You haven't paid us any attention. All moping and weird. You walk around like a zombie rearranging the living room, moving beds, throwing everything out. No one cares how clean the house is. Act normal. Just because you lost your job is no reason to go crazy. Lots of people don't work. You have money. You don't have anything to worry about. Plenty of people in the world are poor. So stop it.   Just stop it." He was near tears, which embarrassed us both. I wanted to hold him, but knew it would only make the situation worse.

And then he sobs. "Be my Mom."

I am doing that. Isn't it in my job description to stop my sons from being involved with girls from bad families? I don't blame Katie. Her upbringing was obviously influenced by a morally repugnant father, but that is no reason to see her entangled with my son.

But his plea tears at my heart. "Be understanding. Be nice. You usually are," he says. He gains control of emotions and the tears stop.

I have thought that same thing about my boys a million times. I have never had the opportunity to say it. I would never say it to them. I haven't been myself lately. I didn't think anyone was paying attention.

"I love you, Josh," I say in my defense. "I care about what you do."

He was kissing someone, it's not the end of the world. I could be mad at him and express my anger without the screaming. I could have done it that way.

"Then show me," he says.

"I might have been more sane," I say.

"You were nicer," he screams at me.

"That may be true. But I still don't want you making out with Katie McIntyre behind the garage."

"That's disgusting," he said. "You shouldn't talk like that."

His face is pinched and red. It reminds me of when he was young and would come home from day camp all sunburned; his skin peeling off his nose. "Talk like what?" I asked.

"Like some hippie from the sixties," he says and cringes. "What is making out? I don't know what that means."

"I think you have a good idea of what making out means," I say. "It's what the two of you were doing."

Max walks in and Josh turns to the wall. And with this gesture my anger drains. I don't want him to continue kissing Katie McIntyre, but I don't want to be the cause of his frustration and stuttering. It's not what a mother should be doing to her son.

"Could you please go upstairs?" I ask Max. I try and keep my tone neutral so as not to embarrass Josh.

"It's a free country," Max tells me. "And I'm a free citizen with the right to choose what floor I want to be on. And right now, I want to be here in the kitchen."

"As a favor to me?"

Max knows something's up. He opens up the cupboard, brings down a glass. He turns on the tap, fills the glass. He takes the tiniest sip, then dumps out the water and sets the glass on the drain board.

"Is Josh in trouble?" Max asks.

I raise my eyebrows. "Please?" I point to the ceiling. "Just for a few minutes? Go?"

Max is capable of being extremely bothersome. He stays. "Is he grounded?"

"Thanks, Max. I appreciate you listening to me on this."

He goes, but not quickly.

And in the end, I'm the one who ends up apologizing. As Josh points out, it's not the message, it's the way the message was delivered. That's what upset him. He has a point.

He gets me to promise that I'll never bring it up again. "And whatever you do, don't tell Dad," he adds and then goes upstairs two at a time. I hear his bedroom door slam.

But I don't give him this. Joe has a right to know what's going on in his own household. I plan to tell him everything, even about our fight, but he gets home late and I forget about it and later it just seems like old news.

I wait for Jane to go back up in her tree.

But when I see her walking home from the bus, she says she's given up.

"No more protesting?"

"No more politics," she declares. "I've joined the unending tide of apathy."

"That's too bad," I say. "I thought you had some really good issues." The Gap protest seemed useless but I thought her attitude on the world leaders was dead-on.

"You aren't going to change the world," she says. "No one is.

She's spending her time renting movies. She and her mother are going to watch every single movie stocked in the local *Blockbuster*.

"What an undertaking," I comment.

"I think I can finish in a year," she says. "But I get tired staying up so late on school nights."

"I can imagine," I say.

She's watching thrillers from the 1970's. "Not a stellar decade," she says.

It seems a long time ago – I'm not sure what she'll gain from that part of the endeavor.

"How's your mother?" I ask.

"How do you think she is?" Jane echoes back.

"Is she okay?" I ask. "Anything I can do?"

"She will be," Jane says. "Give her some time and she'll be just fine." Jane promises and walks on ahead. Head down, the wind kicks up. I watch her disappear into her house, a place that no longer holds any magical power for me.

The other woman is fifteen years younger than Allan, which makes the whole thing a huge uninteresting cliché. I expected more from Allan. I guess Maggie must have too.

"He's marrying her," Maggie tells me. "She's American. Isn't that hysterical?"

The humor is a bit too sophisticated for my tastes. "How is that funny?" I ask.

"Allan abhors Americans," she says. "He thinks they're ridiculous."

"Certainly not all of them," I remind her. "At one time he must have loved you."

She disagrees. "I don't think so. Odd as it may seem, I don't think he ever loved me."

I don't believe this, but I know what she means. No matter what the accent, love that isn't returned fades drastically. It's as if it never was. A heart changes – it loses passion and then it simply forgets.

Chapter Twelve

I read Joe's novel. It's a very different book than when I read the first few chapters. There's a more cynical tone established from the beginning – it rains almost every day – the husband is a bitter man who doesn't trust anyone. The murdered wife is discovered in the garage a few days after an exceptionally brutal rain storm. Winds and rain from a hurricane down south came north and the city flooded. The wife is gone – missing – but only the husband realizes this. It's a weekend, she's not expected at work, the couple have no children and no dinner invitations for that particular weekend. The city streets flood and businesses are closed – there's real destruction, something that keeps everyone occupied. But finally a neighbor notices and questions the husband about his wife. "Haven't seen her in a few days. Hope she didn't drown in all this rain," is the off-hand comment. The husband's reaction surprises the neighbor. "Wouldn't mind if she did," the husband sneers. The neighbor calls the police who come over not to investigate – the wife hasn't officially been reported missing – but just to appease the neighbor who has relatives in the mayor's office.

The husband is the number one suspect from the time the police find the wife's body in the garage. They're suspicious because the husband didn't report the wife missing for several days. He blames the rainstorm, but the police think this is ridiculous. They don't see the logic between the rainstorm and the missing wife. He insists on his innocence. I find the husband strange, but likable. I know the police are wrong – he is innocent – any decent reader can see this. The police finally give up.

They determine it to be a random killing and close the case. Then the point of view switches to the neighbor.

I don't know what it means. My first thought is that Joe knows about Allan and me and then I realize there isn't anything to know. He can't read my mind. I never told anyone except one conversation with Julie and I never told her Allan's name.

I am in the mood for a fight. I have to blame someone for my foolishness. Barbara seems the best answer. I go over to her house. I know she won't answer the external door so I don't even try. Her downstairs neighbor is just coming home. We exchange pleasantries as he holds open the door and I go up the third floor. I knock. There's no answer. I knock again, then turn the handle. It's open. I walk in.

At first I think no one's home. The apartment is dark and disordered.

Lily is asleep on Barbara's bed. She's alone in the apartment.

Barbara is not just flighty or weird, she is disturbed.

She's way off. It's not her personality. It's her mind.

I call Barbara's mother as soon as I get home.

She remembers who I am. "Is something wrong?" she asks.

"Yes," I say right away. "Yes," I say again, this time more forcefully. "Something is very wrong."

"Is it Barbara?"

There is a weariness to her voice, which I have to get rid of. This isn't the same old problem. This is something that has to be addressed.

"I know you can help," I say. "Barbara won't fight you this time."

She sighs. "I'll come down."

The next day I'm home, thinking I should probably call Childhood Protective Services when someone starts knocking on the front door.

The dog barks with the eruption of noise.

"Coming," I call, but the person on the front porch is an impatient sort.

It's Betty, Barbara's mother and she gets right to the point. "Take her."

"What?" I say.

She holds up Lily's hand. "Here," she says simply.

"What are you talking about?" I ask.

"Take her," Betty says. She's nervous, the tension shows in her cheeks – two red spots.

"You asked for my help and now I'm asking for yours," Betty says. "Barbara's not fit to be a mother."

She's got that right. "I should have stopped her from the start," Betty says. "But there's no sense looking back at what should have been. Not when we have Lily to worry about."

I'm speechless. I haven't a clue how to respond to this woman.

She encourages me to take action. "You have to do something."

"She's not mine," I say.

"She should be," Betty says. "You know what I'm talking about."

I do know what she's talking about.

"Then help me," Betty demands. "I'll call the right people. I'll do the right things. With Barbara. But for now, take her. You love her."

"I always have," I say and the emotion of that statement overwhelms me. I kneel to look at Lily, who seems distracted and tired.

"You want to come in and play little Princess?" I ask.

She nods and I take her hand. "Go find Spot," I say. "Tell him to stop all that barking. He'll wake up the entire neighborhood."

"Morning," Lily tells me as she walks past. "Everyone up."

"They are?" I ask.

She curls up beside the dog and puts her head on his back. He doesn't growl or pull away.

"You love her," Betty says. "In the right way. You wouldn't have driven all the way up to see me on Thanksgiving Day, not when you have your family here."

My motives for taking action are misinterpreted, but this no longer seems important.

"I should have done this months ago," she says. But she cannot afford to feel regret.

I'm afraid that Barbara will come and take Lily from me.

"Let's play hide-n-go-seek," I tell her and we go upstairs.

We sit in the bathroom. I lock the door. I know it's paranoia, but I'm nervous and unsure of what Barbara will do when she's angry. And she will be angry.

We're still there when Joe comes home. I explain everything to him

Later after we've had dinner – potato chips and peanut butter for Lily, pizza for the boys and leftover chicken for Joe and me, Joe says we should talk.

I know he's going to tell me that we have to take Lily to Child Protective Services. I stop him before he can speak. "Can you give her some time here? Just so she doesn't feel so unwanted?"

He's looking out the kitchen window. "I think we should do something about making this a permanent situation."

It takes me a few minutes to figure out what he means.

"Really?" I ask.

"Anything else would be cruel," he says. "We can't do that to Lily. She doesn't deserve to be treated that way."

Joe and I adopt Lily. The undertaking is more intimidating than it is complicated. The paperwork overwhelms for several nights, but we get through it. We are assigned a social worker who reviews our case. She spends time with each of us, more time with the boys. When I ask what they talked about the boys shrug it off. "She's just making sure we don't resent Lily," they tell me. "They want to make sure that you and Dad can handle another child."

"Not financially," Max explains. "Emotionally."

"I see." I'm curious how they responded but they don't offer me their reaction on my emotional state as a mother. They do tell me not to worry.

"Worry about what?"

"Lily's a good kid," Josh says. "She'll be fine."

I have to believe this is what they told the social worker.

I worry about Maggie. She was Lily's primary caregiver for months but she's incredibly enthusiastic. "It couldn't be more wonderful," she assures me. She discounts all the doubts and fears.

"You'll be wonderful," she says. I think she is telling me the truth.

I worry that people will mistake me for Lily's grandmother. I worry that we'll be too old to walk at her college graduation. I worry that we'll be dead before she has kids and that our grandchildren will think of us as those old-fashioned people in the photographs over the fireplace.

I worry that Lily is Chinese and I'm not. I worry that people will immediately know she's an orphan and pity her. I worry that she'll grow up to resent Joe and me, that she'll hate us for taking her away from her home, her culture, the one safety net she had.

The social worker tells me this is all normal.

I doubt this. How can all my fears be normal? Some of them must seem foolish.

But she insists that it's true. Then she tells me that doubts are good.

"Besides you're hardly the oldest mother we have adopting," she says. "Not by far."

"How far?" I ask. "How much older are we talking?"

"Five or six years," she says and points to the stack of papers on her desk, which I'm guessing are her other cases though she doesn't say this.

"Five or six years?" I ask.

"We have women nearing fifty who are looking into adoption," she says.

I'm encouraged by this statistic. We wait for our court date.

I wear a pinstripe black suit to court – the first time I've dressed like this since I lost my job. Joe wears the exact same color suit.

"We look like we're in a marching band," he comments.

"Is that bad?" I ask. I want us to look the right part. I want us to look like adoptive parents should look.

"We should wear whistles around our necks. Yellow epaulets," Joe asks. "We could walk in playing our instruments."

My palms sweat; I'm much too nervous to joke. I want to look professional – something I've never associated with watching marching bands.

We're early. The judge is late; the social worker tells us that we've been postponed half an hour. "Not to worry," she says. "It doesn't mean anything." Joe volunteers to walk across the street to Starbucks. He returns twenty minutes later without any coffee. "I didn't think we needed it," he explains. He's eaten a pastry – the crumbs cover the front of his suit. I brush them off his lapels.

The judge checks the forms, checks the home study report; he checks out our financial papers. He asks about the boys. The social worker hands him her home-study report that she did on Josh and Max.

"Do you think they'll have any problems having a new little sister?" the judge asks.

"I think they're looking forward to it," Joe answers.

"Why do you want to adopt this little girl?" the judge asks and I wait for Joe to respond. But the judge directs the question to me.

I fumble, my sweaty palms moving up and down the table leaving huge wet marks.

"Because I already love her." I can't look at the judge so I stare just above his head. I speak the truth – exactly what I feel. "With the boys I had to take a chance and hope for the best. But we know Lily and there's no chance that we won't love her. I have faith in this."

My face is drenched. I take the scarf from my neck and wipe my face. I'm incredibly shaky and feel like I'll pass out unless I can sob.

Joe's hand is in the middle of my back. "It's okay," he says.

I'm a mess. My feelings for Lily are not exactly a surprise, but I'm taken aback by the overwhelming need I have to care for her.

I apologize for my tears, but the judge shakes his head. "Motherhood is an emotional time. You have all the reason in the world to speak with your heart." He flips through the files again, says something to the social worker. They talk for several minutes. Back and forth – quick questions, quick answers.

The judge looks up. He smiles very broadly, but very briefly, then wishes us luck.

I'm still sweating. I turn to Joe. "What do you think this means?"

"It's over," Joe says.

"What?" I ask.

Now he is the one who is crying. "Congratulations, Mommy."

"That's it?" I ask. I look around. No one seems to be paying us much attention.

"That's it," Joe says.

The social worker comes towards us. She's got her hand outstretched so I know the news is good. We have just enlarged our family by one 2½ year old girl.

That night I make rice and beans for dinner. This is what the boys asked for. They roll them up into burrito shells. Lily stands on the chair and sprinkles grated cheese on top and then we microwave them. Joe opens a bottle of champagne and pours out a glass for everyone. Joe makes a toast. "To us," Joe says. "To our new family."

The boys don't like the champagne. They dump theirs into our glasses and grab the gallon of orange juice from the refrigerator. Lily doesn't taste hers, but imitates the boys until soon there is champagne spilled all over the table. I sip slowly, thinking there should be drums and trumpets. Instead it's just us. Us and the messy table.

Though they don't like the champagne, the boys insist on toasts. "Welcome to our family, little Lily," they say and raise their glasses. "Welcome."

Max predicts that Lily's going to have an easier time than they had growing up.

"Did you suffer?" I ask.

"Tragically," Josh says.

"Did you have a bad childhood?"

"It was horrible," Max reflects, then attacks. "You should know. You were here."

Josh agrees with his brother. "It was a terrible time," he says, then he seems to reconsider. "She's a girl. They'll be so easy on her."

I cry periodically. Spontaneous tears when I think about everything that's happened –with everything that will change.

The boys tell me to stop. "Don't be so weird," they insist, but I don't care. I cry. Lily laughs. Joe keeps nodding. "Great. Great."

"Should we be easier on Lily?" I ask Joe.

"Most definitely," he agrees. We're too old and too tired to do much patrolling or policing."

"Okay," I say and raise my glass. "Lily you have free rein to do exactly as you please."

She snorts all the orange juice that is in her mouth out her nose and it sprays across the table. The boys burst out laughing and Lily does it again.

"If you're done with dinner, you may all be excused," I say.

The kids, all three of them now, go upstairs to watch a movie. "Nothing scary," I call up after them.

"Did you think we were going to show her *Halloween 4?*"

"I think you have more sense than to show her that," I say.

"Thanks, Mom," Josh says. "I'm glad you give us some credit."

Joe and I finish the champagne. I know we should be saying profound things to one another, but we talk about the basement, which floods every time it rains.

"Let's just hope for a dry June," he says.

"Isn't there any way to fix it?" I ask.

He shrugs and I imitate him.

"Should we call someone?" I ask.

"That's a good idea," he says, both of us knowing that this won't happen. Not this year anyway.

Later that night, Joe and I are getting ready for bed. He notices that I'm quiet. "What are you thinking?" he asks.

"Honestly?" I ask.

He turns down the duvet cover. "I think that's probably for the best."

"Clothes," I say. I haven't thought about Allan in days. Not in days. Not even a reflection. It's a relief to deal with reality.

"Your clothes?" he asks. "What's wrong with them?"

"Not mine," I say. "I'm thinking about girl's clothes. Little girls' clothes."

He seems a bit confused.

So I explain. "I'm thinking about black velveteen dresses with bows in the back. And white tights. I'm thinking pink shorts and ponytail holders." I have all of this on my mind. "Mary Janes, and fur trimmed boots. A rubber ducky raincoat. "I want to buy things for Lily's room, which right now is decorated with a three-foot Clifford dog – the stuffing coming out of his ears – and some of the boys' discarded hot wheels cars. I want a canopy bed, but I worry she might be afraid. I want a dollhouse and a red table with two matching chairs. Glow-in-the dark stars on her ceiling. And a toy chest. One that won't slam on her hands."

"Should I take out a loan?" Joe asks.

"I won't buy it all at once. I'll drain the account slowly," I promise.

He follows me into Max's room where Lily has fallen asleep in the bean-bag chair. She's curled into a ball and even in sleep is neat – the exact opposite of the way the boys used to fall asleep.

Joe picks her up and carries her across the hall. Her head flops onto his shoulder, her finger goes directly into her mouth and she starts sucking loudly but doesn't open her eyes. I haven't seen him with a child draped over his arms in a long time. "It's good this Little Princess has finally found her castle," Joe says.

He puts her into the bed and I cover her with a blanket. She kicks it away, sucking her finger, eyes shut tight.

I flick on the lamp in the hallway in case she wakes in the middle of the night.

Later, I will get up to go check on her – just to make sure she's still breathing. Joe will check too. Then I'll check once more. Joe will go in before he leaves for the hospital. This pattern of caring returns without effort as if we've simply been on hold for ten years.

I don't fantasize that taking care of Lily will be easy. I've had some experience in child-rearing and know it's best not to think too much about what will happen. It doesn't resemble what one has planned.

There have been such significant changes in the neighborhood – the condominiums built on the empty lot are red brick monstrosities with gigantic garage doors that face the street. Betty took Barbara back up north where she's working on getting healthy. Karen and Greg could never have imagined such a building nightmare. It's worse than anything anyone could have imagined. The units, I've heard, have all been rented. There's some concern that parking will become hopeless after the tenants have moved in. But I've been too busy helping Lily adjust to our family to worry much about the chaos the new neighbors will cause on our street. Raising Lily is not exactly a freefall from the Golden Gate Bridge, but in some respects it's very close.

Over the next year my interest in ginkgo trees decreases dramatically.